Praise for
KILLER DEALS

"A tough and tenacious female PI uncovers fraud and murder within a corrupt circle of Philadelphia real estate developers. So gritty and propulsive, you'll race through the pages to the surprising and satisfying finish."

– Kelly Simmons, bestselling author of nine suspense novels, including *Not My Boy* and *The Shortest Years*

"Chris Quarembo's *Killer Deals* is the real deal, a beautifully written procedural with prose as precise as the investigation by the gloriously overworked and underpaid Andrea Fabiano. Step by careful step, we follow Fabiano into the heart of a twisted case of murder and arson even as we get ever closer to the demons that drive her doggedness and her outsized humanity. A true treat."

– William Lashner, author of *The Barkeep*

KILLER DEALS

CHRIS QUAREMBO

atmosphere press

Published by Atmosphere Press

Cover design by Dhiraj Navlakhe

Atmospherepress.com

For
Margaret DeCicci Quarembo,
my late mother
whose love and encouragement
sustains me.

CHAPTER ONE

The warehouse was a rubble of wood, soot, and ash. Not a single wall remained standing.

I slipped under the yellow tape and switched on my flashlight. Until it had burned out of control the night before, the warehouse had stood, abandoned, in one of Philadelphia's old industrial neighborhoods.

Its insurer, Southeastern PA Financial Group, had hired me to investigate possible arson but when I showed up earlier in the day, the Fire Marshal barred my access calling the site too dangerous. So I returned after nightfall to examine the damage and look for the possible source of the blaze.

I came prepared, wearing thick boots and heavy work gloves. As I moved slowly into what had been the interior, I sniffed the air for the odor of an accelerant but breathed in only the choking smell of charred wood. I picked up a short, blackened plank and carefully probed the debris, searching for the source of the blaze.

The insurer was right to be suspicious. This was the third fire within the last eight months at properties owned by real estate developer Sean McFarland and insured by SEPA Financial.

I had progressed through two-thirds of the site when I came across a mass of debris taller than my five-nine frame. I searched the area with my flashlight, looking for a pathway through, but couldn't find any. Thick beams, likely a portion of the collapsed roof, blocked my progress. I examined the pile, found a foothold, and climbed up. As I did, the beams collapsed under me.

I landed on my back. Pain shot through my leg. It was lodged, up to my calf, in a gap that had opened up. I worked to shift the more massive planks and tossed aside smaller chunks of wood. Finally, I cleared away enough debris to free my leg. I wiggled my foot to check for broken bones. None. The cuff of my jeans was torn, caked in soot and wet with blood. I bent down to point my flashlight into the gap. I saw remnants of burnt wood and a mass of ashes. Barely visible among the rubble was what looked like a charred piece of barbecue. I leaned in closer. It was a finger. I gently brushed aside a layer of ashes surrounding it. Two, three, four more bony fingers. I was looking at the remains of a human hand.

CHAPTER TWO

Back in my car, I called Ian, one of my contacts in the Fire Marshal's office. "I'm at the warehouse site."

"Andrea, we told you to wait until tomorrow. SEPA Financial's investigator or not."

"You should be thanking me. I'm giving you a chance to save face."

"Fresh from one arson course, and now you're a fire expert."

"Suit yourself. I can hang up now, and you can hear about it on the news."

"Don't be a smart ass." Ian exhaled. "Okay, hit me."

"The fire was fatal. You'll find a body buried under the rubble. I made it easy for you. I brushed away the soot from what's left of the victim's hand, and I was as careful as an archaeologist."

Back at my South Philly home, I took a hot shower, applied an antiseptic to my calf, and wrapped it in a clean bandage. The cut wasn't deep enough to require stitches. Over the years, I learned first aid and kept a well-stocked medicine cabinet. It saved trips to the doc or the emergency room. I pulled on a warm robe, made a bracing cup of strong black tea, took Tylenol for the pain in my leg, and curled up on my sofa.

I was dozing off when my phone rang.

"We need to talk." It was Tom. "Now. I'm at the fire scene." Tom was a Philadelphia Homicide Detective. We grew up together when his parents became my foster parents and we remain close. Tom's parents, the Volpes, took me under their wing when my life imploded at a young age. They're the only family I have, that is, besides my late mother's sister, Aunt Roseanne. She's a whole different story.

I gulped down the remains of my tea, dressed, pulled my still damp hair back into a ponytail to keep the pesky waves under control, and drove my Subaru back to the site.

Police, Fire Marshal, and medical examiner vehicles were parked near an ambulance when I arrived. I spotted Tom talking to one of the crime scene guys and started walking toward them, but someone grabbed my arm and stopped me.

Detective Tyrone Lewis, wide enough to be a pro lineman, moved in front of me. He had a deep aversion to PIs. "What the hell are you doing here, Fabiano? You're not allowed at a crime scene."

"Nice to see you too, detective. I was asked to come by Detective Volpe."

Lewis glared at me.

"It's alright, Ty," Tom, tall, slim, dressed in a finely tailored dark suit, called out as he walked toward me.

On the job, Tom's face was stern, almost immobile. But as soon as Lewis left, Tom greeted me with a smile. His dark eyes, as black as his hair, sparkled, and a hint of his kind and generous spirit shined through, at least to me. But only for a moment.

He took me aside, out of earshot of the others. "Keep clear of Lewis. Now give it to me straight. Why did you disobey the Fire Marshal and slip into the warehouse tonight?"

"I do have a right to be here, Tom." I told him about SEPA Financial's concern that this was the third fire at McFarland properties. "The company wants to know if there's any indication that this fire was deliberately set. Besides, if you remember, I was the one who reported finding the hand."

"Fair enough, but we won't know for certain how the fire started until the Fire Marshal completes the investigation."

"First impressions?"

"It appears to be accidental," he said.

"No signs of an accelerant?"

Tom shook his head. "At this point, it looks like the fire

started in a trash barrel. The night was cold. The victim could be a homeless guy who lit a fire to stay warm. We didn't find any ID."

"How did the victim get inside? Wasn't the place locked?" I asked.

"Can't answer that one, not yet anyway. Now I need to get back to work," Tom said.

"Before you go, I have a request. I'd like to have a look at the body."

"Why?"

"Call it professional curiosity. I only saw a hand."

Tom exhaled. "Okay. Professional courtesy this time, but don't push it. Do I have to remind you not to get involved in my investigation?"

"I'd like to remind you that I have a job to do, too," I said.

"We both know our jobs. You stick to the fire investigation, and I'll handle the victim."

"Got it." I figured I'd learn more about the victim anyway while I investigated the fire. But I kept that to myself.

Tom walked me over to the ambulance. The victim, in a body bag, was being placed on a gurney. "Open it up again," he told the two attendants.

I looked at the deformed corpse, part charred flesh, part skeleton. "Nasty way to go," I said as I took a closer look at what looked like a tattoo on the little flesh that remained on the victim's arm. It was circular, with curved lines woven through the circle like a Celtic motif. I took a photo with my cell. I couldn't be sure that Tom would ever let me see the crime scene photos.

"Tom, I didn't notice any surveillance cameras around here," I said.

"Closest is down by the pizza place. We're getting it checked out now."

"Were there any at the entrances to the warehouse or maybe inside?"

"If there were, they've been destroyed."

"Let me know if your investigators find any fragments that might be a security camera."

"There won't be any images even if we do."

"But if McFarland failed to secure his property, it would impact his claim," I pointed out.

"I'll let you know if we learn anything that might help you. And I expect you to let me know if you find anything that connects with my inquiry. Professional courtesy works both ways."

I agreed, thanked him, and walked to my car. I figured I had what I was going to get from him. I didn't want to push it. Cops, like corporate suits and street gangs, protect their turf.

CHAPTER THREE

In my car, I called Nate Warner. He answered on the second ring. "What do you have for me?"

"The firefighters found no trace of an accelerant, and neither did I. But so far, there's nothing official on the cause." Then, I told him about the body.

"How did someone get in?"

"We don't know yet." I told him about the fire starting in a barrel, most likely by the victim. "What caused those earlier fires?" I asked.

"The Fire Marshal's reports found that paint and varnish cans caused the fire at the apartment building, and an electrical spark started the fire at the industrial building near the airport. Both were ruled accidental," Nate said.

"I'll check if the warehouse was locked or if McFarland had security cameras installed. Doesn't his policy require him to protect the site?"

"It does, but you need to check the exact wording with Jim Keenan." Keenan was SEPA Financial's corporate counsel.

"I'll talk to him tomorrow, and then I'll go see McFarland." There was a long pause. "Nate, you still there?"

"Legally, Green Street Ventures LLC is the owner of the warehouse. The attorney of record is Arthur Newman."

"But McFarland would have formed the LLC as he does for all his developments."

"Correct. I'm not telling you not to talk to McFarland, but I'm asking you to talk to Keenan and Newman first."

"Aye, Aye, Chief. Any other marching orders, sir?"

"No joking around. Get to work."

Nate didn't get sarcasm. But it was the only weapon I had to hurl at him if I didn't want to use my fists, which is what I often felt like doing. The man liked to put on the pressure, and I always came through, but he never once thought I delivered fast enough. Even though I busted my butt to earn every penny of my retainer.

It was late, and I was tired, but I drove to my office. Nate had that effect on me. I could hear his voice in my head telling me to get to work.

The office of Andrea Fabiano Investigations is in a mid-rise near Twenty-Second and Chestnut before the bridge over the Schuylkill crosses into University City. In this western tip of Center City, the rents are more affordable than in the glossy office towers near City Hall.

At my desk, I called Jim Keenan's office and left a message requesting a meeting the next day. Then I began my research on Sean McFarland, checking various subscriber databases essential for my work.

Over his years in business, McFarland built and managed multiple properties, each through separate limited liability corporations. I created an inventory of his properties, saved it to a new file folder that I started for the investigation, and then sent the list to my cell to have it handy.

His holdings included three industrial properties near the airport, six mid-rise office buildings, and apartment complexes located in various city neighborhoods. He had recently completed a luxury high-rise condominium along the Delaware River. Several of his properties were undergoing renovations, including the two sites where the earlier fires occurred. Last year he established a mortgage brokerage firm called Mid-City Mortgage, which operated out of McFarland's offices in Center City.

Next, I checked into Arthur Newman, McFarland's attorney. I always like to learn as much as I can before I interview someone, especially an attorney. Newman graduated from Temple University law school and specialized in corporate law. He'd been in solo practice for fifteen years. From what I could learn so far, McFarland seemed to be his principal client. I left a message on Newman's office phone requesting time on his calendar.

By now the pain in my leg had ramped up, so I left for home. As I drove toward South Philly, I considered Newman's career. Fifteen years in practice and I could find only one major client? "Definitely something to take a closer look at," I said to Bella, my faithful Subaru, as we drove along Broad Street.

CHAPTER FOUR

James Keenan, SEPA Financial's corporate attorney, called the next morning while I was at home finishing my second cup of coffee. He agreed to see me at nine a.m. in his office on the 30th floor. Minutes before my appointment, I stood near the elevator bank and started to sweat. The idea of being trapped in a sealed metal box for a ride to the 30th floor made my heart pump as though I'd just finished running a marathon. I decided to use the stairs, telling myself I needed the exercise. But by the 20th floor, my pace slowed to a crawl and my injured leg ached. I didn't expect my energy to slack off in my thirties despite only four hours' sleep. I steeled myself, chewed a piece of gum to ease any nausea, and rode the elevator for the last ten floors.

During my time working for Nate, I had been in only two or three meetings with Keenan, so I wasn't sure how he would react to a fatal fire at an insured site. I took the gum out of my mouth and went up to his secretary's desk to introduce myself.

"Morning. Go right in. Jim is expecting you," she said, smiling.

"Nate's filled me in on what you're working on." Keenan gestured for me to sit in one of his client chairs. Keenan looked to be in his forties, tall, his hair flecked with gray. He wore an impeccably tailored navy suit, which must have set him back at least a thousand.

"What can I do to help?" he asked.

I reached in my back pocket for my cell phone, pulled up my list of McFarland properties, and handed it over to Keenan. "I'd like you to confirm which of these properties, besides the warehouse, SEPA Financial insures."

"I'll check our records. It'll take a few minutes."

While he was occupied, I scanned his office to see what

I could learn. His desk, carved mahogany, and a large green granite pen set looked like objects I'd seen in museums. Classy and *molto* expensive. His impressive Ivy League degrees, framed in wood to match his desk, hung on a nearby wall. The credenza behind his desk displayed photos of him with two teenage daughters, one a female carbon copy of her dad. Another photo showed him and several buddies wearing outdoor vests, caps, and holding fishing rods. There were no photos of his wife.

"We insure his mid-rise apartment building in Old City." His baritone voice jolted me back to the interview. "The office building in University City. And, of course, the warehouse and the two properties that suffered the earlier fire damage." He handed back my phone.

"All these others are viable business properties. Why insure an empty warehouse?" I asked. "It's a ripe target for vandalism."

"Nate and I were not at all pleased when we learned about that decision, especially when the property wasn't scheduled for development any time soon. At least we did protect ourselves. I reread the policy before you arrived, and it requires the warehouse to be properly secured against break-ins and to have at least two surveillance cameras in operating order," he said.

"But since the fire victim gained access, it doesn't look like the place was all that secure," I said. "And, so far, I've found no evidence of any cameras at the site, but I'm still looking into it. Tell me who approved the policy?"

"The senior executive in charge told me the person responsible is no longer employed here."

"Do you know his or her name?"

"I can get that for you if you think it's important."

"I do. Mr. Keenan ..."

"Jim." He smiled.

"Jim, you know I'm on retainer. I get paid the same no matter what work I do for you. So, I'm not trying to boost my income.

But I don't understand why SEPA Financial doesn't want me looking into those previous fires. All three could be connected."

"I would tend to agree with you. But for now, our management committee wants us to concentrate on this fire. In this instance, someone died." Keenan stood up.

"How well do you know Sean McFarland?"

"We met once or twice at those annual charity galas. But that's about it. I know he's been highly successful with his real estate ventures. When can we expect the Fire Marshal's report?"

"In the next week or two at the earliest. I'll keep you posted when I know anything definite."

He walked me to the door. When we shook hands, he looked me in the eyes. The intensity of his blue stare felt electric, and I caught my breath. I was a sucker for blue eyes. The man certainly had charisma and sex appeal. Shaking hands with Nate never felt like this.

As I walked back to my office, I phoned Tom. "I have another question."

"Make it quick."

"I need to know as soon as possible if any security equipment was found among the debris the investigators carted away."

"I'll call you back."

That was the fastest conversation I'd ever had with Tom. I could tell he was pissed. But I wasn't sure whether it was with me or his boss pressing him for quick results.

CHAPTER FIVE

"I don't understand why you couldn't wait until the Fire Marshal's office releases its report." Arthur Newman, McFarland's attorney, had a gruff voice to match his manner.

His digs lacked the classic style of Jim Keenan's office, but like Keenan, he, too, had an appetite for expensive furniture. His Italian-designed chrome desk, leather chairs, and sofa spoke of modern tastes and deep pockets.

"I thought you might be concerned about a fatal fire at your client's property."

"Did Keenan send you here?"

"He knows I've come to talk with you."

"You can tell Keenan that I'll talk to him once we have an official ruling."

"You're not at all concerned that this is the third fire at a McFarland property this year."

"I thought you said you were looking into the warehouse fire. The earlier fires have nothing to do with this."

"Is it possible someone might have a grudge against Sean McFarland and may not be above sabotaging his business?"

"Where did you get that far-fetched idea?"

"I like to be thorough and consider all options."

"You need to do your homework. There was no indication of foul play in those earlier fires, and I'm sure the warehouse fire will prove to be accidental as well."

"You and Mr. McFarland should consider improving the safety and security measures at all his properties. Someone managed to get inside the warehouse, spend the night, and end up dead. I'd say that shows a lack of proper security on your client's part."

"That's your opinion. We'll wait to hear what the Fire

Marshal has to say." He stood up. "Now I do have another appointment."

"Another client?" I asked.

"You know better than to ask that."

"You do seem to do the bulk of your legal work for Sean McFarland."

"He's a valuable client, but the rest of my practice is none of your business."

I walked out, wondering why Newman was so quick to dismiss the idea of foul play if, as he claimed, he was looking out for the interests of his valuable client.

When I got out to the street, my cell phone notified me of a new text. It was from Keenan. "Newman called me to complain. He doesn't want you talking to McFarland."

Newman got to Keenan less than five minutes after I left his office.

CHAPTER SIX

My cell phone rang as I was driving back to my office. Tom's name popped up on the caller ID.

"I've arranged for you to have a look at the forensics. You'll need to go over now."

"Thanks, on my way. Oh, Tom, did you get anything from the surveillance camera down the street near the pizza shop?"

"Nothing. It wasn't working. And Andrea, remember, your job is the fire, not the victim."

"Right." Tom was getting to be a pest, warning me not to cross the line every time we talked.

At the lab, an assistant brought me into a room where the debris from the fire scene was spread out on a table. I put on a pair of latex gloves and began examining a blackened shard of glass.

"That's what's left of a whiskey bottle," the assistant explained. "It was found beside the victim. Cheap stuff. Before you ask, it wasn't used as a Molotov cocktail."

"Have you come across anything that might be a camera lens?"

"None of the glass here is the type from a camera. It's mostly from the windows."

Windows. "Do you have any idea where the windows were located?"

The lab assistant showed me an old photo of the warehouse. The windows were just below the roof. No way could the victim have gotten in that way. The only options were the doors, which should have been locked.

We moved on to an array of charred metal scraps. "These are hinges from the doors." Then he pointed to various pieces of plastic. "Melted pieces of soda bottles and the remnants of a flashlight. No fingerprints."

"Anything that might be the body of a surveillance camera?"

"Nothing like that. But this might be of interest." He pointed to a heavy chain, blackened by the flames, which lay coiled on the table.

"This was found in the alley at the rear of the building. It was hooked around the handle of the back door."

"You think the back door was padlocked?"

"If it was, then the victim could have been trapped," he said.

"Caught between the fire in front of him and a locked door behind him," I said.

"That's about it," the attendant said.

I tried to get the attendant to give me a hint about what the Fire Marshal's report would say, but no luck. The guy had integrity.

I left, considering McFarland's bad luck with fires. It was hard not to consider arson. Knowing Nate, he had similar suspicions but needed to obey the company directive to only investigate the warehouse fire. No one died in the previous fires, and besides, SEPA Financial had already paid out the claims.

But now that a man had been killed, I needed to determine if McFarland had kept his commitment to properly secure the warehouse, other than padlocking the back door.

I was at my desk when Russ Hanley phoned.

"I thought we were meeting for drinks?" he said.

Russ was a newspaper reporter and a jazz pianist who I've dated off and on. Lately, it was more on than off. I'd completely forgot that we agreed to meet at six, and it was six-thirty.

"I'll be there ASAP." I changed into a clean turtleneck and a black jacket that I kept at the office for emergencies. I combed my hair and swiped blusher across my cheeks, added lip gloss, and then walked to Russ's favorite bar on 18th Street where he immersed himself in the atmosphere of the Jazz Age he idolized. I figured if he lived back then he'd have gotten over his love affair with the 1920s.

I spotted Russ's mop of black hair as soon as I entered the downstairs bar. He was at a table sipping an Old Fashioned. He stood, his blue eyes at their most appealing in the candlelit room and gave me a peck on the check. "What are you having?"

"Gin and tonic, with extra tonic."

Russ signaled the bartender, who couldn't mask his disappointment that I wasn't ordering one of their unique cocktails, such as Cat-o-Nine Tails, Day of Atonement, or Sagittarius Rising. The truth was I found the smell of hard liquor a turnoff, even when fancied up in exotic drinks. Like most Italians, I savored red wine with my meal. Especially Chianti from Abruzzo, the province of my ancestors. It was Russ who liked to recapture the ambiance of a speakeasy. At least for a drink or two. The place was too pricey for anything more.

"I have good news." Russ looked at me with a broad smile, like a kid who'd brought home a good report card.

"A promotion?"

"With the state of the newspaper industry? I'm lucky I still have a job." He leaned in toward me. "We have a new bass just in time for our gig in Baltimore. And the guy is a great fit."

Russ and his pal, Gary, a guitarist, had trouble keeping a bass player to fill out their trio.

"You should come down to hear us. It's the weekend after next."

"I'm up to my eyeballs in work. This might not be a good time." The bartender brought my drink. I took a sip and added more tonic.

"So, what's keeping you at the office?" Russ said.

I smiled and lifted my glass in a toast. "To client confidentiality."

"And protected sources." He sipped his cocktail and shook his head. "I guess we'll always be at an impasse."

That pretty much described our relationship, both professional and personal.

CHAPTER SEVEN

The following week, the Fire Marshal's office released its report on the warehouse, concluding that the fire was accidental. As Tom had predicted, the fire started in a trash barrel where the victim likely built a bonfire to keep warm. The flames, however, were too close to a side wall, constructed entirely of wood. When the wall caught fire, flames spread throughout the entire building within minutes. The victim would have had little time to escape, especially if he were in an alcohol-induced sleep. There was no definitive answer on how the victim gained access to the warehouse, but the report did conclude that the back entrance had been padlocked.

In my email to Nate Warner and Jim Keenan, I provided a summary of the Fire Marshal's conclusions, attached the full report, and recommended that I interview McFarland to check out what security measures had been in place at the warehouse.

I received an email back from Keenan telling me to hold off interviewing McFarland. Again. But I didn't have time to argue. I was due at the Criminal Justice Center at ten to testify in a chop shop scam that I had worked on for another client.

I arrived on time but spent the next few hours warming a bench in the hall. Four hours passed before I was called to the stand. When I was finally released from the stuffy, overheated courtroom, I was nearly comatose.

Outside, I walked along Filbert Street, the cool air felt as refreshing on my face as the Atlantic Ocean breezes at the Jersey Shore. Besides being exhausted, my mouth was so dry my lips seemed glued together. The water in the courtroom had smelled and tasted of chlorine and left a sour taste in my mouth.

At the first coffee bar I came to, I bought their tallest cup of hot chocolate with extra whipped cream. I gulped down several mouthfuls and plopped myself into a cushy chair to savor the sinfully rich drink, not caring that it would cost me twenty minutes on the elliptical.

As I indulged, I caught up with my social media, emails, and text messages that I couldn't check while a captive of the court. Nothing seemed urgent. I could grab dinner and then respond. Then I listened to my voicemail. I had four messages from Nate Warner. "Andrea, I need to talk with you. Call me back. It's related to McFarland's business." Then in his following message, "Come see me as soon as you get this." His voice began to show frustration in his third message. "I don't know where you've been all this time. Or why you're not answering your phone. It's bad for business. Call me." In his last call, Nate sounded both tense and angry. "Come see me first thing in the morning. I can't discuss this over the phone." I'd texted Nate the day before, reminding him of my court appearance. Apparently, he'd forgotten.

SEPA Financial's offices were closed by now, but I tried reaching Nate anyway. He often worked until seven. His extension went directly to voicemail, and I left a message. Next, I tried his cell, but he didn't pick up.

I bought a small pizza and returned to my office. As I ate, I responded to my other message, paid bills, and reviewed my accounts. Several clients were late paying me, so I sent them friendly but firm reminders. My bank account would thank me.

I stood up and walked to the window. Something was nagging at me, but I hadn't had time all day to clear my mind and think what it was. I paced around the office, then went to my desk and looked over the Fire Marshal's report once again. That's when it struck me.

I reached for my phone and called Tom.

"I think your victim was murdered."

"Andy, I don't have time to talk to someone who promised to stay out of my investigation."

Tom only called me Andy when he was angry. He knew I hated the name my classmates taunted me with as a child. They thought Andrea was a snooty name. They didn't get it, even though I told them my mother named me after my grandfather. They thought that was funny too.

"I'll just leave you with this thought. When I found the body, the victim was nowhere near any wall. So why light a bonfire in a barrel near the wall and then sleep far away from it if he wanted to keep warm?"

"Don't get involved." Tom hung up.

My cell rang. It was Russ.

"I know I'm not late since we had no plans to meet," I said.

"I'm checking to see if you changed your mind and want to come to Baltimore with me to hear us play."

I had completely forgotten he'd asked. "I'd love to but I'm tied up here with a case." Truth was, I didn't want to go. I preferred to keep our relationship low-key. Going away with him felt like taking another step. A step I wasn't ready for.

CHAPTER EIGHT

At eight-thirty the following morning, I signed in at SEPA Financial's security desk, reached for a Tums to hold off any nausea, and took the elevator to Nate's office on the 20th floor. He usually arrived at eight, but I wanted to give him time to have his bowl of shredded wheat with almond milk before I arrived. For some strange reason, eating cereal that tasted like tree bark made him less irascible.

"I'm afraid he isn't in yet," Nate's assistant Diana said. "I don't have you on his calendar."

"He called late yesterday and asked me to come in."

"Have a seat. He should be here shortly."

While I waited, Diana fielded calls from people wanting to speak with Nate. "I'll leave him your message," she told one caller after another. "I'm so sorry. He seems to be running late," she told others. I watched her usually smiling face grow tenser as a half-hour passed and Nate still didn't show.

Diana made several phone calls, and when she put the phone down, she was frowning. "He's not answering his home phone or his cell. I don't understand. He had a meeting at nine with the chairman. He'd never miss that."

"Did you try his wife?"

She nodded. "I called her at work, but she's not there, and she isn't answering her cell or text messages."

I stood up. "Let me know when we can reschedule." I walked out of her office and then went back. "I'd like to have Mrs. Warner's cell number."

Diana quickly jotted it down and handed it to me as her phone lines began ringing again.

Diana was right. Nate was meticulous about his schedule.

He would never blow off a meeting with his company chairman. He seemed almost reverential toward the company executives. Sitting in my car, I replayed his voicemails. The more I listened, the more tense his voice sounded. He was insistent that I come to his office first thing today. He was clear that he didn't want to discuss whatever it was on the phone. So why wasn't he in his office?

Throughout the day, while I tried to concentrate on working the warehouse case, I contacted Diana, called Nate's cell and home phone, and texted him. No sign of Nate. I tried to reach his wife on her cell but left messages and texts when she didn't respond. As the hours passed, I knew something was wrong. I even called around to area hospitals in case Nate had been in an auto accident. But I learned nothing.

I kept occupied by continuing my research on Sean McFarland. I may have been warned to stay away from him, but no one said I couldn't take a closer look at the man. I don't like being told to back away from talking to a crucial source. Besides, McFarland's attorney, Arthur Newman, seemed too slick and arrogant to trust. God bless databases.

I had already learned a bit about McFarland's business, so I concentrated on building a clearer picture of the man. He was born and raised in Northeast Philly. He was forty-three, a graduate of Penn State. He lived in Chestnut Hill, one of the city's wealthy neighborhoods, where Germantown Avenue, its main street, was still paved with old-world Belgian Blocks. McFarland had started his real estate firm right out of college, and it grew, both in size and revenue, over the years. He and his wife divorced a little over a year ago.

An excellent place to find out about a developer's reputation is through court records. Lawsuits are an occupational hazard for developers and builders. In comparison to others in his industry, McFarland had a relatively clean record. In the early years of his business, he hadn't been sued at all. In the last few years, however, two lawsuits were filed against him for negligence. Those cases were settled out of court with no records of the outcomes. I made a note of the parties involved. Newman had represented McFarland, so I didn't expect to get anything out of him, but maybe I could pry something loose from the plaintiffs.

Like other developers, McFarland conducted business and secured investors for his developments through limited liability corporations, LLCs, established for each of his projects. The LLCs included Green Street Ventures, which owned the warehouse, Spring Garden Investments, Riverfront Enterprises, and Logan Properties. Arthur Newman was the attorney of record for all four.

I called my contacts in the Philadelphia real estate industry to find out what they knew about McFarland. A few didn't want to talk, and I left voicemail messages asking others to call me back.

I brewed a fresh pot of dark roast and tried again to reach Nate Warner on his cell. I got his voicemail again and left another message. When I phoned Diana, his assistant, I could tell she was forcing back tears. "He's not been in, and his wife doesn't know where he is."

Nate had to be in trouble, or he would have contacted his family and his office by now. "Has anyone contacted the police?"

"His wife said she did."

I hung up, ready to head off and look for Nate without any idea of where he could be. My phone rang. One of my real estate contacts was returning my call.

"So, Andrea, what do you want to know?"

"What can you tell me about Sean McFarland? Ever work with him?"

"Our paths have crossed. I know him through our local real estate association. Sean worked hard to get where he is. He didn't come from money."

"Then you admire him?"

"I admire his smarts and his success. He invests in midrise office buildings and apartments, renovates them, and then manages them. He was also smart enough to develop new apartment complexes in up-and-coming neighborhoods close to Center City. But, if you ask me, he bit off more than he could chew with his obsession to build luxury condos."

"Would that be the Riverfront project?"

"Right. Sean thinks he can compete with the major developers in the city. But he lacks the chops for that huge an undertaking. It would be enough of a challenge to build and manage luxury condos, but Sean had the chutzpah to open a rooftop supper club. He doesn't know shit about running a venue like that. The club's got to be a huge financial drain. And rumor is he can't get funding for the second tower he had planned."

"You think he's in financial difficulties?"

"Don't get me wrong. The majority of his properties are money makers. But at this point, he seems overextended. But you didn't hear that from me. Maybe he can ride this out. But I also heard he's been through a rough divorce. That must have cost him."

I placed a second call to a former client, and this time she answered and had time to talk.

"McFarland's ego is bigger than his projects. He wasn't satisfied being a second-tier developer. He wanted to make a big splash. Build a luxury condo complex. Show he could compete with the best. For years, he failed to get financing for the condos on the waterfront. Then two years ago, he had the funds to move ahead with one of two towers. Those condos are on the market now."

"So I hear. Do you know where McFarland got his financing?"

"It wasn't from any of the big banks. They'd want proof that McFarland had signed sales contracts for most of the units. And from what I know, only about a third of the units are under contract since the opening."

"Not good?"

"Let's put it this way. He'll need to sell a lot more for the project to be viable. And if they don't sell, he can give up his dream of a second tower."

I looked at the time. It was nearly six. "Thanks. I appreciate your help."

We promised to meet for lunch soon and hung up. Immediately, I called Nate's home phone. Its voicemail was full. His wife, Helena, was still not answering her cell. So once again, I asked her to call me.

I left my office and drove to the SEPA Financial building to see if I could get a line on what might have happened. I went into the company garage to see if Nate's car was still there. The garage attendant recognized me. "Still driving that old Subaru."

"Too attached to dear Bella to replace her." I asked him to check on Nate's car.

He came back shaking his head. "The car's gone."

"Can I have a look at the surveillance tapes?"

"Sorry, no can do. You'll have to talk to the head of security. We don't have access down here."

Seeing the head of security would have to wait until the SEPA Financial offices reopened the next morning. I drove home. I took a hot shower then fixed myself a frittata with leftover sautéed zucchini and onions and washed it down with a glass of Chianti. Again, I tried to reach Helena. Still, no one picked up.

After I cleaned up the kitchen, I went into the living room, relaxed on my comfy sofa, and pulled a tattered copy of Sherlock Holmes short stories from my bookshelf. My mind, though, kept drifting again and again to Nate. Did he want to talk about something related to the warehouse fire? He said McFarland's business. Something he considered too risky to discuss over the phone? And something worrisome enough to account for the tension that kept building in his voice with each phone message.

I was jolted awake when I heard my phone ringing. I was still on my sofa, the book opened flat on my stomach. I sat up and reached for my cell on the coffee table. It was after midnight and the caller was Helena Warner.

"Andrea? This is Helena, Nate's wife. Sorry to call so late."

"No worries. I've been waiting to hear from you. Is everything alright?" I knew from her voice it wasn't.

She let out a sob. "My husband is missing. My friends and I have been out searching for him. We've called the police in, but nothing so far."

She broke down, and I let her get it out of her system. I expressed my sympathy and concern but didn't mention Nate's phone messages. I figured she had enough to worry about.

"Andrea, I don't think he ever made it home after work. You see, I was in D.C. for business. Just overnight. When I landed back in Philly this morning, I listened to the messages Diana left me telling me that Nate didn't show up for work." She paused. "When I got home, I saw he hadn't eaten the dinner I'd left for him the night before, and he hadn't slept in our bed. I called my mother. Our boys were spending the night with her while I was out of town. Neither she nor the boys heard from him either."

"When was the last time you spoke to Nate?"

"He called me from his office around six to tell me he was heading home. I had a business dinner to attend. I told him I'd be back in my room too late to call him. So, I told him I loved him and wished him good night. I should have called him again."

"Helena, we don't know yet what's happened, so don't go blaming yourself."

"I want you to look for him," she said.

"But you said the police are already on the job."

"They have so many crimes to deal with every day. One missing person isn't a priority."

I couldn't argue with that. "Why me?"

"Nate trusted you. He told me you were the best, and I want the best for my husband. I can pay your fee."

I was speechless. Nate had high praise for me? The same person who kept riding me for not getting results fast enough.

"Helena, let me see what I can find out, then we'll talk again. Don't worry about a fee right now." I couldn't believe I said that. I was giving tightwad Nate a free ride.

When I hung up, I phoned missing persons and reached the Philadelphia detective assigned to the case. Luckily, it was someone I had worked with before.

"He was last seen leaving his office building," she said. "A surveillance camera picked up his car, a blue Toyota Camry, leaving the company garage ten minutes before seven, and he was driving. After that, nada. So far, we've checked accidents, hospitals, and the morgue. No sign of him or his car. You said you worked with him. What can you tell me about him? Could he be a runner?"

"Not the Nate Warner I know. He has the strongest sense of responsibility of anyone I ever met. No way would he run out on his family or his job."

Again, I kept Nate's phone messages to myself. I had a deep aversion to giving too much information to cops. It usually came back to bite me in the ass. Besides, my instinct told me Nate's disappearance was somehow linked to what he wanted to talk to me about. I was clueless about what connection might exist between McFarland and Nate's disappearance, but I needed to find out. Especially when I thought about the charred corpse in the warehouse.

CHAPTER NINE

My first stop the next day was the SEPA Financial security office on the ground floor to look at the video from the garage cameras. "That's Nate's car, and he's driving, but can't tell if anyone else is in the car," the head of security said, pointing to the image on the screen.

I thanked him and left for Keenan's office. I ate two Tums this time before I got into the elevator. It helped my stomach, but not my dizziness. When I got out on the 30th floor, I swayed down the hall like my Uncle Dom when he was drunk.

Jim Keenan was at his secretary's desk when I entered his office. "Please come right on through and tell me what you've learned," he said.

I related my conversations with Helena Warner and the police and what I viewed on the security video. "Helena talked to Nate by phone at about six p.m., and his car left the garage a little before seven. After that, nothing."

"Maybe he was in an accident."

I shook my head. "He'd be in a hospital by now. And he's not."

"Nate's a good man. One of our best. We want to do right by him," Keenan said. "Can you look into this for us?"

My first instinct was to tell him that Helena was already a client. She did offer to pay me. I could revisit my too-quick refusal and ask for a fee. With SEPA Financial, I would only get my retainer.

"I know the police are involved, but that doesn't mean we can't have you looking for Nate as well. You know him better than they do," Keenan said, noticing my hesitation.

I needed to search Nate's office, and Keenan had the authority to let me do the snooping crucial to an investigation.

"I'm in," I said. "I want to talk to Nate's staff and have a look at his office. I suggest you call and let his assistant, Diana, know I'm coming."

Keenan agreed and went to open his office door. "I want you to concentrate on Nate. We'll be able to wrap up the warehouse claim now that we know it wasn't arson."

"You don't want me to find out if McFarland secured the property?"

"Leave that to me."

"By the way, did you get any information on the person who approved the warehouse insurance policy?"

"She married and moved to California."

I decided to put that lead on the back burner. It didn't seem worth my time to track down a person who might not have all that much to tell. I thanked Keenan and headed for Nate's office.

I interviewed Nate's staff, but none reported any unusual problems with their boss or any unusual behavior from Nate. Still, I doubted they would complain to me about their boss. Only Diana hesitated when I asked whether Nate seemed worried or concerned about anything.

"He was always intense when it came to his work," she said.

Intense was one way to put it. Hyper pain in the ass would be more accurate. "But?"

"I don't know. The last few days, he'd close his office door and ask me to hold his calls. He'd be in there, alone, for several hours."

"Was that unusual?"

"Absolutely. Nate always maintained an open-door policy for his staff during office hours. He'd used the time before or after regular hours to do his own work."

"Any idea what he might have been working on?"

"None. I can tell you this, though. When Nate reopened his door the day before he disappeared, his face was flushed red, and he was cursing. He never cursed around me." She considered this for a moment. "He was angry, which was not at all like him."

Diana gave me Nate's keys, security codes, and passwords, and I went into his office and closed the door. I searched his desk, his computer files, paper files, and emails. I inspected his bookshelves and a locked credenza under the window. Nothing. I sat down at his desk again and reread his files on the warehouse fire but learned nothing I didn't already know. There wasn't any clue as to what had prompted Nate to phone me. I rechecked everything, concentrating on documents and calendar notations created in the days leading up to his disappearance.

I found two computer folders created in the last week. One was titled RFLLC and the other Mid-City. I clicked on each one. Pop-up messages informed me both were no longer in the system. Had they been deleted? Or had Nate transferred them to a flash drive? I searched his desk, file cabinets, and credenza a second time. No signs of a flash drive or an external hard drive. Mid-City wasn't an unusual name for a business. But I remembered that McFarland had established a mortgage brokerage named Mid-City. And his waterfront condo project was developed through Riverfront Enterprises LLC. But why would Nate be interested in McFarland projects that, as far as I knew, SEPA Financial was not involved with?

I thanked Diana and left. I chewed another Tums, hit the elevator call button, and kept my attention on my yoga breathing until I was released into the lobby. My therapist called it claustrophobia. I say I don't like being confined.

I drove along Lincoln Drive to Nate's home in the West Mount Airy section of the city, one of the city's successfully integrated neighborhoods.

I knew Helena only from her photos displayed in Nate's office. In them, she appeared smiling, slim, with a pixie haircut, looking younger than a woman in her forties. But the Helena who opened her front door looked like she'd aged several years. She had swatches of deep purple under her eyes, and her face was blotched in red, probably rosacea brought on by stress.

I explained that SEPA Financial also wanted me to investigate her husband's disappearance, so she didn't have to worry about a fee. "If I can take a look at his office, it may help."

"It's down the hall." We walked through the living room, the walls painted a light, cheery yellow and the sofa and chairs, soft and inviting, in fabrics chosen to withstand abuse by two active sons.

Helena opened the office door. "Can I get you anything? Coffee maybe?"

"Thanks, no. I'll be as quick as possible. I don't want to intrude at a time like this."

"Take as long as you need. The most important thing is for you to find my husband. I'll be in the kitchen if you need me."

Nate's home office was as neat and organized as his SEPA Financial office, making my work fast and easy but not very enlightening. His computer and paper files contained household accounts, family medical records, and emails to friends and family. I learned that he volunteered as a math tutor at a program in West Philly for at-risk youth. He had a paid membership at a local gym. And the family had plans to travel to Disney World in the spring. Nothing work-related. No files on either Mid-City or RFLLC. I checked an external hard drive. It contained personal tax and financial records that showed he and his wife were living well within their substantial income. The missing files from the office weren't here.

I found Helena sitting at the kitchen table, crying.

"Where are your boys?"

"They're still staying with my mother." She mopped her tears with a tissue. "I didn't want to upset them any more than they are already."

"Anyone staying with you?"

"I need to be alone."

"You might think about having a relative or friend over. You need support, too."

She smiled. "Tomorrow, if we don't hear anything."

"Nothing from the police?" I asked.

"I called earlier, and they had nothing new."

I sat down across from her. "Did Nate seem concerned about anything recently? Anything pressing on his mind related to work?"

"I don't think so. He seemed fine. His job could be stressful, but over the years, he learned how to handle it."

"He did unmask quite a number of fraudsters in his years at SEPA Financial. Did he receive any threats recently?"

"He would have told me if he did. He'd have wanted to make sure the children and I were safe."

"I'm afraid I have to ask." The one question I always hated asking a spouse. "Were you and Nate having any problems?"

"The police asked me the same question. Nate wouldn't run out on us if that's what you're thinking. We have our difficulties like any marriage, but we're committed to each other. And he'd never leave the children without a word. He loves them and wouldn't hurt them like that. Besides, his passport is still here."

"If you do think of anything that might help, let me know." I handed over my card and got up to leave. "By the way, I'd like to check out Nate's locker at his gym."

Helena handed me a key from a corkboard by the kitchen door, and I went over to the gym to see what I could learn. As it turned out, not much. Nate's locker was empty except for an old pair of sneakers and back issues of Prevention Magazine. Too bad that along with health tips, Nate didn't seek out advice on personal safety. I doubted very much that his disappearance was voluntary.

I headed next to the West Philly nonprofit where Nate tutored kids in math. Traffic was heavy but thinned after I passed the University of Pennsylvania campus. It was then I noticed a black Dodge Charger was still several cars behind me. It had been with me since I left the Schuylkill Expressway.

I made a quick right turn and then another right. The car was still there. I continued anyway and parked in the tiny lot behind the red brick building of the after-school program. The Dodge Charger didn't enter the lot but drove down the street. The car had dark tinted windows, so I couldn't see inside. As it picked up speed, I was able to read the first three letters of the PA license: GRM.

The director of the after-school program, a black woman in her fifties dressed in a gray pantsuit, gave me entirely new insights into Nate Warner. "He's terrific with the kids, especially the ones struggling to learn. He has so much patience with them. And they do learn."

So, Nate could be patient and understanding. Only not with a hardworking PI.

"Nate serves on our board as well. He is a real asset in fundraising. He's been able to get us grants from SEPA Financial and other companies in the city to help keep us afloat."

The idea of Nate as a philanthropist was much harder for me to swallow. To me, he was a tightwad. But then again, I was no longer an at-risk youth.

"Did he keep a desk or a file cabinet here?"

The director shook her head. "We lack the space. We only have a common room for our tutors. You're welcome to have a look."

I surveyed the room and found textbooks, a single computer containing tutoring schedules, student lists, and math exercises. No sign of Nate's computer files.

"I hope and pray you find him. I can't believe anyone would want to harm Nate of all people," she dabbed her moist eyes. "God willing, he comes back to us."

I had no idea what to say. I admired the woman's faith. But somehow, I didn't think it was God's will that we were dealing with here.

When I stopped at a red light a few blocks from the after-school program, I checked my rearview mirror. Sure enough, the black Dodge Charger was there. If Pennsylvania issued front plates as well as back, I could have read the entire registration.

I took a circuitous route through the city, changing course like an out-of-town tourist. Still, the Charger kept with me. A little too close. The driver wasn't experienced enough to avoid being spotted.

When police headquarters came into view, I snagged a nearby parking spot for Bella, then waved back to the Charger as I walked into the building. I checked in with my contact in missing persons to ask about Nate.

"Still no sign of him or his car," she told me. "We had the local police check out the couple's summer home in Avalon. No one was there, and the neighbors haven't seen Warner or anyone near the house. The family hasn't received any ransom requests. But we thought kidnapping was only a slim possibility. There's not a huge income there."

I went over to Tom's unit to say hello, but he was out on the street and not expected back for hours. When I left, I walked several blocks, scanning the streets for my tail, then made my way back to my car once I knew I was clear. I doubted any of my other open cases would attract a tail. Besides, I had picked up the Dodge Charger while checking out leads to Nate's disappearance.

At my office, I tried Tom on his personal cell. "Any ID on the warehouse victim?"

"I thought I warned you not to get involved."

I told him about Nate's disappearance and his voicemail messages to me. "The two incidents may be connected."

"If they are, the police will handle it."

"If we knew who the fire victim was, it might give us the connection. Was the Celtic tattoo any help?"

"What's this 'we' and 'us'?" Tom joked.

"Just tell me if the tattoo helped."

"It seems Celtic designs are popular, and the victim's tat isn't all that distinctive."

"What about the cause of death?"

"Still haven't heard. I'm told bodies are stacked up, and I need to wait my turn."

"If the poor man was murdered, the trail will be cold by the time you get after his killer."

"I don't think we're talking murder here. It's most likely that the death was accidental."

I hoped Tom was right. The same way I hoped Nate would be found unharmed. But I wasn't optimistic.

I picked up the pile of mail accumulating on my desk and began tossing out junk mail offering tree trimming services, hearing aids, and credit cards. Then I sorted new bills by the due dates. Busywork to keep me from thinking about Nate.

One envelope wasn't a bill or an advertising pitch. My name and address were handwritten, and I recognized the cursive from the scrawled notes he often made on my reports. It was Nate's handwriting. The envelope was postmarked the day before he went missing.

Carefully I slit open the envelope. Inside, was a single sheet of plain paper. On it was a brief note. "20R, 15L, 5R. More later. NW." A lock combination, most likely. But no indication where the lock was located.

I phoned Helena. "Do you have a safe in your home?"

"No, we don't. What's this about?"

I told her about the envelope I received from Nate.

"I have no idea what he's referring to. But obviously, you

think it's important."

"I believe Nate wanted to share some information with me and I need to find it."

CHAPTER TEN

I was at my desk, staring at Nate's cryptic note when Tom's ID popped up on my cell phone screen and I picked up on the second ring.

"We found him, Andrea," Tom said. "We're on the third floor of a parking garage on 15th street." He gave me the address. "It's not a pretty sight."

I swallowed hard before I could speak. "Nate?"

"Yes."

"On my way." When Nate disappeared, I thought that his death was always a possibility but I was surprised when tears moistened my eyes when I realized he really was gone.

When I arrive uniformed officers and a crime scene team were already at work surrounding a Toyota Camry that I recognized as Nate's. The car's trunk was open, and blood stained the ground around it.

"You'll have to leave, miss," one of the officers told me.

"Detective Volpe phoned me." I showed my PI license. I spotted Tom speaking with the medical examiner, then he looked up and saw me. "It's alright," he called out to the officer. "I want to talk with her, she may be able to identify our victim."

I slipped under the police tape and walked over to the car.

"I'm sure it's Nate. The car is registered to him, but there's no ID on the body," Tom said. "Are you ready to take a look at him."

I nodded.

"You might want to cover your nose with that scarf you have around your neck."

I did as Tom suggested, covering my nose and mouth. I didn't want to be considered a wuss and get sick at a crime scene.

Inside the trunk, the body of a white male dressed in a business suit was folded nearly in half so that his head touched his socks. Bloodstains were visible on the back of his jacket, and a thick red pool had congealed around his body.

"Bullet wounds?" I asked.

"Correct," the medical examiner said. "Two bullets to the chest."

Tom had the medical examiner turn the body over for me to see the face. Thankfully, it was intact. I nodded to Tom. "It's Nate Warner." I turned away, grateful my scarf masked my gags if not my tears.

"He's all yours," Tom said to the medical examiner. "Make this one a priority." Nate's body was placed on a gurney for the ride to the morgue.

"Wait here for a moment," Tom told me and walked over to talk to the officers and the crime scene technicians.

With Tom out of earshot, I asked the medical examiner, "Any estimate as to the time of death?"

"He's been dead at least seventy-two hours."

That made it around the time he went missing.

"And the shots were at close range?"

The medical examiner nodded. "He might have known his killer. Tell Tom I should have results tomorrow at the latest." Then he headed to the elevator.

I cupped my hands and peered through the window on the driver's side.

"Andrea, stop." Tom was standing next to me.

"I'm not touching anything. I know the drill."

"Listen, I called you in to help identify Nate. That doesn't give you carte blanche to investigate."

I stepped back. "Sorry, I was curious if the killing took place in the car. Any ideas?"

"At this point, I haven't determined where the killing occurred. Only that the body was dumped here."

"How did you find him?" I asked.

"One of the parking attendants noticed the blood on the ground, told his manager, and the manager called it in."

"Why leave Nate's body in his own car in a busy downtown garage? Did the killer want the victim to be found?" I said.

"I'd say the killer was in a hurry to get rid of the body," Tom said. "He or she removed the victim's wallet and ID but left the registration plate for us to identify. This is someone who panicked and wasn't thinking straight."

"What about surveillance cameras? Any help there?"

Tom glared at me. "What did I just say about interfering?"

"I can't help being curious. That's why I'm a good investigator." I smiled.

Tom paused. "You can help me right now. I'd like you to come with me to break the news to Mrs. Warner. I don't want her hearing about this through the media if word leaks out."

In the car on the way to the Warner home, Tom looked over at me. "This is the part of my job I never get used to. I'm about to take away the family's hope that their husband and father will be coming back to them."

I thought about the warehouse fire victim. With no ID on the poor guy, his family didn't know he was dead and would probably never know. "I think if I were the family, I'd want to know the fate of a loved one, rather than be kept in perpetual limbo."

"Perhaps you're right."

He parked in the Warner driveway and we went up the front steps to ring the bell.

CHAPTER ELEVEN

"Andrea, thank you so much for coming," Helena Warner said when I offered my condolences. She was standing with her two sons beside Nate's coffin in the Unitarian Church, greeting visitors before the funeral service.

Helena dabbed her eyes, struggling not to break down. "I know you worked so hard ... trying to find him."

I hugged her, then shook hands with her two sons, twelve and ten. The younger boy didn't try to hide the steady trickle of tears escaping from the corners of his eyes.

The truth was, I never expected I'd attend Nate Warner's funeral. Not only because he'd been a fifty-year-old dedicated vegetarian and fitness nut who I thought would outlive me, but because in the three years I worked with him, we never formed anything resembling a bond. I'm rebellious by nature, and he was a control freak about work. Still, we proved to be an effective team getting results important for both our careers. And I did admire his smarts.

The funeral director had done a great job with Nate. I almost didn't recognize him. The Nate I knew looked a bit rumpled most days, but today he was wearing a dark blue suit, a crisp white shirt, and a maroon silk tie. A single lock of hair, which typically tumbled onto his forehead, was now permanently attached to the rest of his brown hair. He would have looked almost handsome if it weren't for the gray pallor on his dead face.

Tom was leading the murder investigation, but no way would he even consider sharing anything he uncovered. I did manage to learn that the cops had no leads, no suspects, and no motive. Unlike the police, I, at least, had a theory that I intended to pursue. Nate was silenced before he could reveal whatever he had discovered related to Sean McFarland and his real estate business.

In my head, I heard Nate's usual spiel whenever we met on a case. "Andrea, I don't want to be nickeled-and-dimed with expenses. I need quick results." The guy was manic about watching out for SEPA Financial's money, as though it were his.

After the service, I stood outside, watching the mourners assemble for the drive to the cemetery.

"Andrea, I'm glad you were able to come." Jim Keenan reached out his hand. "Nate always spoke highly of you."

I shook hands, speechless once again. Keenan was now the second person to tell me Nate had good things to say about me. When he was alive, Nate never once showed me any sign of approval. Was Keenan telling me the truth, or was he trying to ingratiate himself?

"Could you come to my office tomorrow? I'd like to discuss something with you."

Ah. Keenan wanted to can me. Nate may have been a relentless taskmaster, but he did keep me on retainer. Keenan complimented me so he would seem less an ogre when he gave me the bad news. Hell, no gig lasts forever.

"I can be there at eleven, if that's convenient."

He nodded. "See you then."

I watched Keenan get into one of the limousines with the other suits from SEPA Financial. Shit. I would need to replace my retainer pronto if I wanted to stay in the black. I mentally made a note of other insurers and financial firms I could reach out to. When I got back to the office, I made a list evaluating which firms might be the most receptive to my approach in case I needed to secure another retainer to stay profitable in the new year.

CHAPTER TWELVE

The following day, I once again sat in the client chair across from Keenan's rich, dark mahogany desk that I figured cost more than my retainer would for another three years.

The attorney, not only his desk, exuded wealth and power. He wore what I figured was an Armani suit, slim and classy. His crisp white shirt had his initials embroidered on the cuffs.

He looked me straight in the eye, grim-faced, and I braced for the axe.

"I want you to look into Nate's death for us. Our senior management is appalled that one of our own has been killed. We owe him justice. The police are busy with hundreds of other cases. You, on the other hand, can put your full attention to finding Nate's killer."

I let out a deep breath. Spared the executioner's axe. "It's an open murder investigation, which puts it off-limits to private investigators. You'll want to speak with Tom Volpe. He's the detective in charge."

Keenan's tight lips told me he didn't like my answer. Corporate types always think they can do whatever they want without anyone ever saying no. "But you investigated the warehouse fire."

"Murder is a whole different matter. Only the police are authorized to conduct the investigation." Still, I had a legitimate card to play. "I would suggest I continue looking into the fire."

"We're in negotiations with McFarland's attorney to settle the claim and we should come to an agreement soon."

I paused. "Nate left me several messages on the day he disappeared, asking me to come to his office the next day to discuss something related to the fire." I hedged a bit. I didn't tell Keenan that Nate didn't actually specify the fire, or that he didn't want to talk on the phone. "Since I can't get involved in the murder investigation, I recommend finding out what was on Nate's mind. He was always alert to any potential fraud against SEPA Financial."

"I can't imagine what Nate was thinking. The warehouse fire was ruled an accident."

"Perhaps it wasn't the fire itself, but something else he thought needed further investigation."

Keenan leaned forward in his chair. "You're the expert, as Nate always reminded me. See what you come up with. But for now, let's keep this between us." He took his green marbled fountain pen from its granite holder. The pen's gold nub glided smoothly across Keenan's monogrammed notepad. Elegant and old world, but I couldn't imagine a fountain pen, no matter how expensive, could keep pace with the quick scribblings of a PI. "This is my personal cell number. It's not listed on my business card. Call me to keep me updated."

I left Keenan's office, satisfied that I had at least saved my gig, and took the stairs to Nate's office. The police had the office sealed, and when I called Tom, he refused to let me touch Nate's computer. "Our tech guys will be there this afternoon. I don't need you messing around with anything."

Diana came to my rescue and let me use the computer in the office of a manager on vacation. I searched through SEPA Financial's entire system for any information on Sean McFarland's business but failed to find anything on his properties other than the insurance policies I already knew about. However, when I searched his Mid-City Mortgage Brokerage, I learned that SEPA Financial's commercial loan department approved a loan for the new company at the beginning of the year. When I clicked on a PDF to see the loan details, a pop-up message asked for an ID and password. I tried the passwords I'd gotten from Diana, but none worked. I tried variations of the passwords and got myself locked out for too many failed attempts.

Who was I kidding? I was no hacker genius. I'd have to find a non-tech solution. Like conning the password out of someone in commercial loans?

CHAPTER THIRTEEN

The head of the commercial loan department was Paul Cameron. I took the stairs to his office and identified myself to his secretary. "I'm working for Jim Keenan, and I need to speak with Paul Cameron, please."

Cameron's secretary leaned back in her chair, tilted her head up, sniffing the air as if it had suddenly turned foul. "What exactly is the nature of your business?"

In my experience, secretaries tended to emulate their bosses. If the boss was open and friendly, the secretary was as well. Cameron's secretary was playing sentry guarding the castle wall.

I smiled. "My work with Mr. Keenan is confidential and for Mr. Cameron's ears only." I glanced at my watch. "We don't have much time. I'm expected to report back to Mr. Keenan in an hour."

The secretary looked me up and down and then picked up the phone. "Someone from Jim Keenan's office is here to see you." She turned to me stone-faced. "You can go right in. But he needs to be on a conference call in half an hour."

I forced a smile as I opened Cameron's office door.

"Take a seat and make this quick." Cameron pointed to a client chair, barely looking up from the papers he was reading. Finally, he closed the folder, stared at me, and frowned. "Are you a new attorney?" His voice sounded as stern as Mother Superior's whenever she called me to her office.

"I'm working on retainer for Jim Keenan." I handed over my business card.

He stared at the card. "Andrea Fabiano Investigations. What is it you want from me?"

"We're interested in the loan your department approved

for Sean McFarland's Mid-City Mortgage Brokerage."

"Jim told me you were looking into a warehouse fire. What does that have to do with Mid-City's loan?"

"Nothing perhaps. But I'd like to see the financial statements provided by his company to qualify for the loan."

"I assure you we perform due diligence on all our loan applications."

"Good to hear. But I'd still like to have a look at the loan documents."

"Just what are you fishing for?"

"I don't fish. I investigate. Real estate development is a risky venture. Just how solvent is Mr. McFarland?"

"You're on the wrong track. Sean, Mr. McFarland, is an extraordinarily successful businessman. He doesn't have financial difficulties."

"What was the amount of the loan, and what was he using the funds for?"

"To expand his brokerage business. He's using the funds to open a second office and hire more staff. New jobs are always good for the city." His face struggled into a half-smile.

"I'm sure, but I still need to see the loan application."

"You'll have access next week." He stood. "Thank you for stopping by."

I remained seated. "You didn't mention the amount of the loan?"

"I don't remember the details of all our loans. This department handles hundreds of applications."

"It certainly doesn't take a week to attach the documents to an email or print out a copy for me."

"We'll accommodate you as soon as possible. We're an extremely busy department." He rose and elbowed me out the door. "Thank you for coming by and give Jim my best."

Cameron was stalling, which made me even more interested in the loan application. I tried to talk to several of the staffers, but they quickly brushed me off. Afraid of the boss or his secretary? I went to Jim Keenan's office, thinking I might have better luck there. His secretary was a whole lot friendlier, but Keenan was away from the office and not expected until the next day. I called his personal cell number and left a message.

Back at my office, I researched Mid-City Mortgage. Other than the address it shared with McFarland's office, I found no evidence that the business used the loan to expand or establish a second office, as Cameron claimed. What was McFarland doing with the money?

CHAPTER FOURTEEN

A shiny silver sign outside the apartment building read, "Managed by Spring Garden Investments," one of McFarland's LLCs. Curious, I decided to check out the sites of the earlier fires and started with the apartment complex that was undergoing renovations when a fire started in the basement.

A sole worker in white overalls was painting a wall in a lobby empty of furniture but piled high with floor tiles waiting to be installed.

"Is your foreman around?" I asked.

"Nope."

"Where is he?"

"No idea."

"Is he on the premises?"

"No. Some guy from the general contractor is out back."

I was relieved to learn the guy could speak in a complete sentence. I tried another question. "Any tenants living in the building?"

"It's being worked on." He looked at me like he was disgusted by a stupid question.

I walked around the side of the building toward the rear. Only a single truck was parked at the loading dock while two men unloaded lumber. For a building undergoing renovation, I saw no other workers or equipment. One of the men jumped down from the loading dock when he saw me.

"I was wondering when this building will be finished," I said. "I'm interested in finding an apartment in the area."

"Lady, I can't answer. I was told to unload these supplies, that's all. You'll have to speak to the contractors."

The other guy laughed and jumped down to join us. "If you need a new place any time soon, I wouldn't count on this building."

"Why do you say that?"

"You see any work going on? It's been like this for months." He stepped closer. "I work for the general contractor. I'm only here today to take this delivery. This is the first load of supplies delivered in two months. All the halls, the elevators, and the lobby still need to be done. And work hasn't started on the apartments themselves."

"What seems to be the holdup?"

He shrugged his shoulders. "Lack of scratch would be my guess. But don't quote me."

When the truck left, I walked with the contractor into the lobby. The painter was gone.

"I have to lock up now," the contractor said.

I took out my PI license. "I'd like to have a look around before I report back to my client." I passed him a fifty-dollar bill.

"Not apartment hunting, then?" He grinned. "We'll need to use the stairs."

We walked the hallways. The carpeting was threadbare, the walls, scuff marked and peeling, needed painting, and the brass hardware on the apartment doors was tarnished. Inside the apartments I checked, the kitchen and bathrooms were gutted.

"When did the work start?"

"In the spring."

It was now fall.

"I'd like to have a look at the basement where the fire started, and then I'll be out of your hair."

"No worries, you're paying for my time."

The basement was cleared of debris from the fire, and a new staircase had been installed but was still unpainted. That was the extent of any repairs. The walls, blackened with soot, hadn't been cleaned or repainted. I thanked my guide and walked back to my Subaru. Lack of supplies and the absence of workers usually meant a lack of funds. So, where did the insurance money go that SEPA Financial paid out?

I drove to McFarland's industrial building near the airport, where the electrical fire had occurred. In contrast to the apartment building, this site was bustling with activity. Not only were workers everywhere, but tenants occupied the building. I identified myself to the foreman as an investigator for SEPA Financial. "We expect to complete the job before Thanksgiving," he told me as he showed me around.

"I understand most of the work you're doing is interior?"

"We upgraded the electrical fixtures, the bathrooms were refurbished, the halls painted, and new flooring installed. The new roof was the only exterior work."

"No problems getting supplies?"

"A week or two delay for the flooring, but other than that we kept going."

"You've made the repairs from the fire, then?"

He nodded. "We were lucky there. The fire was in a mechanical closet, and we got to it before it did serious damage to any of our work."

CHAPTER FIFTEEN

Back in my office, I heard a knock on my door and Tom poked his head in. "Need to talk with you about Nate Warner."

"I was wondering when homicide would get around to me." I smiled. "But I figured you'd be questioning me at headquarters."

"For professional witnesses like you, I make house calls." He held two Dunkin' Donuts coffee cups and handed me one. "You wouldn't get this at headquarters."

I took a sip. Dark roast. My favorite. "Come and sit." I led him to my worn but cushy sofa. "You look beat."

"That's because I am."

I handed Tom a throw pillow for his back, which I know can trouble him when stressed. "Need a Motrin?"

"Thanks, the pillow's good."

"What is it that you want to know?"

"I need you to have a look at the names on this list"—he handed me a sheet with photos — "and tell me what you know about them."

"Nate Warner helped put all of these guys away for fraud," I said. "You think one of them might have enough of a grudge to kill him."

"It's a line of inquiry. Any standout to you."

"This guy," I pointed to a man with a scar on his left cheek and a nose broken more often than a boxer's. "He threatened Nate in court."

"Detective Lewis tells me he's still in prison. What about these guys?" Tom pointed to two other men. "Lewis learned these two are out on parole and living in Philly."

"Both were business owners who thought they could get away with scamming the system" I said. "They lived a lavish lifestyle and had huge debts. One had a gambling addiction; the other kept a mistress with extravagant tastes. Frankly, I don't see them going after Nate. Not unless they hired a professional."

"I don't see this as a professional hit. The killer acted without much planning and then found himself with a body he had to get rid of," Tom said.

"Makes sense. What does forensics say?"

"Nate Warner was shot with a nine-millimeter. Only his fingerprints are in the car. It looks like he was shot elsewhere, and the killer used the car to move the body."

"The killer probably wore gloves when he drove Nate's car," I said. "But what about the car seat? Had it been moved?"

"You hit on our one piece of evidence. The killer was much taller than Warner. From the position of the driver's seat, he had to be six feet."

Keenan was about that height. And he was keeping me away from McFarland. But why would he want to murder Nate and then want to hire me to find the killer?

"That's all you have?" I asked.

"I'm concentrating on motive. Now tell me everything you know about Nate Warner."

"I've worked with him for about three years. He's as straight an arrow as you can find. Loyal to his family and his company. He treated his staff fair, and they respected him. I don't see any bad blood there."

"That's what Keenan, the corporate attorney, said, and he's worked with Nate for fifteen years. He also told me that Nate didn't gamble, was careful with money, both his and the company's, and wasn't a heavy drinker. So, no habits likely to cause trouble."

"I'd agree. Nate was tough to work for, but he was an honest, upright guy."

"No affair at work? No irate husband?"

"No way. Nate was extremely loyal to his wife. It was apparent to anyone who worked with him that Nate loved his wife."

"He must have angered someone or he wouldn't be dead."

"Did Keenan say when he saw Nate last?"

"Lunchtime, the day he went missing. Keenan said he was leaving the cafeteria when Nate arrived and he joked that Nate should try the beef stew. Apparently, Nate was a vegetarian."

"He was a health food nut. Ate tofu and liked it. Told me to stop eating sugar. Sorry, I digress. Did Keenan say whether Nate seemed nervous or upset in any way?"

"Not at all. Nate smiled and seemed his usual self."

I took a last swig of my coffee. "I do have a possible motive for you." I told Tom about Nate's frantic messages the day before he disappeared and that he asked me to come to his office the following morning. "But we never spoke. He disappeared that night."

"You think there might be a connection between Nate's death and the fire?"

I nodded. I told Tom about the prior fires. "Work has pretty much stopped on the apartment building renovations. His Riverfront condo project isn't selling fast enough. He could be overextended financially."

"Arson for profit? But we have no proof the warehouse fire was arson. And those earlier fires were also ruled accidental," Tom pointed out. "Besides, I don't see how any of those insurance payments would be large enough to solve the type of financial problems you're talking about. And we don't know for sure that he's having financial difficulties or if they're serious enough to be a motive for murder."

"There is something else," I said. I got up, threw my empty coffee cup in the trash, and filled him in on Nate's note with the combination. "He had information he wanted to share with me, but it was removed from his office computer."

"You think this has a bearing on his murder?"

"I do."

"Let me see the note."

"Nate wanted this to remain confidential. It could have an impact on SEPA Financial."

"Nothing is confidential in a murder inquiry."

"Maybe we could make a deal?'

Tom ran his fingers through his hair. "What kind of deal?"

"Have your tech guys go through Nate's computer and try to retrieve the deleted files. Then share that info with me."

"First of all, it's only a theory of yours, not mine, that these files have a bearing on the case," Tom said. "And second, there's no way I could convince the department to spend our time and money without more proof this isn't just a fishing expedition. And finally, I can't turn over evidence to you if we found any. Whatever you're hunting for, you're on your own."

"Understood." Still, it was worth a try.

"I best be on my way." Tom walked to the door.

"Still no ID on the fire victim?" I asked.

"We can't check dental records. And he doesn't fit the description of anyone reported missing. He might never be ID'd," Tom said. "Anyway, I hope you're still coming to dinner tomorrow night?"

"Wouldn't miss it." I always looked forward to visiting the Volpes. Sal, Tom's father, was the closest I had to a father since mine died in a car accident along with my mother. Spending time with Tom, his wife Julia, their daughter Marisa, my god-child, and her brother John always left me with joy and hope for the future.

CHAPTER SIXTEEN

My phone rang the next morning, and the caller ID read James Keenan.

"I got another call from Arthur Newman complaining that you were harassing workmen at McFarland's properties yesterday."

"I visited the two properties where the earlier fires occurred. And I spoke to a few people. None of them complained." No way did I harass anyone. Not by a long shot. I know when I exert excess pressure. This wasn't about my behavior.

"What were you doing there? We're not paying you to waste time on old claims," Keenan said. "Newman is threatening to have you arrested if you go onto any of McFarland's properties again."

"And you're willing to take those threats seriously?"

"We have to."

"How am I supposed to do the job?"

"Avoid getting called out again by Newman." He hung up.

Arthur Newman was proving a real pain in the ass. Why didn't he want me looking into McFarland and his business?

I thought about Helena Warner. She might be interested in whatever her husband left for me to find. That way, if Keenan and SEPA Financial got too skittish and called me off, I'd still have a client.

I phoned her home, planning to leave a message, but she answered.

"I'm taking leave from work. I need time with my sons."

"I'd like to stop by and see you. It concerns Nate. Is either today or tomorrow good?"

"I'm home. Come see me whenever you can."

I had just hung up the phone when I heard a knock on my

door. It's not locked during business hours, but no one came in. I opened it myself to find a woman in dark Ray-Bans. She took a step back as though startled that I'd answer her knock. She was slim, wore a black light-weight wool suit, and carried a red Kate Spade handbag. The sparkle from the four-carat diamond on her left hand made me want to reach for my shades.

"Ms. Fabiano?" Her voice was soft but shaky, as though she was suffering from stage fright.

I smiled and stepped aside. "Please come in."

"I'm not interrupting your work?"

"What is it that I can do for you? Ms. ...?

"Mrs. Kramer. Nan Kramer. I think I need your help."

As I led her to a client chair, she removed her sunglasses. Her eyes were red and puffy. I estimated her age to be around forty.

"I can make fresh coffee if you would like some."

"No, thank you." Nan Kramer gave me a tight smile.

Most potential clients call and make an appointment. It's rare for someone to walk in off the street. When that happens, it's usually because they're scared, desperate, or both.

"How about tea? A nice hot cup of tea helps the conversation."

She nodded. I went over to the credenza and put water on to boil in my electric teapot.

"Do you live in the city, Ms. Kramer?" I asked, mostly to get her to relax a bit.

"We live in Bryn Mawr. And it's Mrs."

I nodded. A traditionalist from the wealthy Main Line. "A lovely area." Once the water boiled, I prepared the tea and brought two cups to my desk along with a sugar bowl. "Sorry, no milk at the moment." I handed over her cup.

I sat in my desk chair, leaned back, and smiled.

She sipped her tea, and the tension in her face eased.

"How did you hear about my firm, Mrs. Kramer?"

"I talked to a friend. You helped her recover coins and jewelry stolen from her home. She said you were reliable."

"Nice to hear I have satisfied clients."

I waited, but Nan Kramer still didn't tell me why she came to see me. My phone rang, and I ignored it.

"Don't you need to answer that?"

"I have voicemail. Right now, I want to hear what you have to tell me."

Nan Kramer started to cry, quietly at first, but then let out a wail as if she were in agonizing pain.

I handed her the box of tissues on my desk. "Tell me about it when you're ready."

She dried her tears and gulped down another mouthful of tea. "My son Jason is missing. At first the police considered the possibility Jason was being held for ransom. You see my husband is the CFO at an investment firm."

That explained the rock on Mrs. Kramer's finger.

"But now the police consider Jason a missing person," I said. "I've seen the news media coverage. He's sixteen is that correct?"

Mrs. Kramer sobbed. "He's so young. It's been two weeks and the police have nothing. I want to hire you to find him. We can pay you and you'd have more time than the police to look for Jason."

I opened my notebook. "When was the last time you saw your son?"

"Like I said it was two weeks ago on the Monday night. Jason and his father were in the living room, and when I walked in from the kitchen, I saw Jason leaving by the front door. I called out to ask him where he was going. You see, it was eight o'clock on a school night. He looked back at me. I could tell from his face that he was angry. The last thing my son said to me was 'Away from here.'" She began to cry again. "I've been calling his cell phone, but it isn't connected."

"Why did Jason leave that night? What happened between him and his father?"

Mrs. Kramer fiddled with the clasp on her handbag and

didn't look me in the eye. "I don't know."

I didn't believe her.

"I want you to find him," she said. "I can't sleep worrying about him."

In the last few years, I found myself handling an increased number of runaway cases. Sometimes I found the missing kids living on the street or being pimped but alive and willing to go home. Other times, the streets had hardened them, and they wanted nothing to do with their parents. The worst were the times I was too late and had to tell the parents that their child was dead from an overdose, a bullet, or stabbed in a street brawl.

"I need you to send me your son's cell phone number, his social media accounts, email address and a list of his friends." I handed her my business card.

"I have a picture with me and can get you the rest of what you want." Mrs. Kramer opened her handbag and handed me a color photo of her son. It was the same picture the police had released. Jason smiling, wearing a soccer team uniform, and holding a ball under his arm. He was a good-looking kid, thin but muscular.

"I took that at the beginning of the school term when he got his new uniform," she said. "He was so proud. He made captain. And I liked the photo so much I had it developed and framed."

"Then Jason was doing well at school?"

"Oh, yes. He loves his school and has good friends there."

Finally, Mrs. Kramer was composed enough to give me some basic information.

The family lived in Bryn Mawr, a leafy suburb on Philadelphia's posh Main Line. Jason, an only child, was a junior at Penn Wynn prep, an exclusive private school for boys. All this sounded like the ingredients of an idyllic life, but kids don't storm out of happy homes.

I tried once more to get a straight answer. "Why do you

think Jason ran away?"

"I've been a good mother." She broke down again.

Nan Kramer was a much too defensive and clearly uncomfortable with the truth. I decided to switch subjects and get back later to the night Jason left.

"Was Jason bullied at all? At school? Online?"

"Jason's popular at school. He's an A student, and his friends are good kids. We're close, and he would have told me if he was having trouble with bullies," she said.

"We all hear of cyberbullying. Do you monitor your son's involvement with social media?"

"I check from time to time. Jason and his friends talk about soccer, school, and what they're doing on the weekend. Nothing troublesome."

"Did Jason and his father get along?"

"Steve can be tough with Jason, but he does have his son's best interest at heart."

"But Jason left right after he spoke with his father. Were they arguing?"

"I wasn't in the room then. I came in when Jason was leaving. I only know I need you to find him and bring him back."

She wasn't giving me the complete picture, and we both knew it.

"Surely, your husband told you what he and Jason talked about."

"He didn't want to discuss it. I'll pay whatever you want to find my boy," she said.

"At this point, Mrs. Kramer, I need more information about your son. You need to tell me everything you know that could help me find him."

"I'm doing my best."

"Your husband didn't come with you. How does he feel about hiring me?"

"Steve is terribly busy at work, or else he'd be here."

"I would like to speak with him. Is he free in the evenings?"

"I'll let him know." Her tone was tentative. She twisted her diamond ring around her finger. "I'm sure he'll make the time."

I wasn't at all sure. There was a great deal more to this story than I'd learned so far. We settled on a fee thirty percent higher than my usual. I use a sliding scale based on the client's income and figured the Kramers could cough up my price with little effort. Besides, I wanted to be paid for my time digging up the info that Mrs. Kramer was withholding.

We completed the contract, she signed it and wrote me a generous check and left.

I phoned the local police and spoke to the cop in charge of Jason's case. "Nothing so far," he told me. "We checked into accidents, the area hospitals, and the morgues, so he's not been hurt or killed. We've notified PDs in Philadelphia and the surrounding counties and sent out the kid's picture to media outlets. Hopefully, we'll get some sign of the kid soon."

My cell phone pinged that I had a new message. It was Nan Kramer's email with the info about Jason I asked for.

I phoned Jason's cell and it was still turned off. When I checked Jason's Facebook, Twitter, and Instagram posts, there was no evidence of bullying. As his mother had told me, he and his friends, male and female, exchanged the usual teen banter about school, sports, music, movies, and video games. Nothing put out any alarm signals. I called Jason's school, and the headmaster agreed to see me as soon as I could get there.

Before I left the office, I responded to phone messages, emails, and texts.

The sun had finally reappeared after two days of gloomy clouds, and the air felt fresh and crisp. The day was perfect for a scenic drive along the river. I drove around the traffic circle at the Philadelphia Museum of Art and took the entrance to Martin Luther King Drive, a tree-lined parkway along the west bank of the Schuylkill.

I rolled down my window and kept my speed at a leisurely

pace, enjoying views of the city's nineteenth century Grecian-style waterworks, historic Boathouse Row, and the scullers gliding across the water as they trained for the next regatta.

I arrived at Penn Wynn Prep with my mind refreshed.

Penn Wynn's headmaster was about fifty, with a pleasant face and a manner that was relaxed and welcoming. "The police have been here. Jason was the last young man I'd expect to run away."

"He had no problems here at school?"

"Jason is among our best students. He's focused on his studies to keep up his GPA to be accepted into a top university. He's the captain of our soccer team, and the other players respect him. I don't think anything at school drove him away."

I didn't either. "I'd like to speak to Jason's teachers, his classmates, and to these students." I showed him Nan Kramer's list. "Maybe he opened up to them about whatever was troubling him."

"We'll arrange for you to speak to them. There's a small conference room you can use."

"One more request. I'd also like to talk to the school psychologist."

"I'll let her know, but you do understand we must maintain the confidentiality of our students. She may not have much she can tell you."

I smiled. "I do need to cover all the bases."

I spent the next three hours talking to both teachers and students. They were all polite and well-groomed, the male teachers and boys in jackets and ties and the female teachers in pantsuits. All of them expressed concern about Jason. But no one, not even his friends, could shed any light on why Jason bolted.

"Jason never came to see me," the psychologist told me, "so I'm afraid I can't be much help."

I was checking emails when I heard a knock on the conference room door. It opened partway, and in slipped a kid with freckles and acne. "I heard you were asking about Jason." He quickly closed the door.

"That's right."

The kid shifted his feet back and forth as if he needed to use the bathroom.

"Please have a seat. My name is Andrea."

"Ethan." He was one of the kids on my list of Jason's friends.

I shook his sweaty hand. "What was it that you want to tell me, Ethan?"

Before his rear end touched the seat, Ethan's words spewed out of his mouth like bullets. "Jason stayed at my house the night he left his parents." Then he stopped, waiting for my reaction. Perhaps thinking he was in trouble.

"He must trust you, then."

Ethan nodded. "He made me swear not to tell his parents. I kept my promise, but now I'm scared something bad happened to him. The police have been here."

"Did you tell the police?"

Ethan shook his head. "I was too scared."

"But your parents must have known Jason was staying with you."

Ethan lowered his head. "I let him in through the basement door and he stayed down there. My parents didn't know he was in the house and I didn't say."

"You're doing the right thing telling me." I smiled. "Did Jason tell you why he left home?"

"Not really." He paused. "Jason had a black eye but wouldn't tell me how he got it. The next morning, we left together for school. But when we passed the Bryn Mawr station, the train to Philly pulled in. 'Remember your promise,' he called out to me and ran onto the train."

"Have you seen or heard from him since?"

"No texts, nothing."

"Can you remember what Jason was wearing when he hopped the train?"

"Shit, I forgot." His face reddened. "Sorry, we're not supposed to curse at school."

"No worries."

"I should have known he wasn't coming with me to school. He was wearing his Philadelphia Union hoodie, sneakers, and jeans. We wear jackets and ties here."

It would have been a whole lot easier to find a kid dressed for prep school than one wearing the uniform of every teenager in the U.S. Then again, the Union logo might be of help. "What color was the hoodie?"

"Dark blue." He paused. "I think he might have had his Union hat. That's the same color."

"You've been extremely helpful, Ethan. Now you leave Jason to me and the police. Don't worry. But if he does contact you, call me." I handed him my business card.

"I don't think he will. He's afraid his parents will find him, and he doesn't want them to. It's funny, though. He never really talked to me about his parents before. Even when I ragged on mine."

Ethan left as quietly as he came in.

CHAPTER SEVENTEEN

In my car, I phoned Helena Warner. "I'm on my way to you now. I should be there in half an hour."

When I arrived, her sons were doing their homework at the dining room table. Helena showed me through to the kitchen.

"I like to be around in case they need me," she said. "Can I get you anything to drink? I'm having coffee."

"A glass of water would be great."

I showed Helena the note with the combination that Nate had mailed to me. "I think he came across something he thought was important enough to share with me. And he put that information in a safe place for me to find. But I haven't been able to locate it.

"You see, it's possible that this information might help explain why he was killed," I said. "I can't be certain, but it's an avenue I can't ignore. I'll need your explicit authority to continue my search. SEPA Financial isn't interested."

"Right now, money is tight. I'm not sure I can pay you."

We signed an agreement with a nominal fee that miserly Nate would have been happy with.

When I returned to my office, I opened my notes on Sean McFarland and phoned the attorneys who had reached out of court settlements on the negligence suits they filed for their clients. Both declined to talk. There were nondisclosure agreements in place. I completed a background report on an executive candidate for a New Jersey pharmaceutical company and hit the send button by my five o'clock deadline.

I was tired and wanted to go home, but realized I needed to send out invoices if I wanted to get paid. I hated administrative tasks, but I loved seeing my hard-earned fees piling up in my bank account. I also completed monthly expense reports for the clients who had me on retainer. When I finished, the thought of a hot shower and a warm meal sounded appealing. But then I considered Jason, my teen runaway, who was out on the streets somewhere.

I decided to make the rounds of the city's homeless shelters. Jason might feel as tired and hungry as I did and head to a shelter for a meal and a cot. I packed my tote bag with two energy bars, a bottle of Propel water, and a stack of flyers with Jason's picture that I printed out on my color printer. Then grabbed my jacket and headed out into the city night.

I distributed Jason's photo to the staff at the shelters I visited. "He's probably wearing a Philadelphia Union hoodie," I said.

"I haven't seen him," a director at one shelter told me. "But I'll keep his photo and let you know if he shows up."

That was what staffers told me wherever I went. I had even less luck with their clients, who didn't trust a woman coming around asking questions. After hours of no hits, I felt tired, hungry, and frustrated. One of the volunteers ladling soup at my last stop heard my stomach growling and offered me a bowl of beef barley. The soup smelled appealing, but I declined, figuring the homeless needed it more than I did. I could go back to my warm home and heat up leftovers.

CHAPTER EIGHTEEN

The next morning, I stared at the map of the city on my office wall, considering where Jason Kramer was likely to be and what would be the fastest route to finding him. Sister Emily popped into my mind. She had recently opened a shelter for homeless teens. I knew her through her work with female prisoners and wasn't surprised she had taken on yet another task. She lived and worked among the city's disadvantaged and jumped in wherever she thought she might make a difference.

I called her and we chatted for a few moments to catch up. "I'm searching for a runaway." I told her about Jason Kramer. "I just emailed his photo. Can you take a look and tell me if you've seen him? I'm working for his parents."

"Hang on. I'm checking my in-box. Got it. He's not been here and I haven't seen him around the neighborhood."

"Please let me know if you do. When he ran away, he was wearing a dark blue hoodie with a Philadelphia Union logo."

"Any indication he was abused at home?"

"I won't know the answer to that until I find him."

"I'll keep an eye out and let you know if he shows up."

Back when I started my firm, I had to learn to balance more than one case at a time if I wanted to get results and keep my clients happy.

But with these two cases, I was spinning my wheels. I sat at my desk, chewing on a soft pretzel slathered with peanut butter. Protein might give me a burst of energy.

To fight my lethargy, I rechecked Philadelphia court records to see if any new complaints were filed in civil court against Sean McFarland. And *ecco*. Another civil suit popped up.

I clicked through to the complaint and downloaded it. It

was a negligence suit against McFarland, his company, and the general contractor on the Riverfront condo project. The lawsuit was on behalf of two construction workers who were injured when scaffolding collapsed at the site. One lost a leg, and the other suffered a concussion and a compound fracture of his arm, requiring numerous surgeries. In addition to McFarland, the lawsuit also named Robert Regan, a McFarland employee who oversaw the site. I put a call into the attorney for the injured workers, Michael Shea.

"What is this in reference to?" his assistant asked.

"I'm a private investigator. I'd like to talk to Mr. Shea about the Riverfront lawsuit."

"Please hold on," she said.

Minutes later, she came back. "I'm sorry. Mr. Shea has no comment at this time."

"I'm afraid you misunderstood. I'm not a reporter. I'm an insurance investigator and would like to get time on his calendar."

She jumped in. "I'm afraid it's you who doesn't understand. Mr. Shea does not wish to speak to you."

I never take rejection personally, especially after only one contact. I made a note to call again.

I left my office to continue my search for Jason Kramer. This time I tried other city's teen shelters. Jason might not have gone to Sister Emily, but a kid from the suburbs, not used to city streets, might gravitate toward kids his age.

My theory sounded good. In practice, it failed to yield any results. No one claimed to have seen Jason, neither the staff nor the teens. I left behind the flyers with Jason's photo. Then I continued down my list of area churches that dished out dinners to the homeless each evening. But no sign of Jason. I headed to a shelter on Arch Street where a childhood friend of mine, Vinnie Mazzo, volunteered as a cook. "Hey, Andrea, didn't expect to see you 'til next week," Vinnie called out when I entered the kitchen. "You makin' a surprise check?" He was loading the dishwasher.

I shook my head. "Another runaway case." I showed him Jason's photo. "His name is Jason Kramer. He's sixteen."

Vinnie stared at the photo. He had an excellent memory for faces, and I kept my fingers crossed.

"*Cawfee?* Just made some fresh."

"Might help." I sat down on a kitchen stool. I always wore comfortable boots for my feet, but my legs felt stiff by this time of the night.

He poured a mug for each of us and tapped his finger on the photo. "The kid looks familiar. I'm not sure why. I don't think I've seen him here. But I have seen this face."

"Posters are up around the city, on TV and on social media. Could that be where you've seen him?"

Vinnie shook his head. "I saw him in the flesh. But not here. And he wasn't wearing this team uniform."

"Was he wearing a dark blue hoodie with the Union team logo, maybe?"

"Not sure." Vinnie walked over to turn on the dishwasher then sat down on a stool next to me, still examining the picture.

"Keep it. It could help jog your memory. You staying out of trouble?" I asked.

"Hey, if I didn't want to stay clean, which I do, seeing the guys around here puts the fear of God in me."

Vinnie was a former heroin addict. His mother, Theresa, was a friend of my late mother. Their mothers came from the same Italian town, Pescara in Abruzzo along the Adriatic. Whenever Vinnie went on his binges and disappeared for days at a time, his mother would ask me to find him. Which I did gratis more times than I could count. When Theresa died, she left behind a surprisingly substantial portfolio of investments for a grocer's widow. She left everything to her only son on the condition that he stayed off drugs and got a job. And she left me a bequest, large enough for me to make a substantial down payment on my South Philly duplex, which meant a low mortgage payment I could afford. Her largesse came with conditions. I was required to monitor Vinnie to make sure he complied with the terms of her will. I visited Vinnie regularly and made sure his blood tests were clean.

I finished my coffee, left the kitchen, and went to talk to the others on the staff and the homeless men eating their dinners. Again, no one acknowledged seeing the missing kid. I stopped at three more soup kitchens, but I found no sign of Jason or anyone who had seen him. All I could do was leave more flyers behind. In my car, I phoned Jason's mother to give her an update.

"I've found someone who thinks he saw Jason in the city. But nothing definite yet."

Mrs. Kramer sobbed. "I can't sleep worrying about him."

"Any word from the police?"

"I called, but they have no news."

I tried my best to calm her, but we both knew the longer he was gone, the worse the prospects were of finding him.

CHAPTER NINETEEN

The phone on my desk was ringing as I opened my office door the next morning. I got to it on the third ring. "Fabiano Investigations."

"Hey, Andrea." It was Vinnie Mazzo. "I remembered where I saw that kid you were asking me about last night. He was talking to Father Kevin after Mass at St. John's."

"Good work, Vinnie. When was this?"

"Couple days ago. The noon Mass. I wanted to talk to the Father, but it looked like he and the kid were into something deep, so I decided I'd catch Father later and left. By the way, the kid looked scrawny, like he hadn't eaten in a week."

Vinnie took after his mother. They loved to feed people.

"Sure it was Jason?"

"Yep. He was wearing a hoodie like you said. I couldn't see the logo. But he was definitely the kid in your flyer."

"Thanks, buddy."

"Sure. You comin' over tomorrow?"

"Nice try. You'll see me when you see me."

Vinnie laughed.

Father Kevin looked over the picture of Jason I handed to him.

"Yes, that's him. He didn't give me his name. He was sitting alone in the back of the church and seemed to be crying. He was still there when the rest of the worshippers left. So, I went over to talk to him."

"What did he tell you?"

"Not much. He looked scared, and I could tell he was living rough. He had cuts and bruises on his face, and his hands were scratched up like he'd been in a fight."

"Did he tell you how he got his injuries or anything about how he was living?"

Father shook his head. "I tried to get him to talk. I told him he could use the bathroom in the sacristy to clean up. He thanked me politely, but he wouldn't accept my help. I'm afraid all those sex abuse scandals create mistrust. I can't blame any kid for that. I can tell you he was well-spoken, and he used correct grammar, so he was educated."

That fit with Jason's prep school education. "Do you remember what he was wearing?"

"A dark-colored hoodie."

"Any idea where he went when he left."

"I directed him to a free clinic on Race Street where he could get his cuts cleaned up."

"If he shows up again, Father, please give me a call." I gave him my business card.

At the clinic, I showed Jason's photo around to the staff, but the supervisor refused to betray patient privacy. I, however, noticed a hint of recognition in the eyes of one of the nurses, which told me he had sought treatment there. By now, Jason knew he was vulnerable to everyday violence on the streets of Philadelphia. I could use that as leverage to convince him to return home. That is if I could find him. And he was still alive.

Outside, the autumn air was brisk. I lifted my face, letting the coolness wash over me. As I walked, I realized I hadn't eaten since coffee and a biscotti at seven that morning. I decided I needed comfort food. I headed to Marathon's on Sixteenth Street, got a table, and ordered the meatball platter with mashed potatoes and mushroom gravy.

My stomach satisfied, I continued walking along the city streets, imagining myself a teenage runaway. Where would I go to feel safe? Jason chose a church. Checking out thousands of churches throughout the city would be onerous. I needed a plan of attack.

Back at my office, I checked in with missing persons. They had nothing new to report. I checked my city map, located St. John's where Jason was last seen, and drew a mile radius around the church. This would be a more manageable search area to work with. And may finally produce the results I wanted: finding Jason and getting him off the dangerous city streets.

CHAPTER TWENTY

My Aunt Roseanne waved as I entered the visitors' room, always crowded on Sundays with mothers, husbands, and children. Correctional officers were there, too, watching everyone.

"*Cara Mia.*" My aunt embraced me. Through her cardigan, I could feel her ribs beneath a thin layer of skin. Her hair was more gray than brown now. Her face was pale, with deep furrows on her forehead and sagging cheeks. At sixty, she hadn't aged well, confined to Muncy State Correctional Institute.

I sat across from her, wanting to hold her hand but knowing I wasn't allowed. I could only touch her when we greeted each other and when it was time for me to leave.

"Last night, I dreamed of your mother, and we were in her kitchen eating roasted peppers." My aunt chuckled. "I could almost taste the garlic, the olive oil. Let me tell you, prison food is even worse than hospital food."

Aunt Roseanne had only just returned to prison after being hospitalized for a heart attack. I wished I could bring her good wholesome food. The prison diet wasn't helping her cholesterol levels or high blood pressure.

"If it wasn't raining, we could go outside," I said.

"I'm used to being in here."

"Are they getting your medicine to you every day?"

"Don't worry about me, Andrea. I'm taking my medicine, and I'm doing fine. Tell me how you're doing."

I gave her a brief, censored version of my life and work. Then I handed her my cell phone. "I have new pictures of the children." The Volpe children were guaranteed to spark a smile on my aunt's face. She had no children of her own and oohed and aahed at John, eight, and Marisa, ten, posing on their bikes, eating ice cream cones, and hamming for the camera.

"Tom and Julia are lucky." Aunt Roseanne let out a sigh.

I figured it was time to bring up a subject she didn't want to talk about. "Auntie, your parole hearing will be coming up soon."

"They're never going to let a murderer walk out of here."

"I don't agree. And neither does Sonny." Harrison "Sonny" Waite, one of the city's top defense attorneys and a friend, was handling my aunt's case. I only wished my aunt had been represented by half as good a lawyer when she was convicted nearly twenty years before. "Your health is compromised. You're not a threat to anyone. They're likely to let you out this time."

"Don't hold your breath."

"You're being negative again, Auntie."

"*Cara Mia*, I gave up all hope the moment I got locked up in this godforsaken place. And maybe I deserve to die here for what I did."

"You don't. And if you don't want to fight, I won't stop until you're back home."

"What home? That's over and done with. I have no home."

"You'll come to me and live in my upstairs apartment."

"I don't want to be a burden to you, and I would be if they let me out."

"You're never a burden. You're my only family, and I love you."

Aunt Roseanne's eyes grew moist, and she stood up. She reached out and hugged me and hung on as though she was never going to see me again. We both knew I had to leave, but I didn't want to.

"You have a long drive back," she said as she released me. "It's too much for you to come all this way."

"I want to see you and know how you're doing."

She smiled. "I'm the same. Nothing much changes here."

I was out of breath from running. Trying to catch up to a man far off in the distance, but the faster I ran, the farther away the figure receded. I called out. "Wait. Slow down. I need to talk to you."

The man didn't want me to catch up. But I had to. It was for his own good. Why didn't he understand? I yelled out, "Nate! Stop! It's Andrea!"

He turned to face me. His face was covered in blood. Then the face was no longer Nate's but Uncle Dominic's, blood pouring from knife wounds all over his body. I looked down at my white sweater and watched it turn red. Aunt Roseanne was shaking me. "It's okay. It's better he's dead."

I woke sweating and breathing as hard as I had in my dream. But I was also trembling with cold. I went to the bathroom, changed into a clean nightshirt, and held a warm washcloth to my face, but the shivering wouldn't stop. I wrapped myself in a soft terry robe, went to the kitchen, and poured myself a finger of Scotch. I curled up on my living room sofa, covered myself with an afghan, and sipped the Scotch, slowly, trying not to inhale the smell. "Fabiano, just think of it as medicine." I lay back and prayed for morning to come.

CHAPTER TWENTY-ONE

Monday morning, I overslept by two hours. The more than three-hundred-mile round trip to see my aunt, my nightmares, and the extra hours I was putting in at work were taking their toll.

Before I left home, I checked emails and phone messages. Russ had left several messages. I decided to call him later. I called the shelters I'd already visited and checked in again with Vinnie and Sister Emily. Still no sign of Jason.

Rather than head directly to my office, I decided to visit churches in an eight-block radius around St. John's for any leads to Jason. But luck wasn't with me. No one at the churches or rectories had seen him. I left behind my business card and Jason's photos, then stopped at a deli to pick up a sandwich to-go and went to my office.

Around five p.m., I caught myself dozing off at my desk. I had been staring at the numbers Nate Warner had written down for me as if they were suspects who could open their traps and talk to me. 20R, 15L, 5R. It seemed logical to me that whatever records Nate wanted to share with me should have been at his office, since that's where he asked me to come. But I had found no safe, cabinet, or anything else with a combination lock either at his home or office. So, where would he keep records that he wanted to remain safe?

What if Nate took his stash with him when he was killed? It was possible his murderer had it. But no, I didn't believe Nate had the information with him. He had put whatever he had behind that combination, somewhere secure, somewhere I could find.

Investigations require putting together a puzzle when you don't know what the finished picture looked like. So far, the few pieces I had didn't resemble any image I'd ever seen.

I called Helena Warner.

"The Warner residence," a male voice answered my call.

A voice I recognized. "Tom?" I could hear competing conversations in the background. "Has something happened?"

"A burglary."

Immediately, I thought about Nate's documents. Someone besides me could be searching for them. The person in the Dodge Charger? Nate's killer?

"No one was injured, I hope."

"The family's fine. Why are you calling?"

"I want to speak to Helena."

"You're working this case when you specifically said you wouldn't interfere."

"I'm still searching for those missing documents of Nate's that I told you about. They're not at the SEPA Financial office, so I thought Helena would let me have another look around Nate's home office."

"If you happen to find what you're looking for and it's connected to his murder, I want to know in nanoseconds."

"You've told me that before. And I said you'll be the first to know."

"Promise."

"What do you want me to do? Sign it in blood?"

"If I thought it would help, I'd insist."

"How long will you guys be there?"

"What's the real reason you called?"

"I told you. I want a second look around for the docs. Now that you told me the house has been burglarized, I may not be the only person looking for them."

"See you when you get here."

The last time I visited the Warner home, I remembered how cozy and welcoming the living room felt. Now when I entered,

I saw slashed sofa cushions, family photos yanked out of their frames, and houseplants dumped out of their pots, strewn across the carpet along with potting soil.

"The rest of the house looks as bad," Tom said. "I don't think you're going to find anything the burglars missed."

"Now you have to agree that Natc had incriminating evidence related to McFarland. The murderer or murderers didn't get what they wanted when they killed Nate."

"Possibly. Whoever turned this house over didn't steal valuable jewelry or silver. The TVs and expensive cameras are still here. But the computers are gone."

I shook my head. "I already checked those out. Nate's laptop contained only personal stuff, nothing work-related. The other computers belong to the children, and Helena."

Tom and I walked to Nate's home office. He rubbed his temple, his tell when he was stressed out. "You have my okay to look around for anything else that might be missing. Mrs. Warner was too upset to be of help right now."

"Where is she?"

"She and the children are staying with neighbors and when we're done here, we're taking them to stay with Mrs. Warner's mother."

"When did all this happen?"

"Sometime during the day when Mrs. Warner was at work and the children at school. We're canvassing the neighborhood in case anyone saw anything."

Nate's office had been trashed as violently as the rest of the downstairs. The contents of his desk were strewn across the floor, and books were torn at their spines. His laptop was gone, but I could have told the burglar it wouldn't be any help. Prints from the Philadelphia Museum of Art had been removed from the walls and torn from their frames. Whoever did this was frantic and angry.

I found Tom in the kitchen. "You're right. The job was thorough. But I'll wager if these clowns were looking for Nate's stash, they didn't find it. Nate knew how to protect data.

But why did he give me the combination without telling me where the god-damned hiding place is?"

"He thought you were smart enough to figure it out?" Tom said.

"Sounds like Nate. He never made things easy."

CHAPTER TWENTY-TWO

Sean McFarland remained my prime suspect in Nate's murder. He owned the warehouse, as well as the mortgage brokerage and condo complex that Nate showed interest in. But McFarland's attorney would get me fired if I went anywhere near his client. I needed to consider my approach carefully not to jeopardize my ongoing relationship with SEPA Financial.

The time was right to go into surveillance mode to see if I could shake something loose without seeming to be doing anything.

For three days, I tracked McFarland and his movements. Each weekday morning at seven, the wannabe mogul left his stone mansion in Chestnut Hill, one of the city's elite zip codes, and drove his Mercedes into town where a valet parked his car for him. He wore double-breasted suits, expertly tailored to hide a growing girth. His hair was thinning, but his mustache was thick and bushy.

Promptly at one o'clock each afternoon, he and three male staff members ate lunch at restaurants within walking distance from his office, preferring the city's expensive steak houses. After lunch, he either remained in his office or visited managers at the office buildings he owned. He left to drive home around six and spent his time in his Mercedes making phone calls. Distracted driving is dangerous, but for me, it meant he wasn't likely to pick up my tail. When McFarland arrived home each night, the lights were already on inside. A housekeeper left an hour after he came home. And McFarland stayed in until the upstairs lights went out around eleven.

I became so bored with his routine that I spent too much time eating Three Musketeers bars, TastyKake chocolate cupcakes, and biscottis washed down with chocolate milk. My comfort foods since childhood. Then on day four, I was wiping icing from my lips when I looked up and saw McFarland walking briskly along Market Street, heading west. I hadn't noticed him exit his building. Distracted by too many chocolate fixes.

The clock on my dashboard read eleven-thirty. McFarland changed his routine. I followed on foot, taking along my tote containing my camera with a zoom lens. He turned down Eighteenth Street, and when he reached Rittenhouse Square, he stopped at an outside table at Parc, a popular French bistro. A man in his thirties with sandy hair, wearing a tan leather jacket, was already seated, drinking a glass of beer.

I crossed Eighteenth Street, walked into Rittenhouse Square Park, and chose a bench where I could watch them without being in their direct line of vision. I took pictures, making sure I got a clear shot of the guy in the leather jacket. Their encounter seemed perfectly normal. Two guys meeting for lunch, taking in some fresh air and sunshine before the cold weather set in. But my sixth sense told me I was about to learn something important.

The waiter served Leather Jacket an omelet but only a glass of white wine for McFarland. Sure enough, once the waiter was out of earshot, McFarland leaned in toward Leather Jacket, his face in a scowl. Each word he spoke was punctuated by his index finger pumping toward Leather Jacket's eyes.

Leather Jacket dropped his fork, pushed his chair back, and moved across the table toward McFarland with his back to me. I jumped up from the bench, expecting a fistfight. But, instead, Leather Jacket slammed his napkin onto the table, toppling McFarland's wine glass, and stormed off, leaving McFarland to pay for the uneaten omelet.

I followed Leather Jacket, my adrenaline pumping.

He entered an office building on Walnut Street, flashed an ID to the security guards at the front desk, and headed to the elevator bank. However, visitors I observed needed confirmed appointments before the guards allowed them through. I had to be content with studying the posted directory of tenants. A familiar name popped out. McFarland's Riverfront Enterprises had offices on the fourth floor.

"Can I help you?" A security guard stood beside me.

I smiled. "I must have the wrong building. Sorry." I decided not to stick around so I wouldn't be recognized when I showed up again.

Back at my office, I looked over my case notes on Sean McFarland and his buildings as I munched on a Golden Delicious apple, my antidote for the chocolate binge. My instinct told me something wasn't legit, but I still had no idea what it was.

What was the argument between McFarland and Leather Jacket? And did Leather Jacket work for McFarland's Riverfront Enterprises? That was one of the entities Nate was interested in. I thought about the scaffolding accident at the Riverfront project. But the negligence suit was filed after Nate's murder. Still, I decided to learn more about that accident—the sooner, the better.

CHAPTER TWENTY-THREE

After five calls to Michael Shea over two days, I got the message he didn't want to talk to me. Good thing he wasn't the only game in town.

I parked outside the Port Richmond rowhome where one of the injured workers lived. According to the lawsuit, the scaffolding accident at the Riverfront site had permanently injured his arm, ending his ability to work construction. He was forty-two. Probably wondering what kind of job he would qualify for now.

A stocky man with a receding hairline and a cast on his right arm answered the door.

I identified myself and showed my PI license. "I'd like to talk to you about Sean McFarland."

"My lawyer told me not to talk to anyone."

"I'm not here about your lawsuit. I'm not involved in that at all. It's Sean McFarland I'm interested in. Him and his operations."

He opened the door wider to let me into the living room. The soft fragrance of lavender permeated the room, decorated in warm, soothing colors that gave it a homey feel. He pointed me to one of two floral chairs, worn but not abused. Like my office sofa. "My wife just left for the hairdresser. Can I get you something to drink?"

"I'm fine, thanks." I sat down. "How are you doing?"

"I'm seeing my docs next week. They're doing everything they can for me."

"Good to hear. I am sorry that you're going through all this."

"Thanks." He nodded. "What did you want to know about McFarland?"

"Did you get to know him at all when you worked for him?"

"He came around but I only knew him by sight. He never talked to me or any of the workers. But he argued all the time with the contractor. I remember one day I could hear Regan, McFarland, and the contractor from inside the office trailer, yelling at the top of their lungs."

"Any idea what the argument was about?"

"Mostly about the work being behind schedule. That's all I could make out. McFarland's man was tough and didn't get along with the contractor's guys."

"What was the name of McFarland's man?"

"Regan. Bobby."

A Robert Regan was named in the suit Shea had filed.

"I read the news accounts about the collapse of the scaffolding. And saw that other workers were also injured, not only the two of you who filed suit."

"I heard a couple of others reached settlements. But I don't know if Doyle did. He was on the ground below. Paddy's a crazy guy." He laughed. "Always cursing about the abuses the workers suffered under the capitalists. The bum's a Commie."

"Do you know how I could reach Paddy Doyle?"

"Our union rep might know."

I thanked him and walked to the front door. He followed behind.

"I remember there was another guy alongside Paddy that day," he said. "Name of DeMarco. Joey DeMarco. Not sure what happened to him, but I hear he may have been hurt, too."

"I appreciate your help," I said.

"I wish I could be of more help, but like I said, I never got to know McFarland. He didn't mix with us workers."

I sat in my Subaru and phoned a union business agent who knew my late father.

"Fabiano, what the hell do you want?" The voice was gruff, but I knew he had a smile on his face.

"Nice to talk to you, too. I'm looking for two men who

might be among your members."

"Give me the names."

"Joey DeMarco and Paddy Doyle. That's probably short for Patrick."

"Hold on."

He came back on the line five minutes later and gave me their addresses. DeMarco lived in South Philly. Doyle's address was in the Northeast.

"Thanks. Appreciate the help."

"No problem, but it will cost you."

It always did.

"I'm sending you two tickets to our fundraiser for the families of our injured workers."

That meant a hundred bucks. "Good talking to you."

"Just put the check in the mail."

CHAPTER TWENTY-FOUR

Joey DeMarco lived in a modest rowhouse in a narrow, one-way street east of Broad. Parking was always tricky in South Philly, where the houses were built before the onslaught of automobiles. So, I arrived early in the morning, knowing residents would leave for work, pulling out of the scarce parking spaces.

I drove past DeMarco's house. Lights were on downstairs. Hopefully, DeMarco was in. I managed to snag a parking spot a block away when a woman drove off in her Honda.

A man in his thirties, about six feet with a mop of curly dark hair, opened the door when I rang the bell. He wore jeans and a tee shirt that showed off well-toned biceps and tattoos so dense they could have been another layer of clothing. He held a large mug of coffee in his hand. The aroma told me it was top-grade.

"Mr. DeMarco?"

"Who wants to know?"

I held up my PI license. "My name is Andrea Fabiano. I'm an insurance investigator."

He moved to shut the door, but I held it open with my tote, heavy enough to stop a bus. "I'd like to talk to you about a scaffolding accident you were involved in."

"I don't have time. I can't be late for work."

"This won't take long." I stepped inside.

He showed me into the living room. Like many homes in the area, no wall separated the living room from the dining room. DeMarco's dining table was piled with mail, work tools, and dirty dishes. He sat down on a plaid sofa and reached over to remove a tattered pair of jeans from an armchair so I could sit.

"What do you want to know?"

"What do you think caused the accident?"

"Don't really know. I got a nice settlement for my injuries. I got no complaints."

"You seemed to have recovered."

"I had cuts and bruises mostly, nothing serious."

"Not like the poor guys who filed the lawsuit."

"Yeah, I heard they got pretty banged up."

"And you're back to work now?"

"Right. I need to leave in a few minutes."

"Where are you working these days?"

"A redevelopment job by the airport."

"Would that be another McFarland property?"

"Yeah, it would. What of it?"

"Nothing. I'm happy to hear you have a job. What can you tell me about Sean McFarland?"

"Why do you want to know?" I saw a slight twitch in one cheek.

"I'm looking into several matters connected with him."

"I don't really know the man. Construction workers like me don't get to mingle with the big bosses."

I stood up. "I wondered if you happen to know Paddy Doyle? He was hurt in the accident as well."

"Don't know him either." Again, a facial twitch.

DeMarco was lying. But he wasn't good at it. Too many tells.

It was approaching nine, and I had an appointment at nine-thirty with executives at a Center City financial firm looking to hire an investigator. The meeting took over an hour. One of the executives told me they were interviewing other candidates and would let me know. I was always on the lookout for new clients, but this meeting might have been a waste of my time when I needed to move ahead with the caseload I was already working on.

On my way back to the office, I picked up a veggie wrap. While I ate it at my desk, I looked up the phone number for Doyle's address. The name listed was L. McCarthy. I called and got voicemail. "The McCarthy family is busy. Leave a message." I left my name and number and said I wanted to contact Paddy Doyle. No sense traveling all the way into the Northeast until I knew if Doyle still lived there.

I checked state records. Doyle didn't have a driver's license. Joey DeMarco's driver's license was expired. And there was no car registered in his name.

From the moment I laid eyes on Joey DeMarco, he had the look of a guy who served time. Turned out my hunch was correct. Pal Joey had a long record for burglaries, armed robbery, aggravated assaults, and weapons violations. He did a five-to-seven-year stretch in state prison and was paroled late last year. I called an assistant warden I knew who worked at the new Phoenix State Correctional Institution, built to replace the old prison.

"Hey Fabiano, how's it going?"

"Great. How's your new digs?"

"Okay. What can I do for you?"

"I'm working on a case and one of your former inmates by the name of Joey DeMarco cropped up. Whatever you could tell me about him, I'd appreciate." I gave him DeMarco's current address.

"Hang on. And let me see what I got."

While I waited, I checked my texts and emails. I was about to reply to a text when the assistant warden came back on the phone.

"DeMarco wasn't a model prisoner. He tried to stay out of trouble by keeping in shape, but the guy had a short fuse. He got into scraps with the other inmates and was written up quite a bit. We had to move him around. But the last year he was here, he was in with Dave Miller, the arsonist, and they seemed to get along."

My ears perked up at the mention of an arsonist. "What can you tell me about Miller?"

"He kept to himself and stayed out of trouble. Miller the Griller is how he's known. Seems to be proud of his skills."

"Is he still in prison?"

"Miller got paroled earlier this year."

"Then DeMarco and Miller knew each other. And they're both out on parole."

"You got it."

"You're the best. I'm treating you and your wife to a romantic dinner. The check will be in the mail today."

"You don't have to do that, but I won't say no to treating my wife."

When we hung up, I looked up Dave Miller's record. Just looking at his face, I knew he was a dangerous man. He had convictions for arson and was sentenced for nearly killing a man with his bare fists when he worked as a bouncer at a Philly nightclub.

I drove to the west side of Broad Street to the South Philly address I had for Miller. His house was on a tree-lined block, up-market from DeMarco's neighborhood. The window shades were lowered. A wreath of dried fall flowers decorated the front door, which was painted dark green. A feminine touch? I rang the doorbell. No response. I rang again, waited and then rapped on the door with my fist. No response. I slid my business card into the mail slot along with a note on the back to call me.

I noticed a curtain move next door, and a woman peered out her front window. I rang her bell. "You lookin' for the Millers?" she asked, standing in the doorway.

"Yes, I am."

"Police?"

I shook my head. "It's a private matter."

"She's at work. Him, I haven't seen for days. But that's not unusual. He's been in and out of prison since they moved here. He might be back in."

"I hope it wasn't for anything violent. Not with you living right next door."

"Don't know. But rumor is he's mobbed up. So, I stay away from them both."

"When was the last time you saw Dave Miller?"

"Couple of weeks ago. He was driving away in that big new car of his."

"What kind of car?"

"One of them SUVs. Dark. Don't know the make."

"Thanks for your help." So sometime after the warehouse fire, Dave Miller was seen driving away in his SUV and hadn't been seen by his neighbor since. Somehow, I didn't think that was a coincidence.

CHAPTER TWENTY-FIVE

That evening, I attended my ongoing self-defense class. My friend Maggie Connors, an assistant U.S. attorney, taught the course and encouraged me to come to keep up my skills.

I arrived late. Maggie, in her heavily padded model mugger suit, was working with a new member of the class who was having a tough time attacking.

"You're not going to hurt me," Maggie explained. "You're here to learn to defend yourself. So, come on, I want you to practice the moves from last week."

The woman broke down in tears.

"Okay. Why don't you go sit down for now and watch the others?"

Maggie worked with the class, having them practice basic skills, going for her nose, and stomping on her foot.

"Okay, Andrea, you're up," Maggie said.

She put both hands on my shoulders, and suddenly I was back in the kitchen with my uncle. My anger swelled. I inhaled deeply and reminded myself it was Maggie in front of me, not my drunken uncle. "Come on, show me what you got." Hearing Maggie's voice brought me back to the present. I aimed for her nose, kicked her knee, and then stomped on her foot.

"Good," Maggie said. "You acted fast and kept up your attack. Okay, who's up next?"

An hour later, the class was over, and the students were gone. Maggie and I went to the showers.

"I'd like you to start teaching the class with me," Maggie said. "You have the experience, and I could use your help."

I never expected her to ask me. The image of me assaulting a student popped into my head. I only joined Maggie's class after she insisted that I needed to practice my self-defense skills, considering my line of work. "Let me think about it," I said.

I entered the shower and let the water pour over my hair and body. My mind brought me back to the day my uncontrolled anger got me thrown out of the Philadelphia Police Academy.

The rage rose out of my stomach, into my chest, then erupted like hot lava.

My peripheral vision was gone. I saw only my attacker, his face close, his arms tight on my shoulders, using his upper body strength to try to push me to the ground.

No way was I losing this fight. I reached for his throat with both hands and tightened my grip.

He gasped for breath. I increased the pressure.

A loud voice penetrated my bubble. "Stop. Training's over."

From behind, two massive hands grabbed mine and pulled me away. "Enough. I said the session's over."

I turned to face him. I pushed him back, kicked him in the stomach, and punched him in the nose, hearing a bone crack.

Suddenly I was on my back, restrained by more arms than I could count, struggling to break free.

"This time, you've gone too far, Fabiano. You're out of here."

"What's taking you so long in there?" Maggie called out. "I need my coffee and chocolate."

I started to breathe normally and turned off the water. "Be right out."

At a nearby coffee shop, Maggie ordered her usual cappuccino. I chose chamomile tea.

"Why herbal tea?" she asked.

"It will help me sleep." The truth was my queasy stomach couldn't digest anything heavier.

I snagged a table and sipped my tea while Maggie waited for her coffee.

Maggie sat down and placed a piece of chocolate cake between us. "It looks sinfully rich." She took a forkful. "Yum. Have some."

I picked up a forkful and placed it on my napkin.

"Andrea, aren't you feeling well? First the tea, now no interest in chocolate. What's going on?"

I didn't want to discuss the replay in my head and switched to another subject. "I'm not making much progress in one of my cases."

She wiped chocolate icing from her top lip. "Is that what's bothering you?"

I nodded, staring down at the chocolate cake but seeing myself assaulting a fellow police trainee. "Tell me, Maggie, what do you know about LLCs? And how I can get to see their financials?"

"LLCs are private. They don't have to file with the SEC."

"That I know. I was thinking of other ways."

"Subpoena for probable cause is the only way I know. Do you have evidence that could get a subpoena?"

"I'm trying to get enough to see if anything isn't quite kosher." Other than breaking in and searching McFarland's office, I wasn't coming up with a viable plan that wasn't against the law and likely to get me caught.

"In one of my cases, I was able to turn the accountant," Maggie said. "They always know the score."

CHAPTER TWENTY-SIX

That night I dreamed I was training at the police academy. I woke in a sweat at two a.m. In my dream, I killed my opponent. The only real damage I had caused back then was breaking the instructor's nose, but it wasn't for lack of trying. Before I was dismissed, I had a session with a department shrink. The diagnosis was uncontrollable anger when I felt physically threatened. I went to my own therapist, got a PI license, and stuck to investigating white-collar crime, a safer bet against physical attacks.

I turned on the lamp and drank the entire glass of water on my nightstand. Then I turned my mind toward how I could get to McFarland's accountant. Maggie was right. A CPA would know every aspect of a client's finances.

I got out of bed, put on a robe, and turned on my laptop. I searched the client lists of the larger accounting firms in the city, but McFarland's company didn't appear. I searched media reports on McFarland and his company. I rechecked the company's website and its press releases. No mention of his accounting firm. I needed a better method, but my mind was blank. Frustrated, I put McFarland aside, showered, dressed, and made a thermos of coffee. I drove to my office at four a.m. It was cold and dark, and light rain made the chill seem rawer. The building's heat hadn't turned on yet, so I kept on my jacket and grabbed the blanket from my sofa to wrap around my legs.

I still couldn't think of another angle to finding McFarland's accountant, so I turned to the problem of finding Nate Warner's stash. As I sipped coffee to warm my insides, I looked over a map of Center City. An idea flashed into my brain. I could take a similar approach I used looking for Jason. I had checked out churches in the area where Jason was seen. Now, I made a list of post offices, banks, and private mail stores within a two-mile radius of SEPA Financial's office. Places where Nate could have secreted his information.

It was a little after six, way too early to start down my list, but not too early for a hearty breakfast at a nearby deli to warm me up.

When I returned to my office, the heat was on, and I dove into paperwork and timesheets I had been avoiding. At nine o'clock, I left the office again.

I visited banks and post offices. The banks refused to tell me if Nate had rented a safe deposit box. Ditto at the post office. The records were confidential, and no matter what story I gave, I failed to con them into coughing up any info.

I grabbed a quick lunch, stopped at an office supply store where I bought a manila envelope, wrote Nate's name on it, and then visited a for-profit mailbox store.

"I have a piece of mail for Nate Warner. Could you put it in his mailbox?"

"We don't usually do that sort of thing," a pimply teenager said.

"Could you check your records? I'm sure he has a box here."

She searched her computer. "No one by that name has an account here."

"Are you sure? Nate Warner."

"No, not on our list."

I tried my phony envelope trick at three other stores. None had rented a box to Nate. By now the rain was heavy, turning store awnings into waterfalls and crosswalks into mini lakes. I opened my umbrella, pulled up my jacket collar against the damp, and walked back to my office. At my desk, I answered voicemails and emails, trying to take my focus away from my failure to find Jason or Nate's stash.

My phone rang and interrupted my sulking. The caller ID read "private."

"You stop pokin' around where you don't belong. Back off before you land in the hospital with more broken bones than you know you got." The caller hung up.

I shivered even though the heat made my office toasty warm. I didn't recognize the voice, but it was male with a classic nasal Philadelphia accent. His tone was even, and he spoke in a whisper. But the threat was clear enough.

Outside, the downpour continued, and wind rattled the windows. I felt exhausted since I had gotten little sleep and had been at work for fourteen hours. I took my brass knuckles and a can of mace from my desk drawer and stuffed them into my jacket pockets.

I raced to my Subaru, spooked by the caller. Once inside, I locked all the doors and burnt rubber exiting the lot. "Sorry, Bella." I didn't inhale a normal breath until I collapsed onto my living room sofa.

Who had I ticked off enough to threaten me? Newman, McFarland's attorney, who had warned me off? DeMarco, the ex-con and construction worker? The tail I had picked up? Whoever it was had me all wrong. I wasn't about to give up, no matter how they tried to frighten me, even though they were succeeding. The tail and the threat were signs that I was on the right track. I was making more progress than I had thought.

CHAPTER TWENTY-SEVEN

I had finished my comfort food dinner—soup, warm Italian bread, and red wine—when my cell phone pinged. I had a new email message. It was a nasty note from Steve Kramer telling me he was prepared to fire me. "You have one more week. Then you're out."

He seemed more interested in concealing his abusive behavior than finding his son.

I was tired and wanted to deal with this in the morning, but instead, I took a quick nap, then drank two cups of coffee. By this time, the rain had calmed to a light drizzle.

I drove to the Kramer home in Bryn Mawr. It was a two-story federal-style brick, set back from the road, screened by tall fir trees. A red Jaguar and a black BMW sat in the circular driveway. To keep from giving Bella an inferiority complex, I parked my Subaru a good six feet away from the luxury cars. I patted her hood. "It's alright. I still love you."

Nan Kramer answered the door when I rang and stood as rigid as Lot's wife turned into a pillar of salt. The shocked look on her face, however, was all too human.

"May I come in?" I asked.

She seemed to recover herself. "You have bad news about Jason."

I shook my head. "Not bad news. But I do need to speak to you and your husband."

"What's this about?"

"I'd prefer to discuss it with both of you."

Mrs. Kramer led me down a hall, past a spacious living room, and into a den with a sixty-inch TV. Both rooms were empty.

"Is your husband home?"

Mrs. Kramer held her mouth like she was about to puke on the carpet. "He's upstairs."

I smiled. "I'll wait while you get him."

Shortly after she left, I heard voices upstairs. The male voice was harsh, almost staccato, but I couldn't make out what he was saying. Then the house grew quiet until the sound of uneven footsteps pounded down the stairs. Suddenly I had a lump in my throat, expecting Uncle Dominic to walk through the door. Instead, Mr. Kramer appeared, his eyes glassy, his gait uncertain.

"We haven't met. I'm Andrea Fabiano." I held out my hand.

"I know who you are." He ignored my hand, but I noticed a slight tremor in his.

"This is my husband, Steve." Mrs. Kramer forced a smile.

"My wife is paying you top dollar, and you haven't found my son. I want to see results, or we get someone else."

Mr. Kramer was drunk despite his best efforts to mask it. After living with an alcoholic uncle, I picked up the telltale signs.

His wife put her hand on his arm. He pushed her away. "Don't try to shut me up." He turned to me. "I already told you in my email that you have one more week. I'll not have you bleed us."

I sat down. Mrs. Kramer followed suit.

I gave my report. "I tracked down a priest who talked with Jason. Your son is alive and living on the city streets. If he remains in the city, which I believe he will, I'm optimistic that we can track him down, but it will take time. I've distributed his photo to shelters and churches around the city. Lower Merion police are working with police in Philly and the surrounding counties. Jason's picture has been on TV and posted on social media. We'll find him."

"Not good enough."

This guy was right up there with the late Nate Warner, demanding results while wanting to pinch pennies.

"I've worked many missing person cases over the years," I began.

"Ms. Fabiano has an excellent track record," Nan Kramer jumped in. "That's why I hired her, hon." Mrs. Kramer's voice, soft and soothing, had the perfect pitch for a meditation tape. She seemed to have gained lots of experience in calming down her volatile husband.

"Certainly, it's up to you whether or not you want to continue with my services," I said. "But any honest investigator will tell you that it takes time and persistence to locate a runaway. Especially one who doesn't want to be found."

I turned to Nan Kramer. "I've asked you several times what motivated Jason to run away on that particular night. I still haven't gotten a direct answer."

"It's none of your god-damned business," Steve Kramer said. "We're not paying you to pry into private family matters."

"Unfortunately, Mr. Kramer, it's usually a private family matter that leads a teen to run off."

Mrs. Kramer intervened once again with her melodious tones. "Why don't I talk with Ms. Fabiano? You're tired and have so much on your mind at work. Go on upstairs and rest."

Hit the bottle was more like it, I thought. Still, I was with her. Get this man out of the room. I wanted to learn something useful. Before I got fired.

He turned on his heels and tripped. "Have it your way."

Once he left, Mrs. Kramer attempted another tight smile. "I must apologize. Steve is under tremendous pressure at work and now this."

"No need." I figured the poor woman spent enough time making excuses for her husband's behavior.

"Can I get you something to drink?" She caught herself. "Soda? Coffee or tea?"

"Thanks, no. Let's talk about Jason."

"I told you, he's smart. He excels at school."

"Why do you think he ran away? He's jeopardizing his

school grades when he wants to get into a top university."

"I don't know." Mrs. Kramer fought back tears.

"How does he get along with his father?"

"Fine. Steve has high expectations for Jason."

"I can understand that." After seeing Mr. Kramer's behavior, I could guess how he might parent his son. "But can you be more specific about their relationship?"

Nan Kramer's shoulders slumped, and she looked down at her hands folded tightly in her lap. "Steve knows how tough it is to get ahead in the business world. He wants Jason to be prepared. He tells Jason that he'll never be a successful man unless he toughens up."

Way to go, Steve. Question your son's manhood when he's a confused teen.

"It sounds like your husband has been aggressive with Jason for some time. So why did Jason run away that specific night?"

A tear trickled down Mrs. Kramer's cheeks.

"I see this is painful, but you want your son to come home, don't you?"

She nodded.

"I know Jason left here with a black eye."

"How do you know that?"

"It's my job. And I know when someone is trying to hide the facts."

Nan Kramer lifted her head. Her face lost its tenseness. Finally, she seemed ready to level with me. "Steve had arranged for Jason to attend military school. That night Jason pleaded with him. He loves his school and does so well there. He didn't see why he had to leave Penn Wynn. I didn't either. But Steve insisted that Jason needed more discipline. Needed to toughen up, as he always says. I can't say I blamed Jason for not wanting to go."

"Mrs. Kramer, there's something I need to ask you. It may be unpleasant. But your husband's drinking. How bad has it been?"

She started to sob quietly. "Earlier that night, I tried to talk him out of the military school, but he was drinking. He gets even more stubborn when he drinks." She wiped a wet cheek with the palm of her hand.

I handed her a packet of tissues from my tote. "Is that why his confrontation with Jason turned violent?"

She nodded. "By the time Jason came home from soccer practice, Steve had been drinking for hours. He told Jason he had no choice but to obey. Jason said he didn't want to toughen up and become as inhumane as his father." She muffled her sobs with her tissues.

"Steve slapped Jason across the face. And Jason hit him back. Jason should never have done that, no matter how wrong Steve was. It made my husband furious. He grabbed Jason by the shoulders and kept slapping his face again and again. I tried to stop him, but he pushed me away. But then Jason's nose started bleeding, and Steve finally stepped back. His hands were shaking. That's when Jason ran out the front door. I begged him not to go." Mrs. Kramer began to cry again, this time not trying to mask her sobs.

"Had your husband been violent before? Has he harmed you or your son?"

Mrs. Kramer wiped her eyes, blew her nose, and stood up. "I've said enough. Steve will not be pleased with me talking about our family this way."

"If you want your son to live here, I'd say you need some outside help to deal with your problems."

"I want you to find him for me, not analyze our family. I have nightmares about Jason living on the street among criminals and addicts. I want him to be safe."

"The question you have to ask is whether Jason is safe at home."

"I love my son, and he'll always be safe here. I'm paying you to find him, not play family counselor," she snapped at me.

I left the Kramer home feeling angry and conflicted. Did I

want to find this kid and bring him back to this toxic home? Steve Kramer was a nasty piece of work who drank too much. I doubted it was the first time he was violent with his family. Nan Kramer seemed a decent sort, but she was in denial that her family needed help. I could see why Jason didn't want to live there. Neither would I.

CHAPTER TWENTY-EIGHT

I was procrastinating. Instead of working, I was going through my mail and eating chocolate bars. Earlier, I had called the McCarthy home looking for Paddy Doyle, but my call went to voicemail again. The family still seemed too busy to answer the phone. I checked in again with my police contact regarding Jason Kramer. "No sign of the kid. At least we haven't found a body." I called Tom to learn his progress on Nate's murder but got his voicemail.

I leaned back in my chair, glancing through a travel brochure that I received in the mail from Smithsonian Journeys, dreaming about seeing far-off destinations at prices I couldn't afford. Frustrated I stood up and paced around the office, kicked over my trash basket, battered a pillow, and punched a wall. Working long hours following up lead after lead brought me no closer to solving either of these cases. And now I had a week to find Jason or the Kramers would pull the plug. But my temper tantrum did nothing for me but build up a sweat. I sat down and bit into another piece of dark chocolate with sea salt.

Snap out of it, Fabiano. Stop wallowing in self-pity. Persistence is what you claim is your best tactic as an investigator. I picked up the trash strewn across the floor and righted the basket.

Suddenly, my office door was pushed open. A man with a mass of salt-and-pepper hair came barreling through, slamming the door so hard my coatrack nearly toppled over. I sat up straight and dropped my chocolate bar into a desk drawer. I recognized him from his picture on his website. It was Michael Shea, attorney for the men suing McFarland.

"Why the hell were you poking around my client behind

my back?" He didn't bother with any social niceties. "SEPA Financial isn't the insurer for the Riverfront condos. What game are you playing?"

"No game. If you returned my calls, you'd know I'm working on a separate matter which isn't connected, per se, with your lawsuit."

He took a deep breath. "Does it have anything to do with the three fires at McFarland's properties?"

"I expected you to be well informed, but I didn't realize you knew about the fires. Most people haven't made the connection."

"I'm not most people."

"Which is why I want to talk with you."

"You went to see my client, knowing it would piss me off enough to get a reaction."

"It seems to have worked. I wanted you to answer my calls. And here you are visiting me personally." I smiled. "Happy to meet you, Mr. Shea." I held out my hand.

Shea laughed as he gave me a firm handshake.

I opened the bottom drawer of my desk and pulled out my half-filled bottle of Dewar's. "Drink?"

"Why the hell not?" He sat down in a client chair. "If I ever need to hire a PI that I know will make a pest of themself, I'll keep you in mind."

I poured two glasses and handed him one. "Cheers."

He took a swig and placed his glass on my desk. "Okay, let's talk. You first."

I took a sip to be friendly, trying not to breathe in the smell. "Is there any indication that the scaffolding at the condo site was sabotaged?"

"What makes you ask? I'll grant you McFarland was penny-pinching on the project and jeopardizing the safety of the workers. But I can't imagine why he would deliberately sabotage his own project."

"What if it wasn't McFarland but someone who had a

grudge against him, a serious enough grudge that led to sabotage and possibly arson?"

"You're not implying it was one of my clients?"

"Not at all. But I wouldn't rule out the other workers at the site. I've spoken to one of the men who settled out of court."

"Who was that?"

"Joey DeMarco, an ex-con."

"And he worked at the Riverfront site?"

"He did, and he wasn't at all cooperative."

"He likely signed a nondisclosure agreement. I'm telling you the accident was caused by negligence. And I'll prove it in court." Shea took another swig of his Scotch.

"I have no doubt you'll do a good job for your clients. Tell me what you know about Robert Regan, who you named in your lawsuit."

"Regan's worked for McFarland for years," Shea said. "They've been buddies since high school. He was McFarland's clerk of the works at the Riverfront site."

"And he still works for McFarland?" I asked.

"He's a manager with Riverfront Enterprises. They have an office downtown."

"I know the building." I didn't mention that I'd followed Leather Jacket there. "Would you happen to have the names of the investors in the Riverfront project?"

"McFarland's lawyer hasn't turned over that information, not so far." Shea drained his glass and got up to leave.

"One other thing." I followed him to the door. "Do you know the accounting firm representing McFarland?"

"What kind of investigator are you? I'd have thought you would have found that out by now."

"You do know, don't you?"

Shea grinned. "The firm is Hayes and Osborne. I saw the name of Caroline Hewitt on some documents."

"Appreciate it." I handed over my card. "Do let me know if

I can ever be of help to you in your work."

He inspected my card, smiled, and shook his head. "It's been an unusual treat meeting you."

CHAPTER TWENTY-NINE

Once Shea left, I poured the rest of my Scotch back into the bottle.

Then I phoned the accounting firm, Hayes and Osborne, and asked to speak with Caroline Hewitt.

"Sorry. Ms. Hewitt doesn't work here any longer. I can transfer you to another accountant."

"Do you know where she's working now?"

"I'm not allowed to give out that information."

Through the Pennsylvania Institute of CPAs, I learned that Caroline Hewitt now had her own practice in Narberth, a tiny borough west of the city with a high percentage of married couples with children. Not my kind of neighborhood. I had only ventured there once to attend a friend's wedding at St. Margaret's church. Now seemed as good a time as any for another visit.

Caroline Hewitt was tall and slender with ash blonde hair. She wore a jade green jacket sweater, a pale taupe pencil skirt, and beige three-inch heels.

"Good to meet you, Ms. Fabiano." She led me into her office, its furnishings sleek and modern like its occupant. "I understand from my secretary you wanted to discuss an accounting issue."

"Actually, I'm a private investigator and already have an accountant." I showed her my license. "I want to talk to you about your experience working on the Sean McFarland account."

Her cheeks grew rosy, and it wasn't from blusher. "I don't

appreciate the subterfuge. Besides, I can't reveal confidential information to you or anyone else."

"But you've left your former employer Hayes and Osborne. Why was that?"

"I don't have to explain my career decisions to you. Now I need to get back to work. Since you aren't here to hire me."

"You're not at all curious why a private investigator is asking about McFarland's financial records?"

"I'm not interested." Caroline Hewitt stood up. "Now, I'm swamped. My secretary will show you out."

"You might want to reconsider and talk to me." I tried a bluff. "What do you think could happen to you and your practice when Mr. McFarland goes down for fraud?" I left my business card on her desk, moved to the door, then turned around to face her. "I can help you as much as you can help me."

"Just go."

Strikeout. I thought about searching Hewitt's office after hours. The bummer these days is the widespread use of surveillance cameras, electronic security systems, and computerized records that require passwords. None of which Philip Marlowe or Sam Spade ever had to deal with.

Rather than return to my office, I drove to the Northeast to visit the McCarthy home. If Doyle wasn't there, the McCarthys might know where to find him.

The Northeast section of the city is referred to as the Great Northeast. My reading is that the name refers to its size, not its status. It's a sprawling area of rowhomes, track housing, and strip malls. It's home to the city's middle and working class.

The McCarthy home was in the center of a block of houses built after the Second World War to meet the needs of returning GIs and their new families. A white and green aluminum awning hung above the front door.

A woman with a mop of brown curly hair answered the bell. I identified myself.

"And you are?" I asked.

"Sue McCarthy. You're the one leaving messages all the time."

"I'm looking for Paddy Doyle."

"He isn't here. Hasn't been for months. My husband doesn't like him around our kids."

"You're related then?"

"He's my brother."

"Do you know where I can find him?"

Mrs. McCarthy let out a deep sigh. "Paddy's had bad problems since he came back from Afghanistan. I'm sure you've heard these stories before in your line of work."

"Drugs? Alcohol?"

"Both. Paddy's living on the streets somewhere. He comes here from time to time, but like I said, my husband doesn't want him. Nobody wants him. It didn't use to be that way."

"May I come in?"

"Sorry for forgetting my manners." She opened the door wider to let me in, and we stood in the foyer. "I get upset whenever I think about my brother."

"I understand he was working on a construction project recently."

"He did mention something about that the last time I saw him."

"When was that?"

"Not sure. Sometime in the summer. He was so thin I almost didn't recognize him. He stopped by one afternoon when the kids were at day camp, and my husband was at work. He knows he makes them uncomfortable. He showered, shaved, and put on the clean clothes I kept for him. He ate lunch and then left. Paddy told me he was working at a construction site down near the waterfront. He worked as a laborer on and off. He couldn't keep a steady job. Not with the drugs and all. Still, I told him I was glad he was working."

Sue McCarthy walked into the living room, and I followed. She reached into the drawer of a side table and showed me a photo. "This is from some years ago. Before he went to war, he spent a week with us in Ocean City that summer. This is how I like to remember him."

A smiling tanned young man in bathing trunks looked back at me. His curly hair was damp from a swim, and he had a tattoo on his arm. I looked closer. I had seen the same tattoo in the same spot before. On the victim at the warehouse fire.

"His tattoo is a Celtic design."

Mrs. McCarthy smiled. "Paddy's always been big on his heritage."

"Did he ever mention any accident at the construction site?"

Mrs. McCarthy shook her head.

"He didn't complain of any injuries?"

"He was thin and pale, like I said. But I didn't see any bruises." She paused. "He did seem nervous and a bit shaky, but I figured he hadn't gotten his heroin."

"Could I have a look at the room he uses when he's here?"

"What's this really about?"

"I may know where your brother is, but I need to be certain."

"What's the mystery? He's one of the city's homeless?" She started to cry.

"Please, would you show me?"

Sue McCarthy took me to the basement. It was paneled and carpeted. One side of the room contained a sofa, a floor lamp, and an electric heater. The other side was a jumble of children's toys and sports equipment.

"That's a sleep sofa," Mrs. McCarthy said. "I try to make Paddy feel comfortable whenever he comes to see me. Unfortunately, he came less and less these past few years."

I noticed a suitcase near the floor lamp. "Is that your brother's?"

"He keeps it here, and I leave fresh clothes in it for whenever he shows up," she said.

"May I have a look?"

"I don't see why." She hesitated. "But I guess there's no harm."

Inside the suitcase were neatly folded tee shirts, boxer shorts, and a pair of pajamas. I felt something between the folds of the pj's. It was a plastic bag containing a wallet and a driver's license, both caked in mud. The name and photo on the license weren't Doyle's. It belonged to a Greg Saunders. I held up the plastic bag for Mrs. McCarthy to see. "Have you seen these before?"

She shook her head no. "If Paddy stole those, you won't tell the cops?"

"No worries. When was the last time you put clothes in here or looked inside?"

"I don't remember exactly. Paddy had changed here, so I put clean underwear on top after his visit. I had to throw out the ripped jeans he came in wearing."

"And you didn't see these?"

"I didn't move the pj's. And I don't go through his stuff. I figure he deserves some privacy."

I put on latex gloves and opened the plastic bag to take a closer look. The wallet was empty of cash but contained Saunders' license and credit cards. I took photos of all the items, placed them back into the plastic bag, and slipped the bag back where I found it. Then I unzipped the inside pocket across the top of the suitcase. I found three pairs of men's socks, bulging with whatever was stuffed inside.

"What's that?" Mrs. McCarthy said.

I reached into one sock, and hundred-dollar bills came out in my hand.

His sister let out a gasp. "Oh, my God."

"Any idea where this money came from?"

"None."

I emptied the other sock in the pair. Besides more cash, stuffed inside the toe was a folded piece of paper. It was a note. "Sue, if anything happens to me, this is yours. For all your kindness and for putting up with me and my bad habits. Love, Paddy."

"This is for you." I handed over the note, and while his sister read it, I found money in all three pairs of socks, which totaled four thousand dollars. Had Doyle been compensated for his injuries at the construction site?

"Did your brother gamble?"

"Never. Paddy spent his money on drugs and alcohol. He might have stolen it if he was desperate enough for drugs." Mrs. McCarthy rubbed her forehead.

"But then he wouldn't have left it here for you." Neither of us could explain the money. "I'm putting all of it back where I found it," I said.

When I got back in my car, I called Tom. "I may have identified the warehouse fire victim."

"I don't suppose I should ask how you managed that when you were supposed to stick to investigating the fire."

"As luck would have it, I was following up on the fire and this information fell into my lap. Do you want what I have or not?"

"Give it to me."

"Patrick 'Paddy' Doyle, a construction worker and addict. He served in the military, so they'll have records. In a picture at his sister's home, he has a Celtic tattoo on his arm. Same place and design as our victim. His sister, Sue McCarthy, lives in the Northeast." I gave Tom the address.

"Thanks. We'll get on it."

"Tom, Doyle worked on McFarland's Riverfront condo project. And he might have been among the workers injured in a scaffolding accident there. Several men reached settlements with McFarland's firm, but it's not clear if Doyle did as well. That may or may not be significant. Two of the others injured filed a negligence lawsuit, but Doyle is not one of them."

"You have been busy," he said.

I didn't mention Doyle's pile of cash. I had to leave something for the cops to think they discovered first.

CHAPTER THIRTY

Caroline Hewitt, McFarland's former accountant, would be my ideal source to learn the inner workings of McFarland's business operations. Still, no matter how hard I tried to push her, she wasn't talking. It was time to turn to my next best source. Former spouses. They always knew secrets their exes preferred to keep hidden.

The divorced Mrs. McFarland could be just the person to help me determine what, if any, relationship her ex-husband had with the late Nate Warner. She lived in an older condo building on Washington Square in the city's historic Society Hill neighborhood, pricey and close to Independence Hall. And she worked in administration at the University of Pennsylvania. When I reached her at her office, it took time to convince her to talk to me, but not much.

"I can meet for coffee after work," she finally told me.

Mrs. McFarland was already at a table when I arrived at Starbucks, and she rose to shake my hand. She wore a light gray cardigan, black pants and turtleneck, and a silver pendant. Her chestnut brown hair was shoulder length, layered to take advantage of its natural wave.

"I appreciate you agreeing to talk to me." I gave her my business card.

She smiled. "I can't say I'm surprised a private investigator would be interested in Sean, but I confess to being curious about what exactly you suspect him of doing."

I told her about the fires, the death of a homeless man, and the murder of Nate Warner. "I believe they may all be connected to your husband, Mrs. McFarland."

"Ex-husband. And call me Jeanne. I prefer Jeanne." She tucked a strand of hair behind an ear. "I can believe him capable of anything that could advance his business. But not murder." She paused. "Sean was always ambitious. It was one of his traits that I admired at first. He wanted better for his family. But he changed over the years. He became more and more obsessed with making as much money as possible."

"You've been divorced for about a year, I understand."

"Fourteen months."

"I've been told you received a substantial settlement."

She grinned. "Sean likes to make himself out a martyr. I made certain he took care of his three children and their college education. I asked for alimony only until I found a job. I didn't want to be dependent on him."

"Any indication that your ex-husband is having financial difficulties?"

"He's been late with his child support payments. And earlier this year, he called me and gave me a sob story about cash flow problems. He told me he could either pay child support or my alimony, but not both. I didn't believe him, but I didn't want the stress of another court hearing. I told him to take care of the children. But I wasn't being generous. I was starting this job the next week."

"You mentioned you wanted to be independent. Is that the main reason you divorced?"

"Where to begin?" She looked up at the ceiling. "Sean became distant not only with me but with the children. When he was home, he stayed in his office and even ate his dinners there. Then there were his affairs."

"Other women?"

"Too many to count. Sean wasn't interested in our marriage any longer. So eventually, I wasn't either."

"I'm sorry."

"No need to be. My children and I are doing very well. You see, Sean was no longer the man I married. Or maybe I just didn't see things quite so clearly at the beginning. I'm ashamed to say that Sean wasn't entirely ethical in his business dealings. I knew he bought older apartment buildings to renovate. But later, I learned he forced out the old tenants and raised the rents when the buildings reopened."

"How do you know that?"

"I received a phone call one night while we were still married. It was an elderly woman. I could tell from her raspy voice. She told me the elevators weren't working in her building. She had a heart condition and couldn't manage the stairs. She said Bobby told her the building was old and she couldn't expect the conveniences of a modern building. And he more than suggested she find another place to live. When I asked why the super wasn't helping, she said he had moved out and wasn't replaced. I told Sean about the call. He brushed me off and said I didn't understand the business. 'I need to clear that building if I want to make money on it.' It sounded sleazy to me."

The more I learned about Sean McFarland, the less I liked him. "You mentioned a Bobby?"

She nodded. "Bobby Regan. Sean and Bobby have been tight since high school." She laughed. "I was about to say they're as thick as thieves. Bobby is one tough guy. I never liked him."

Regan was named in Shea's negligence suit. "Can you tell me anything else about your ex-husband's business?"

"Such as?"

"Do you remember his dealings with SEPA Financial?"

"Just that the company insured some of his properties. I didn't know until you told me that SEPA Financial insured the buildings that suffered fire damage." She paused. "I'm not a fan of Sean at this point, but it's hard for me to believe he'd commit arson."

"Did he ever mention the name of Nate Warner? He was an executive at SEPA Financial?"

She paused again, then shook her head. "I never heard the name. But I remember one night shortly before we separated, Sean was talking to Bobby in our kitchen. Bobby said something like, 'My guy at SEPA Financial told me he couldn't chance doing any more favors for us. Not now anyway.' Sean slammed his fists on the table. 'Christ. After all I did for the bastard.' When I walked into the room, they stopped talking."

"And you're sure it was Bobby who said he had a contact at SEPA Financial?"

"I'm certain," Mrs. McFarland said. "If you ask me, that man is trouble. He always has a scheme going to make a quick buck."

"But you didn't hear the name of the person he referred to?"

"I didn't hear it, but I'm not sure he used it." Jeanne McFarland then leaned across the table toward me and lowered her voice. "Now, Bobby is someone I'd look at if I were you. He'd be capable of killing anyone who got in his way."

That night I left my office late, after the parking lot had emptied out. While I was unlocking my car, a bullet struck the back door of my Subaru. I gasped and ducked down, then made my way slowly to the passenger side, remained crouched and didn't move. I scanned the lot for any movement in the dim light. I listened for any sound. Nothing. Another bullet whizzed over the car roof. The shooter was using a sound suppressor, and the shots came from the direction of Chestnut Street.

I carefully lifted my head just enough to take a quick look toward the street. Cars drove by as usual. Pedestrians weren't running for cover. I checked the roofs of the surrounding buildings. No signs of a shooter.

I slipped through the passenger door, climbed into the driver's seat, and floored the gas pedal, speeding out the lot's rear exit. I took evasive actions, turning left then right through the city streets. No one seemed to be following me. I drove home slowly, keeping an eye on my rearview mirror.

When I parked in my driveway, still panting to get back my

breath, I got out to check the damage to my faithful, reliable Subaru that I've owned for fifteen years. "You'll need a new rear door, my dear Bella," I patted her roof, "but no internal damage as far as I can tell. I'll get you fixed up, and you'll be back to your usual self."

I walked onto my porch, but before I could unlock the door, a bullet buzzed past my ear, knocking out my porch light. My reflexes were faster this time. I ducked behind one of my porch chairs. Now I was more angry than scared. Who the hell was shooting at me? I peered out from behind the chair and saw a car speed off. It was a black Dodge Charger like the car that tailed me when I went to the West Philly after-school program. It was too dark for me to see the license plate numbers, so I still only had a partial ID.

My hands were trembling as I unlocked my front door. I sank down on the sofa and slid under my afghan. Gradually the warmth of the wool stopped my shaking. But I knew now that my investigations were putting me in greater jeopardy than I had imagined. "I could have been killed tonight," I screamed.

I got up, poured a thimble-full of Scotch, and managed to get it down without gagging. Then realized I drank more Scotch these last few days than in my entire life. I didn't want to get used to the stuff. I went into the bathroom to take a warm shower, then got into bed, drawing my comforter up to my neck. I woke up an hour later and sat up. The shooter had ample opportunities to kill me. He was either a lousy shot or he only wanted to scare me. Hell, he had succeeded in terrifying me. But he had also unleashed my anger. Now it was his turn to be scared.

CHAPTER
THIRTY-ONE

Early next morning, I dropped my injured Subaru off at the body shop and picked up a rental. Then I phoned the handyman I hired for jobs around my house and asked him to install new, more powerful lights on my front and back porches.

I tried reaching Caroline Hewitt again, but she didn't take my calls.

I wanted to call Tom, but I decided to put it off. He'd give me one of his lectures about quitting the PI business and going back to finish law school. Besides, I didn't have enough evidence yet on the shooter.

It had to be my SEPA Financial investigation that was attracting the gunfire. But no way did I think McFarland would get his own hands dirty. He'd hire someone to come after me. Dave Miller didn't seem to be in town. And as far as I knew, he drove an SUV. And he was more likely to be hired for his skills as an arsonist, not a stalker and gunman. I scratched him off my list for the time being.

Joey DeMarco was a more likely candidate. He knew more than he coughed up, and those tics of his told me he had something to hide.

I drove over to DeMarco's house. Before I could park the rental, DeMarco came out of his front door and started walking down the block. I followed in my car. He didn't look back but kept walking. If he had been my tail, at least I was driving a different car, and he might not make me.

I waited at a four-way stop sign until I saw him cross into the next street. I let two cars go through the intersection before me. By this time, DeMarco was halfway down the next block. He stopped and got in on the driver's side of a black car. I drove into the block, parked near a fire hydrant, and waited.

When DeMarco pulled out, he was driving a black Dodge Charger, and this time I got his complete license plate number. I tailed him to Passyunk Avenue near the Melrose Diner. He found a parking spot and entered the restaurant.

I parked blocks away and walked back. Inside, DeMarco was giving his order to a waitress. I sat down across from him.

"What the hell are you doing here?"

I stared at DeMarco but didn't speak.

He avoided eye contact.

The waitress returned, smiling. "*Cawfee* for you both?"

"Please," I said, returning her smile.

"What else can I get for you?" she asked me.

"She's not eating," DeMarco barked at the waitress.

"The coffee is fine."

When she walked away, I stared at DeMarco. "Don't you know it's against the law to drive with an expired license?"

DeMarco remained silent.

"But then again, you have something more serious to worry about. I know you've been tailing me, threatening me, and shooting at me. And that Charger isn't registered to you. Did you steal it, Joey?"

DeMarco's eye twitched. "My brother-in-law let me use his car. And I don't know what the fuck you're talking about."

"Don't even try to lie. I want to know who hired you to come after me."

"Don't make me laugh."

"It might go easier on you if you talk to me rather than the cops."

"Do you think I'm a sucker for that crap?"

The waitress placed an omelet with ham, cheese, onions, and peppers in front of DeMarco.

"More *cawfee*, folks?"

"Yes, please." I smiled and she poured refills for both of us. DeMarco grunted as she left.

It was tempting to reach for a forkful of his omelet, but I

didn't want to touch this guy or his food. DeMarco looked at me, sneering. "Lady, let me eat in peace before you give me *agita*."

"Who hired you?"

"You don't hear so good, do you? I told you I don't have nothin' to say." He shoveled a forkful of omelet into his mouth.

"Then you're a fool, Joey. The cops know it was you who attacked me," I lied.

"It's only a matter of time before they arrest you for attempted murder."

"You're the one that's stupid for giving me a heads-up."

He wasn't denying it.

"I'm offering you a deal. Talk to me, help me out here, and I'll help you out by not pressing charges. Otherwise, you'll go back inside. Goodbye to restaurant breakfasts."

Silence. But he didn't leave the table and chewed his omelet.

I tried another approach. "Then let's talk about Paddy Doyle. How did you know him?"

DeMarco's eyes widened, and both ears turned beet red.

"I can see you did know him, so don't even try to deny it. Doyle was killed in a recent warehouse fire, or should I say arson."

DeMarco's ears were still red, but now his face lost all its color.

"When the cops catch up with you and your pal Miller, you'll both be going down. Miller the Griller is what I believe he's called. Tell me what you know about him and Doyle, and maybe I can help you."

"Not in here."

We got up to leave. I paid the bill and left a tip.

"Where's your car?" DeMarco said.

We walked to my rental. Once he was seated in the passenger seat, DeMarco took out a pack of cigarettes. He lit one and offered me the pack.

"I'm set, thanks." I opened the windows partway. If I was driving Bella, she wouldn't like the smell, but then neither did I. "Now, let's have it. Tell me about Doyle."

"He worked on the Riverfront construction site. Day labor, not any skilled jobs. All I know is that he drank on the job, but he was clever at hiding it from the bosses."

"You're not telling much I don't already know."

"I hardly knew the guy."

"Doyle was in the same scaffolding accident you were. Did he receive a settlement like you did?"

"I don't know any of that legal shit."

"How much of a settlement did you get?"

"Four grand."

"That's quite a haul for minor scrapes and bruises."

"McFarland's the generous type."

"Or else he was paying you for something else entirely. Like an arson job?"

"I got nothing to say."

He didn't have to. The tic in his left cheek had kicked in.

"Let's get back to Doyle."

"I'll give you this much. Doyle had a grudge against McFarland. He called him a cheat and a criminal. And before you ask, Doyle never gave me any details."

"Then Doyle and McFarland knew each other before Doyle came to work on the Riverfront site."

DeMarco nodded. "Could be." He took several drags of his cigarette. "I swear I only knew he died when I read in the paper that the cops identified the body in the warehouse. And no way did I have a reason to want him dead."

"But you think McFarland did?"

"I don't know. Maybe."

"Miller seems to have disappeared. Any idea where he is?"

"I can only tell you about Doyle."

"You might want to rethink protecting Miller. He's a convicted arsonist. He was the one who lit up the warehouse, wasn't he?"

"I don't know nothin' about him."

"Don't try to con me. You two shared a prison cell."

"My life'll be crap if I talk."

I wanted to tell him his life was already crap, but that wouldn't get him to help me.

"What can you tell me about Nate Warner?"

"Who the fuck are you talking about now? You said you wanted to talk about Doyle. Then you bring up Miller. Christ, now you bring up a guy I never heard of."

"You sure you didn't hear his name come up? Could McFarland have mentioned it?"

"McFarland's the big boss. Do you think he talks to me?"

"Who do you deal with then? Bobby Regan?"

DeMarco turned his head away, looking out the window. "I want you to leave me alone. You're the craziest broad I've ever met."

I laughed. "Wise up, Joey, or you'll be in jail while your pals can still inhale fresh air."

"You going to turn me into the cops?"

"I'll keep my offer open on two conditions. One, you don't come after me again, and two, you decide to tell me what you know about the warehouse fire. Don't look so downcast. You just got a free breakfast, didn't you?"

"Fuck you." DeMarco opened the car door.

"I'll be in touch, Joey."

CHAPTER THIRTY-TWO

When I got to my office, I phoned my contact in missing persons to check if the cops were having any better luck than I was locating Jason Kramer. They weren't.

I spent an hour responding to emails, phone and text messages, and preparing invoices.

After lunch at my desk, I rechecked other churches in the area. But no one had seen the kid. It wasn't difficult to disappear in a city of millions. Especially a teenager with no credit cards and no working cell phone.

Since my search for Jason was proving fruitless, I switched gears to look for Nate's hidden stash. I tried other private mail stores, using my envelope with Nate Warner's name as bait, but none of the stores I visited listed him among their customers.

My cell phone rang as I was walking back to my office. It was my handyman. "I installed LED lights in your new fixtures. They'll do the job for you."

I thanked him and asked him to put his invoice in my mailbox.

"Sure thing. Say, do you want the bullet I dug out of the wall?"

He said it so casually, like a bullet was nothing unusual to find.

"Apparently you're not new at this," I said.

"In this city? It's not the first bullet I've dug out of a wall, and it won't be my last."

On my way home that night I drove to his shop to pick up the bullet that he had placed in a plastic baggie. I locked the bullet in the safe in my home office and grinned. More leverage to use on DeMarco.

I had finished dinner and was washing the dishes when my cell rang. The caller was Vinnie Mazzo.

"Your kid's here," Vinnie said. "Come as fast as you can."

When I arrived, Vinnie took me into an area of the shelter marked Staff Only. "A doc volunteers here," he said, as he knocked and opened the door to a room halfway down the hall.

The runaway I knew through photographs was sitting on the doctor's examining table, wearing a paper hospital gown, and getting stitches on his left arm. His cheeks were scraped raw, and both feet were bandaged.

Jason Kramer stared up at me, his brown eyes wide, filled with fear.

Vinnie introduced me. "Andrea's here to help you. She helped me out when I needed it."

"My parents hired you, didn't they?" Jason's voice was hoarse.

I nodded.

"I have nothing to say to them or to you. I won't go back home."

"You don't look like you're in a position to go anywhere but a hospital."

The doc smirked. "Good luck trying to get him treated, let alone admitted without ID or insurance. And if you don't mind, please leave. You're disturbing my patient."

In the corridor, I asked Vinnie. "Any other way out of here besides the front door?"

"There's a back door to the alley," he said. "If you stay right here you won't lose him."

"Thanks, Vin." He left to get back to the kitchen.

About ten minutes later, the doc came out. "You can go in now."

Jason was lying on the examining table covered with a thin blanket. "I don't want to talk to you." He turned his head away.

"Then just listen to what I have to say."

"Do I get a choice?"

I took a deep breath to clear my head, hoping to choose the right words to build trust with him.

"It was your mother who hired me, not your father. I know he's an alcoholic who gets nasty when he's drunk. And that you two don't get along. How am I doing so far?"

Jason nodded.

"It's tough," I continued. "But living on the streets is no solution, and it looks like you've learned that already. You're getting abused out there too. Jason, you're a young man with brains and talent. You'll waste all that if you don't go back to school. Do you agree?"

Jason said nothing.

"I feel like a comedian dying out here before my audience."

Jason laughed, held onto his cheek, and grimaced. "You're not funny."

"No worries, I'm keeping my day job." I looked around. "Where are your clothes?"

"They were all torn and bloody. The doctor threw them away."

"Even your Philadelphia Union hoodie?"

"You know what I was wearing?"

"If I didn't, I wouldn't be much of a detective, would I?"

Jason nodded. "Vinnie said he'd find me something to wear. What did he mean by saying you helped him?"

"I'll let Vinnie tell you about that. All I'll say is that Vinnie cleaned up his act, has a nice house, a girlfriend, and a job. He volunteers here because he knows what it's like for people on the street."

I heard a knock, and the door cracked open. "Okay to come in?" It was Vinnie. "I made my mom's recipe for mac and cheese." He brought two bowls. "I'll bring some clothes when I come to pick up the tray."

Jason scarfed down a bowl. "Aren't you going to have some?" he asked, pointing to the second bowl.

"Go for it," I said.

After he ate, Jason leaned back in bed and closed his eyes.

Vinnie came in. "Is he okay?"

"He's resting."

Vinnie placed a packet on the bed. "Inside is underwear, a sweatshirt, a pair of chinos, faded but cleaned and ironed, and a cardigan. Best I could do," he said.

"Can you tell the doc I want to speak to him?"

"Sure thing," Vinnie left with the tray of dishes.

When the doctor came back to the room, we stepped out into the corridor.

"I'll be looking after Jason. What do I need to know about his condition?"

"He doesn't have a concussion, and there's no sign of internal injuries."

"Did you give him something for the pain?"

"Tylenol. I don't believe in opioids." The doc handed me a prescription. "He needs to take a course of these antibiotics. Can you manage the cost?"

"No problem. What's with the bandaged feet?"

"Someone stole his sneakers and socks. His feet are badly bruised and lacerated."

While Vinnie helped Jason get dressed, I drove my rental around to the back door. Jason was wobbly, so Vinnie and I eased him into the back seat.

"Where are you taking me?"

"For now, you're coming to my house."

On the way, I stopped at a pharmacy for the antibiotics. When we got home, I helped him out of the car and supported him as he limped into the house.

"Tell me why you ran away?" I asked once he was settled on my sofa.

"None of your business."

I sat down on an armchair. "My money is on a dispute with your dad. He wanted to send you to military school, and you didn't want to go."

Jason snickered. "My dad needs to dry out at rehab. And stop bullying Mom and me. He slapped me hard across the face. I slapped him right back." He laughed and shook his head. "You should have seen the shock on his face. He landed on his ass."

A detail Nan Kramer failed to mention.

"When he managed to get off the floor, he slapped me around and gave me a black eye. Dad said I couldn't live at home until I learned respect. I shouted something like I didn't want to live with him ever again. Then I bolted."

"Had your dad hit you or your mother before?"

"He's always in a bad mood and reams us out all the time. The last few months he was getting worse with the drinking and his rages. But so far, he hasn't touched Mom. She pampers him and soothes his ego. I think she's afraid of him and wants to hide his drinking from everyone. The night I left was the first time he got physical with me."

I felt relieved. Verbal abuse was terrible, but in my experience, broken bones were worse. "Can I get you anything else to eat?"

"I'm all set."

I stood up. "Then you need to get some rest. We'll talk more tomorrow."

"Thanks. Vinnie's right. You're okay."

"The bathroom's down the hall. Take a shower. You're still a bit ripe from the streets. Clean towels and bandages for your feet are in the hall closet. You can use the terry robe on the hook in the bathroom."

While he was in the bathroom, I made up the sofa bed in my home office and left him a pair of Russ's sweats. On a side table, I placed a pitcher of water, his dose of antibiotics, a soda, and pretzels.

I woke up to the sound of crying. It was coming from my office where Jason was sleeping. My first instinct was to check on him, but I waited. I didn't want to embarrass him. Then I heard a bloodcurdling scream. I ran barefoot to his room.

Jason's face was covered in sweat. He was tossing, turning, throwing off his sheets. I thought he had a fever, but when I felt his forehead, it was cool.

"Run. Keep running. I can't let him get me." Jason jumped upright in bed and saw me.

"You had a bad dream. Are you okay? Anything I can help with?"

"I'm fine. I need to get back to sleep." He turned his back to me.

Early the next morning, I checked on my patient. He was sleeping quietly. The water, antibiotics, and the snacks I had left were gone.

I took my laptop from the desk and went into the kitchen. I made a pot of oatmeal for Jason, brewed my coffee, and responded to emails. Russ had left a text asking me to meet him for dinner that night. I texted back, begging off using work as an excuse. I was checking voicemail when I heard the toilet flush, and then Jason's bandaged feet shuffled down the hall.

"I made you breakfast," I called out.

Jason appeared at the kitchen door wearing the terry robe. He didn't look much better than the night before, but his appetite was healthy. He ate a big bowl of oatmeal and drank two glasses of water.

"Do you drink coffee?"

He shook his head. "Water is fine."

"It's good to drink lots of fluids when you're taking antibiotics."

"That's what the doc said."

"Jason, do you remember calling out in your sleep last night?"

I noticed a hint of shock on his face, but he recovered quickly and shook his head.

"Maybe you were having a nightmare?"

"I don't remember."

I walked over to the kitchen counter to pour myself more coffee. "You might be able to recall it later."

"I don't have nightmares," he nearly shouted.

"Okay. By the way, I found some clothes for you. They're on the chair in the living room."

When Jason returned to the kitchen a short time later, he had showered and was wearing a pair of Russ's jeans and a plaid shirt. Both were too big for him. "I put the other clothes in the washer," he said.

"Good. Your mom trained you well."

"I can't go back to my parents," Jason said, his voice low. His lips curved up in an attempted smile, but the attempt was weak.

"It's okay. You're safe here." I smiled.

"I need some fresh air."

I tilted my head toward the kitchen door. "The back porch will have to do for now. Take the afghan from the sofa. It's a good idea to keep warm while you're healing."

Jason gave me a look any teenager would give his mother, but he went to get the afghan.

I'm no psychologist, but I could see Jason was a traumatized young man. He had been having a rough time with his father. During his time on the streets, he'd been beaten up at least twice that I knew of. But I sensed that wasn't the whole story. His screams at night told me he was afraid of something or someone. I still had more to learn about Jason Kramer.

After lunch, Jason went to rest, and I finished preparing three background reports for my pharmaceutical client. I was doing sit-ups in the living room when I heard Jason scream out. I ran into his room. His hands were balled into fists, and he was calling out. "Where's the door? I can't find the door. I need to get out." Then he shouted, "Don't shoot." And woke with a jolt.

I smoothed the damp hair from his face and took hold of his hands. "You're safe. You were having a bad dream."

"A man is dead, and I should have saved him."

Whatever I had expected Jason to tell me, it certainly wasn't that.

"Is that the reason you ran away, not your father?"

Jason shook his head. "No, it happened after I ran away."

"Talk to me. You need to tell someone, and I'm here to listen, not judge."

Jason began to sob. I put my hand on his shoulder. "Go ahead. Get it out."

His whole body shook with anguished sobs. When his tears subsided, I handed him a box of tissues, fluffed his pillows, and helped prop him up in bed. I poured him a glass of water.

"Trust me." I pulled a chair up next to the bed.

He gulped down the water but remained silent.

"Whatever you have to say won't shock me. Not in my line of work. I hear a lot worse than a priest in a confessional."

His lips curled up in a half-smile.

"Jason. At this point, I'm all you have in your corner."

"He died, and I should have saved him."

"Who died?"

"Some homeless guy in an old warehouse."

"Tell me more."

"I spent a night at a warehouse in a neighborhood north of Center City. I was asleep but woke up when I heard two guys talking." Jason stopped and rubbed his forehead. "They lit a fire and then torched one of the walls. The fire reached the ceiling, and I must have screamed. There was so much smoke. I heard someone coming toward me. He shot at me but the bullet missed, and I ran out as fast as I could. The guy with the gun chased me all over the neighborhood but I managed to get away from him. Only I couldn't save the other guy who was asleep."

"What other guy?"

"He was sleeping under a blanket."

I poured Jason another glass of water and waited until he drained it.

"I'd like to ask you a few questions. Is that okay?"

He nodded.

"Did you get a look at the men who started the fire?"

He nodded again. "There were two of them. White. Tough looking."

"Would you recognize them if you saw them again?"

"I see them in my dreams."

When I had him describe the building and the neighborhood, I knew he had witnessed the fire at the McFarland warehouse.

CHAPTER THIRTY-THREE

I bought Jason a new pair of sneakers, larger than his usual size to accommodate the bandages, and two pairs of socks. He packed up the few clothes he had, then I drove him to Sister Emily's. "You'll be safe here until I get back."

When I spoke to Sister by phone earlier, she reluctantly agreed to keep Jason under wraps for a day or two after I explained that the police wanted to interview him as a witness to a crime.

I dropped off my rental and picked up my Subaru. I patted Bella. "You look wonderful, all shiny and healthy." The mechanic eyed me as though I had something contagious.

Then I went to see Tom.

"I found a witness to the warehouse fire." I was standing in front of his desk. "And he can prove it was arson."

"Where's your witness?" Tom looked around.

"Things are a bit complicated." I told him about Jason running away. "He may be in some danger and need protection." I related that the arsonists had seen Jason, chased him, and tried to shoot him. "His picture has been all over the media as a runaway. If the arsonists recognize him, he could be in danger. He's safe at Sister Emily's for now, and I see no reason he can't stay there."

"His parents might not see it that way."

"Could you help convince them? We need to keep him away from the arsonists and the alcoholic father who abused him."

"I want to talk to the kid before I make any commitments. If he has the goods and I'm convinced he's in danger, I can put him in protective custody."

"I'll arrange for him to come in."

"First, you need to go tell the parents their son is safe."

I took the Martin Luther King Drive along the Schuylkill and drove to the Kramers' Bryn Mawr home. It was one o'clock in the afternoon, so Steve Kramer would be at work. I could talk to Nan Kramer without the bully's interference.

When I told Mrs. Kramer that her son was alive and safe, she smiled for the first time since I met her.

"Why hasn't he come back with you?"

"I'm afraid there are some unusual circumstances." I explained that Jason was a witness to arson and murder. "The police need to interview him."

"The police can't talk to him without Steve and me present. I know that much."

"A Detective Volpe will be calling you to set up a time."

"I want to see my son. If you don't bring him back home, I'm certain my husband will take you to court."

"Mrs. Kramer, Jason has been traumatized by what he saw. And the police want to keep him safe. He could be in danger. He's a witness to a crime and his picture has been all over the media as a runaway."

Nan Kramer let out a gasp and held her hand over her mouth.

"If you love him, let him stay where he is. He's off the streets. He's safe. Besides, the last thing he needs right now is to live with an alcoholic father who gave him a black eye."

Mrs. Kramer flinched but remained silent.

"It's true, and you know it."

"I want you to leave. Thank you for finding my son. But his father and I will decide what's best for him."

"I'm returning your fee." I took a check out of my pocket and laid it on the hall table then stormed down the steps and slammed my car door as I got in. "Sorry, Bella, but I'm pissed."

I wanted to shake the woman, get her to see reality. She was so busy covering for her husband that she was ignoring her son's welfare. She was likely terrified her husband's company would find out about his drinking, and she'd have to wave goodbye to her deluxe lifestyle. Funny. Aunt Roseanne wanted to protect what she had and look where it landed her.

I started the ignition and burned gravel as I pulled out of the driveway. I drove faster than was prudent, weaving in and out of traffic on Montgomery Avenue, until I nearly sideswiped a white van. I pulled Bella into a metered space outside a Starbucks but didn't go inside. I sat there inhaling and exhaling until my breathing evened out. "Didn't mean to put you in harm's way again, Bella." I patted the dashboard.

As I drove, I forced myself to look at things from Nan Kramer's viewpoint. She'd been married for decades. More than enough time to be cowered into submission. An abusive husband can do that. On the other hand, she was also a mother. Why couldn't she find the courage to stand up for her only son, even if she was incapable of helping herself?

CHAPTER THIRTY-FOUR

Steve Kramer burst into my office, his face contorted like a Notre Dame gargoyle. "I paid you to find my son, and now you're hiding him from me. I can sue you for breach of contract," he shouted.

I remained seated and did my best to imitate his wife's dulcet tones when she tried to calm him down. "I've already returned my fee to your wife. I'm concerned about Jason's welfare at this point, and maybe you should be too."

"Arrogant bitch."

In a nanosecond, he was standing on my side of the desk. I stood up to face him. Up close, I saw his bloodshot eyes, the broken capillaries in his cheeks, and smelled the foul odor of strong liquor. For a moment, I saw Uncle Dom's face. Nausea hit my stomach, hard.

But then a stinging slap across my face jolted me back to reality. Kramer struck with such force I struggled to keep my balance. My jaw throbbed, and my eyes watered from the blow. My first instinct was to punch the bastard in his soft, fleshy, decidedly flabby stomach. A quick, strong jab would bring him to his knees. I don't take abuse from anyone, not anymore.

I hesitated too long. Kramer slapped me, harder, across my other cheek. I felt blood dripping from my lips. Now my anger took over. I put my hands on his shoulders and shoved him away. He teetered and began to sway like he was keeping time with music he could hear in his head.

I grabbed him by his shoulders again. "No one gets away with slapping me around." This piece of shit was asking for a beatdown. I closed my fist and gave it to him in the gut. My punch sunk deep into flab. Too much booze and no exercise. He doubled over. I pulled him up and was about to slam my fist

under his chin when I thought of Jason. If I beat the crap out
of his father, I'd be making a tough situation worse. I dropped
Kramer into the nearest chair.

"Now I'm going to charge you with assault," he said, holding onto his belly.

"I could do the same. Tit for tat? Or do we both want to
concentrate on what's best for your son?"

"Keeping him from his parents. Is that what you think is
best for him? You have twenty-four hours to bring my son
home."

"That will be up to the police, not me."

"This is your doing, not the cops. If you don't hand over Jason, I'll charge you with kidnapping. Then any assault charges
against me will be chicken shit." He stumbled to his feet and
came toward me, his eyes burning with rage. I prepared for
another assault, but instead, he turned, headed to the door
and slammed it so hard my Phillies cap flew off its peg.

When I figured Kramer was out of the building, I went
down the hall to the bathroom and washed my face in cool water, cleaning the dried blood from my lips and nose. Kramer's
handprint was visible on my cheeks, soon nasty bruises would
become visible. I began regretting my decision to be the adult
in the room. I should have given the bastard a dental bill that
would have taken him years to pay off.

CHAPTER THIRTY-FIVE

I was mulling over where to hunt next for Nate Warner's missing files when Tom called to let me know that Jason Kramer's interview was scheduled for the next day.

Just as I hung up, my phone rang again. It was Caroline Hewitt. "I have to talk to someone I can trust."

"I'm on my way."

"Those scoundrels." That was the first thing Caroline Hewitt said to me once she closed her office door and led us to the upholstered chairs around a glass coffee table. She said it with more venom than I expected from a woman who epitomized self-control. "I don't want them to get away with it."

I reached into my tote, pulled out a Three Musketeers bar, and handed it to her.

"Chocolate always makes me feel better. What about you?"

Caroline laughed. "This was my favorite when I was a kid." She ripped the wrapping and took a bite, then another, until the bar vanished.

"I can see you enjoyed that."

"Very much." She leaned back in her chair. "I was happy working at Hayes and Osborne. I enjoyed my clients and my colleagues. I was getting great reviews and a top salary." She paused and sighed. "Then I was asked to assist with the Mc-Farland account."

"Sean McFarland?"

She nodded. "I didn't know what I was getting into."

I wanted to poke and probe but decided to let her give it up in her own way.

"For the first few months, there were no problems. Then one day, I was asked to join the partners for lunch with Mc-Farland. He flirted with me, but I ignored it. Then he started showing up at the office and asking me out to dinner. He'd remark about my clothes, my hair, how attractive I was. It made me extremely uncomfortable, and I told Hayes. McFarland backed off.

"But there's much more. Soon after I started on the account, I discovered I didn't have access to all the McFarland files. When I asked, I was told I was assisting, so I was assigned only to specific accounts, not the entire portfolio.

"That should have been a red flag, but I ignored my gut and continued to work on the account. It wasn't until tax time that I found out the firm was keeping two sets of financial records for McFarland."

"You're sure?"

She nodded.

I moved forward in my chair. Two sets of books usually pointed to one thing: fraud.

"I found two separate financial reports for the same LLC for that year. I had worked on one of the reports, but Hayes had worked on the other. When I compared the two, it was clear that the Hayes report showed a great deal more revenue and profit than my report. It wasn't hard to figure out. I used my figures to prepare the tax filing. In that case, McFarland would pay fewer taxes, and his investors would receive distributions based on lower profits than actually existed if the Hayes report was authentic.

"Why would the firm put you on the McFarland account and risk you discovering the fraud?"

"They needed help with the volume of work on the account and they did restrict my access to the McFarland records." Caroline rubbed the nape of her neck. "But tax time is extremely hectic. I don't think I was meant to see that second report. Hayes must have misfiled it and placed it into the folders I had access to, rather than folders that he kept private."

"Then you're telling me you suspect that McFarland cheated his investors out of their rightful distributions and likely falsified his tax filings with the help of his accounting firm?" I asked.

"Right."

"How do you know it was Mr. Hayes who worked on it?"

"All the accountants in the office have ID numbers that appear on the templates we use. That way we know whose work it is," Caroline explained.

"Which LLC are we talking about?"

"Logan Properties," Caroline said. "It owns office and industrial buildings."

"Is that the only LLC you found proof of doctored financials?" I asked.

"I only saw that one report from Hayes. I was so concerned I made copies of both my report and his. I can't be sure, but my instincts tell me the firm kept two sets of books for all the McFarland LLCs," Caroline said.

"Did you confront the partners?"

"Before I could decide what to do, Hayes called me into his office. He must have known I'd seen his report, but he never brought it up. Instead, he told me I could make more money working full-time on the McFarland account if I were a team player. I told him I'd have to think about it since I enjoyed the other clients I'd been working with. That night I took the reports home and locked them in my desk. The more I thought things over, I knew I had to quit.

"I thanked Hayes for his offer but said I had to cut down on my work hours or my ex-husband would fight me for custody of my children. I'm not sure he believed me. But after tax season, I gave notice and they had me sign a nondisclosure agreement, which was okay with me."

"I'd like to see those reports."

"I don't have them in the office."

"Do you still keep them at your home?"

"They're in a safe place."

"And where might that be?"

"I'll keep that to myself for the present. It's my insurance."

She reminded me of Nate. Always wanting protection against risk. "Have the partners contacted you or threatened you?"

"They've left me alone so far," she said. "But I'm still scared. Could I be in danger like that executive?"

"Which executive?"

She poured a glass of water. "Would you like some?"

"Thanks, no." What I wanted was to hear the rest of her story. My pulse quickened.

"I received a call from an executive at SEPA Financial. He wanted to talk to me about McFarland," Caroline said.

"Do you remember the name of this executive?"

"Nate Warner."

"You're sure that was his name?" I asked, knowing in my gut that's who it must have been.

"I'm certain. I told him I had left Hayes and Osborne and was no longer on the account. But he still wanted to talk. I told him I couldn't discuss a former client. And I hung up."

"Can you remember exactly when he phoned?"

Caroline went to her desk to check her calendar. "He called a number of times, in mid-September."

After the warehouse fire. "How many calls were there?"

"He called maybe four times and left messages. But I never returned his calls."

"So, you never actually spoke to him about McFarland?" I asked.

She shook her head. "Then I read about his disappearance and murder."

"And you think his death might be connected to McFarland and his finances?"

Her hands trembled as she drank her water. "It may seem crazy, but I can't help thinking it could be."

Neither could I.

"The articles about his murder said he was in charge of

fraud investigations at SEPA Financial," Caroline said. "And McFarland was the person he wanted to talk to me about."

If Nate suspected McFarland of fraud, why didn't he go to Keenan, the company attorney, with his concerns? Why reach out to Caroline Hewitt?

Then I recalled what Jeanne McFarland overheard in her kitchen. Bobby Regan, McFarland's right-hand man, said he had a contact at SEPA Financial. Could Nate have suspected someone at the insurance company was involved in fraud? That would certainly explain why he kept his information away from the office.

It never made sense to me when Keenan instructed me more than once to stay away from McFarland, a man I was investigating. Of course, having a corporate attorney on your side would be a clear advantage if McFarland did commit fraud. But what type of fraud involved SEPA Financial? As Tom had already pointed out to me, the insurance payouts on the fires were too paltry to warrant murder. But the loan to Mid-City Mortgage was another matter entirely, especially since the amount of the loan could be substantial. If McFarland was indeed in financial difficulties, how did he qualify for a loan? And why was SEPA Financial stalling turning over the loan application to me?

"If it will make you feel more secure," I said to Caroline, "I can check out your office and home to be sure you and your family are as well protected as possible."

She smiled. "I would feel a whole lot better, especially for my children's safety."

Once we finished talking, I surveyed Caroline's office and recommended installing surveillance cameras above the front and back doors. A security alarm system was already in place.

We drove to Caroline's house, located on a tree-lined street only blocks away. Like her office, her home had a security system. I checked the perimeter of the house and recommended cameras for the front and back of the house and the installation of more powerful floodlights around the entire property.

I went out to my car and reached into a box of supplies in my trunk. "Keep this with you. It's the type of personal alarm police recommend."

"Appreciate it. Thanks for your help."

"I would like to see those financial records."

"I have to think about it."

"Do that. Let's stay in touch."

On the drive back to my office, I mulled over whether Nate could have been Bobby's contact at SEPA Financial. And Nate wanted out of whatever scheme they had going but got killed instead. No way, though, could I reconcile the Nate I knew being involved in anything illegal or even remotely dishonest. After all, he did reach out to Caroline Hewitt and took steps to give me access to the information he had. No, I knew now that I was on the same trail that Nate had followed before me.

CHAPTER THIRTY-SIX

That night I parked Bella on Green Street in the city's Fairmount neighborhood where Bobby Regan lived. I was lucky to snag a space close enough to watch his house but far enough away so he wouldn't spot me.

It was after seven now. No lights were on inside the house. Since I arrived, the only change was that the front porch light came on. On a timer. I'd already eaten a protein bar, a soft pretzel, and was onto my chocolate fix. A milk chocolate bar with caramel filling.

When I did a background check on Regan, I recognized him from his drivers' license as Leather Jacket, the guy who had met McFarland at the Parc bistro in Rittenhouse Square. Regan had no substantial criminal record, only one conviction for drunk driving.

Regan could be out for the evening. I decided to wait another half hour and then use my lockpick on his back door if there were no signs of an electronic security system. But, not ten minutes later, a man approached the house. When he climbed the front steps, his face was visible in the outdoor light. Regan was wearing the same leather jacket he wore when I tailed him from the restaurant to the offices of Riverfront Enterprises.

He entered the house, and a light went on inside. I left my car carrying my tote bag and walked around to the rear alley. I counted off the houses and then crept slowly into Regan's backyard. The light was on in the kitchen, and the blind on the window was halfway up. I crouched down and moved closer. Regan was guzzling a bottle of Heineken and setting the table for two. Then he left the room and returned accompanied by a woman.

She had deep auburn hair and a teal sweater that fit like a second skin. She placed a bag of takeout Chinese on the table. She turned to face Regan, they embraced and locked lips. The smooching went on and on.

I stepped back into the alley, took my camera with a zoom lens out of my tote, and began shooting. Regan removed her sweater, then her bra. I snapped more photos. Then the two left the room. I felt relieved. I really didn't want to spy on what was to follow. Too bad I couldn't reach through the window and grab the bag of Chinese. I was hungry, and by the time they returned, the food would be cold.

CHAPTER THIRTY-SEVEN

"I have an appointment with Bobby Regan at Riverfront Enterprises on the fourth floor." I lied and beamed at the security guard. Since I didn't need to be at police headquarters for Jason's interview until that afternoon, I decided to see what I could learn about the work Regan did for McFarland.

The guard pointed to the sign-in sheet. I wrote "Philippa Marlowe." He looked to be in his early twenties, so I figured he wasn't familiar with classic detective fiction.

I stood at the elevator bank along with six other people. When the car arrived, they all stepped in. I considered waiting for the next elevator. Just thinking about being confined with all these folks clustered around me made me hyperventilate. But I saw the guard at the security desk staring at me. I didn't want to draw attention to myself, so I inhaled deeply, stepped inside, and ate a Tums, grateful that the ride would be short.

The car stopped at each floor on the way to four, making for a bumpy ride. By the time I got out, I was nauseous and sweating. I popped another Tums in my mouth, wiped the perspiration from my forehead, and walked down the hall to Riverfront's office.

A receptionist sitting behind the desk with a nameplate that read Tanya Powell was painting her long nails with a fuchsia-colored polish. There were no visitors in the waiting area. Tanya had deep auburn hair, and instead of the sweater that she wore last night at Regan's house, she had chosen a teal wrap dress that clung to all her curves. Teal must be her favorite color.

"Morning, Ms. Powell, I'm here to see Bobby Regan. My name is Andrea Fabiano."

"Mr. Regan isn't in right now," she answered and leafed

through her appointment book, careful not to smudge her nails. I noticed a wedding band on her left hand. "He could see you next Tuesday. He does prefer if you send your resume and audition video before the interview." She smiled.

"Excuse me?"

"You are talent applying for a gig at our supper club, aren't you?"

"Afraid not," I smiled. I showed her my PI license. "At the moment, I'd rather talk to you."

The smile disappeared from her face. "What's this about? Why would an investigator want to talk to me?"

"What is it this company does?"

She stared at me. "Not that it's any of your business, but we have nothing to hide. We book talent for the Riverfront supper club. I answer the phone, schedule appointments, and assist Bobby, er Mr. Regan."

"I see." But I didn't. Why would Regan, who oversaw construction jobs, be booking talent for McFarland's supper club?

"Now I have to get back to work," Tanya said.

I looked around the empty office. "I can see you're terribly busy. And you haven't finished putting a second coat on your nails."

Tanya didn't appreciate my sarcasm. She rose from her chair and wiggled her way to the door. "I want you to leave now."

I held up the screen on my phone and showed her the photos I'd taken through Regan's kitchen window the night before. Her face turned almost as red as her hair.

"How did you get these?" She reached out to grab the phone, but I pulled it away.

"Why don't we sit down and talk."

Tanya fell into the chair at her desk. "Christ, you're working for my husband, aren't you?"

"I don't do matrimonial work. I told you I'm here about Bobby Regan. Is he expected anytime soon?"

"He's out of town. I don't expect him back today."

"I'm interested in what you can tell me about him."

"I got nothing to say."

I pulled out a chair and sat down in front of her desk. "If I were you, I'd ask myself why a PI is interested in Bobby and whether his troubles could spill over and become your troubles?"

"If you're interested in Bobby, why take those pictures of me."

"In my business, it's called leverage."

"You want me to tell you about Bobby, or you make trouble for me with my husband. I call that blackmail."

I ignored her comment. Probably because she was right.

Tanya swallowed hard.

"We can go somewhere else to talk. A coffee shop nearby?" I suggested.

She hesitated. "Not now. I need to think about this. I don't want to jam up Bobby. He's been good to me. But I don't want trouble with the law or my husband."

"Smart thinking." She was teetering, but not ready to jump. I decided to give her some space, then come back and push hard. "I'll be in touch." I handed over my card. "In case you want to call."

CHAPTER THIRTY-EIGHT

At police headquarters, Jason Kramer sat next to me and across the table from his parents. Tom Volpe was at the head of the table, a set of official folders in front of him.

From where I sat, Steve Kramer seemed sober. At least his eyes weren't glassy while he sent death rays in my direction. I had slathered liquid foundation on my face to hide my bruises, but I couldn't mask my anger. I glared right back at him.

"That woman has no right to keep my son from me. You're the police. Why don't you charge her with kidnapping?"

"I found Jason. I didn't kidnap him." I snapped back.

Kramer stood up, leaned across the table, and got in my face. "I'm going to sue you for every cent you own. You bitch."

Under the table, I gripped my hands into a fist, so tight that my nails dug into flesh, as I fought back every instinct that I had to deck the SOB. Tom had warned me before the Kramers arrived that he'd throw me out on my ass if I made trouble.

Tom Volpe held up both palms. "That's enough. We're not here to watch you two go at each other. We're here to listen to what Jason has to tell us about what he witnessed."

"What's she doing here?" Kramer asked.

"Ms. Fabiano is here at my invitation. You both stay as long as you behave."

"I have a right to be here to protect my son," Kramer said.

"While you're in this room, you need to sit down and be quiet, Mr. Kramer." Tom spoke with the force and authority of a cop stopping a street fight. "If you don't keep your emotions under control, your wife will be the only parent looking out for Jason's interests here."

Kramer opened his mouth to say something but Tom shouted, "Enough!"

Mrs. Kramer touched her husband's hand. He sat down and clammed up. I wanted to hug Tom but managed to restrain myself. Tom would deliver on his promise and toss me out if he found me remotely disruptive.

Tom turned to Jason. "Okay, son, I need you to take us through what you saw at the time of the warehouse fire."

The room was quiet. All eyes were on Jason. But he sat mute.

"You said you wanted to talk. Now is the time to get this off your chest. Come on, let's have it," Tom said.

Jason nodded. "I was spending the night in an abandoned warehouse. A couple of guys I had met the day before told me about it and said it was one of the safer places to crash at night."

"Did you break in?"

"A side door was unlocked."

"Can you tell me the address?"

"I don't know exactly. It was north of Center City. There was an auto body shop down the street and a pizza place in the next block."

"Was the name of the auto shop Ferguson's?" Tom asked.

"Yes, that's right. The place had a huge sign above the garage door. How did you know?"

"I know the neighborhood. As best as you can remember, what night did you stay at the warehouse?" Tom asked.

"I ran away on the Monday. So, it was Wednesday night."

Tom and I exchanged glances. Jason was in the warehouse on the night of the fire.

"I found the place, and it was like the guys said," Jason continued. "An old guy was curled up under a blanket. He was asleep, and I saw a bottle of whiskey next to him. But otherwise, the place looked empty. I decided to stay, and I ate the burger and soda I bought with the last of my money. I must have fallen asleep. But I woke up when I heard voices."

"Do you know what time that was?" Tom asked.

"No idea." Jason paused. "I kept my cell phone off. I didn't want to be tracked. But it had to be late into the night."

He took a swig from his bottle of water. "Two guys were standing over a bonfire near the sidewall. I thought that was strange since it wasn't all that cold. But then I saw one man dip a plank of wood into the barrel, and when the flames caught, he held it up against the wall. The fire spread so fast. I got scared when I saw smoke. It was getting hard to breathe. I must have cried out, and they heard me. I heard someone coming toward me, then I heard a shot and I ran as fast as I could."

"Oh, Jason," his mother cried.

"I wasn't hurt. I managed to outrun the guy who chased me." Jason stopped and gulped down more water.

"Then I remembered the old guy. I ran back once I figured the guy with the gun was gone. By that time, the flames were shooting up into the sky, and firefighters were hosing down the place. A crowd was watching, but the police pushed everyone to the other side of the street. I tried getting their attention, only I couldn't. Oh, I remember I heard a guy in the crowd saying it was two in the morning and he was going back to bed.

"I got scared when I noticed the other guy. Not the one who chased me but the guy who set the fire. He was in the crowd. I ran away before he could spot me. That poor old man died. And I should have saved him."

"Jason, those men are responsible for his death, not you," Tom said. "Now tell me anything you can remember about the men who set the fire. Any description would help."

"They were both big guys. White. One was tall, maybe six feet. He was the guy who chased me. The other one was shorter and heavier. He was a real mean-looking dude. He was the one I saw when I went back to the warehouse. His hair was thin like he was going bald, and he had a beer belly."

"You saw his face well enough to identify him?" Tom asked.

"I have nightmares about him." Jason glanced at me. "He

could be in a horror movie."

"You were an idiot to go back," Steve Kramer said.

"I told you already." Jason's face flushed red. "I wanted to try to help the old guy."

"I'm asking the questions, Mr. Kramer—don't interrupt again," Tom said. He turned to Jason. "Did you get a good look at the man who chased you?"

"I got so tired from running that I found a place to hide. I looked out and saw the guy standing near a streetlamp. His hair was thick and curly, and I could tell he needed a shave. I didn't move until I saw him walk away in the opposite direction of the fire."

"Would you recognize him if you saw him again?"

Jason nodded.

"You've done fine, Jason," Tom said. "The next step is for you to work with one of our sketch artists. See if we can come up with a composite to help us identify these men. We'll need to set up an appointment. Do you think you can do that for us?"

Jason agreed. "I'm so sorry I couldn't save that poor man."

"You're doing the right thing now by helping us find his killers." Tom gave Jason a pat on his shoulder.

For the first time, Jason looked at his father, and then said to Tom, "I don't want to go back home."

I kept my gaze on Tom. "Why not?" he asked.

"I don't want my parents at risk. My mother's been through enough. I don't want these guys coming after her."

"That woman put you up to this, didn't she?" Steve Kramer stood up, thrusting an index finger toward me. "There's no reason to believe they know who you are or where you live."

Tom intervened. "Sit down, Mr. Kramer. One more outburst and you're out of here. Your son was shot at running away from a crime scene. You're right, we don't know for certain if they have identified him, but I doubt these men would hesitate to come after him if they did. They might have seen the publicity about his being missing and recognized him. They have nothing to lose."

"I see what you're doing," Steve Kramer said. He pointed to me again. "You're trying to protect her from a kidnapping charge by creating this so-called need to protect Jason. Those men don't know who Jason is." He turned to his son. "Admit it. She put you up to this stunt, didn't she?"

Nan Kramer cut in. "We need to do what's best for Jason."

"The best thing for him is not to get involved in any of this." Steve Kramer stood up again. "I'm going to take my son away from here. I had planned to enroll him in military school anyway, far away from this city. He'll be safe there."

"Haven't you been haranguing him for years about what you called his lack of guts?" Nan Kramer said. "I'm proud of Jason. He's shown he has courage."

I wanted to cheer. Finally, Nan Kramer was standing up for her son.

Tom pounded his fist on the table. The room grew deadly silent. "Listen, and I'm only going to say this once. Mr. and Mrs. Kramer, I don't do family counseling. I do crime. Jason here is our best chance to catch and prosecute these guys. I want to place him in protective custody. And that means he won't be going back home right now."

"He's underage," Kramer said. "If I want to take him away, there's nothing you can do about it."

Tom and I knew he was right.

I stood up and moved between Kramer and his son. "You don't find it ironic that you were angry at your son for running away from home, but you have no problem encouraging him to run away from assisting the police?"

Kramer lurched forward, his fist raised to slug me. Tom grabbed Kramer by the shoulders, pinned his arms around his back, and moved him to the door. "Okay, that's it. You don't try to assault someone in my presence. Leave before I charge you."

The veins in Kramer's temple visibly throbbed, and his face grew crimson. "Get your hands off me. You'll be hearing from my lawyer."

"Wait a minute." Jason walked toward his father. "Dad, I'm no wimp. I'm old enough to decide that I want to get these guys. They hurt people and they need to face the consequences."

Nan Kramer embraced her son. "I'll support whatever you want to do, Jason."

Steve Kramer looked as if he'd been punched in his ego.

Tom motioned to the officer outside the door. "Mr. Kramer is leaving. He can wait for his wife in the lobby."

After her husband left, Nan Kramer turned to me. "I apologize for my Steve's behavior." She opened her handbag and handed me a check. "As far as I'm concerned, you did your job. And don't worry about Steve's threats." She leaned over and whispered in my ear, "If he even tries to sue you or force Jason into that school, I'll threaten to tell his company about his drinking."

Tom took me aside after Mrs. Kramer left. "I told you to keep your mouth shut. But you did help to resolve things. Just don't do it again."

"You know me. I don't make the same mistake twice."

"True, you try something else. Listen, the kid looks exhausted. Have him get some rest. We'll bring him in again as soon as we can get an artist."

"When will that be? I don't think I can get Sister Emily to keep Jason much longer."

Tom smiled. "We don't have unlimited resources, but I'll do my best to speed things up."

I called Sister Emily and asked if she could keep Jason for another day or two.

"Andrea, as much as I'd like to help, I can't keep this house locked up. It's a home for these young men, not a prison. I would destroy the trust I'm building with them."

"I understand."

I phoned Father Kevin at St. John's. "He can stay with us during the day, but I'm afraid we can't keep him overnight."

Tom was not pleased with my suggestion that Jason come back to my place. "I can watch out for him. And he's been there before, so it's at least familiar. You can't keep this kid in lock-up." I didn't mention the drive-by or the bullet in my safe. I was taking a risk bringing Jason with me, but a lock-up was the last place this kid needed to be. He'd had enough violence out on the streets.

"Okay, but only for one night while we find an alternative. I'll have a patrol car come by to keep an eye out," Tom said.

I motioned to Jason, who was drinking a soda and talking to Detective Lewis. "You're coming with me."

"Are we going back to Sister Emily's?"

"Not tonight. I'm taking you back to my place."

We walked together to my Subaru.

"What happened to the new Toyota?"

"It was a rental while my dear Bella was in the shop."

"Bella? You actually have a name for this heap of junk."

"I'd prefer if you didn't disparage my faithful, reliable car. It hurts her feelings."

Jason gave me a wary look like he just discovered I was mentally unstable.

"You're not the only one who doesn't understand my affection for Bella. We've been through a lot together."

He raised his eyebrows.

"Just get in."

While Jason rested, I rechecked the locks on all the windows and doors, including my upstairs apartment, vacant since last month when my tenant accepted a job at a New York law firm. I scanned the street for any unfamiliar cars. All the cars belonged to neighbors. No sign of a black Dodge Charger.

I was putting plates and napkins on the table when Detective Lewis called.

"Tom asked me to let you know we have the sketch artist scheduled for tomorrow."

"Jason will be there."

"He's a good kid and a credible witness," Lewis said.

"He's a brave young man. He's resting now."

"I thought you brought him to Sister Emily?"

"She didn't want to jeopardize the safety of the other kids."

"Volpe won't like this."

"He knows. It's only for tonight. Tom's sending a patrol car around to check on us."

"Keep your gun handy. We need to make sure this kid remains safe if we want to nail those bastards." He hung up.

Lewis didn't know that I didn't own a gun. I hadn't wanted to touch a firearm since the Academy, let alone keep one in my home. But tonight I was attempting to protect Jason without a weapon.

I took a casserole of my homemade lasagna out of the freezer to heat. I figured Jason could use a hearty meal with beef to build his strength. Then I opened the drawer to take out flatware. My eyes fell on a sharp carving knife. It could serve as an effective weapon in the absence of a gun. I held it in my hand and immediately gagged. The image of Uncle Dominic, a knife in his back, blood pouring onto the kitchen floor, seemed as real as if it were happening all over again. I dropped the knife back into the drawer. No, I'd never be able to stab someone.

I needed something that could inflict what coroners call blunt force trauma. I found my mother's old wooden rolling pin tucked behind my cookware. And in the hall closet, I pulled out a plank of wood leftover from repairs to my back porch. I placed the rolling pin in my umbrella stand by the front door. I propped the plank alongside the corner cabinet in the kitchen.

Jason moved his food around his plate but ate little. I considered pouring him a small glass of the Chianti that I was enjoying hoping to perk-up his appetite, but quickly dismissed the idea. I didn't want to be accused of serving liquor to a minor. Not with Steven Kramer on my back.

"Don't like it?"

"What?"

"My lasagna."

"It's fine. I'm just not hungry."

"Want to talk about what's bothering you?"

"You sound like my mother. Why do you think something's bothering me?"

"I don't know. The fact that you witnessed a crime, that someone took a pot shot at you, that your father threatened you with military school. Any of the above?"

Jason grinned.

"That's better. I always recommend keeping a sense of humor in a crisis."

He put down his fork. "I feel guilty. I saved myself, but I left the old guy to die."

"I get that. I'd be worried if you didn't care about the loss of human life. But Jason, I learned a long time ago that we can't save everyone. If you stayed, you would have died in that fire, too. Or been shot. It's going to take time for you to come to terms with all this. You're carrying a heavy burden."

Jason began to sob. He got up from the table and ran to his room.

I gave him a few moments alone, then followed.

He was sitting on the side of the bed. When he saw me, he walked over to face the window.

"No reason to be embarrassed." I handed him several tissues and put my hand on his shoulder. "You're a courageous young man. You're head and shoulders above that bullying father of yours."

He wiped his tear-stained cheek and blew his nose.

"Feeling better?"

He nodded.

"How about I warm up some of that lasagna for you? You need to eat and gain weight."

This time Jason ate two helpings. "This is good stuff."

I smiled. At least color came back to his face. I cleaned up the kitchen, and then joined Jason in the living room where he was playing a game on his phone.

"I suggest you get to bed soon. Detective Volpe has the sketch artist lined up for tomorrow."

When Jason went in to take a shower, I placed an extra blanket on his bed. The night had turned chilly.

I camped out on my living room sofa under my afghan with tea, a Kind bar, and my rolling pin.

CHAPTER
THIRTY-NINE

While Jason worked with the sketch artist, Tom filled me in on the arsonists he was checking out.

Dave Miller was on Tom's list. I kept my mouth shut. If this case went to court, I didn't want to be accused of influencing the cops or the witness.

I glanced over toward Jason. He was pointing to the artist's sketch pad and shaking his head. "His chin was broader."

An hour passed, and I needed a caffeine boost since I had stayed awake all last night, rolling pin at the ready. I grabbed my jacket and was about to go for a coffee run when the artist called out. "We're finished."

The man in the sketch had close-cropped hair, pockmarked cheeks, and a nose that looked like it had been broken once too often. Miller the Griller stared back at me.

"You saw this man at the warehouse?" Tom asked.

"Yeah," Jason said. "A scary-looking guy. He set the fire."

"Take a break," Tom said to Jason.

Tom and several officers began pulling together mug shots of men who resembled Miller. When Jason got back, Tom showed him the array. "Do you recognize any of these men?"

I watched Jason's face, saw a flicker of recognition, and then he pointed to Miller's photo.

"Dave Miller," Tom said. "Tell me where you saw him and what he was doing."

"Like I said, he's the one who set the wall on fire," Jason said. "And he was on the sidewalk when I went back to try to tell the police about the guy inside."

I gave Jason a high five. We had Miller cold.

"Good job, Jason," Tom said. "How about you go to lunch with Andrea, and when you get back, we'll get to work on a sketch of the guy who chased you?"

Jason agreed.

"I need a quick word with Andrea before you two go," Tom said to Jason.

Tom took me aside. "Miller's got a violent record."

"I saw. I don't think he'd hesitate to go after a witness."

"No way can Jason continue to stay with you," Tom said.

"I agree, but what are the options?"

"I'll see what I can do. We'll talk again after you take Jason to lunch."

Walking along Broad Street to the restaurant, I kept a watchful eye on Jason while trying not to be obvious and scare the poor kid.

"That Miller guy is dangerous," Jason said, as though reading my mind.

"I can't lie to you. He is. But you have me and the police looking out for you. It'll be alright." How good a bodyguard was I without a gun?

Back at police headquarters, Jason and the sketch artist went back to work. This time I was smart enough to bring a large Dunkin back with me.

Tom took me aside. "I talked to an Augustinian brother I know at Villanova." Tom was a graduate of the university. "Jason can stay in one of the dorms. He'll be safe there."

"Sounds like a good plan." I felt relieved that I wouldn't be responsible for putting Jason in danger if DeMarco or another goon came after me again. While I caught up with email and texts, I could hear the artist and Jason discussing noses, hairlines, and eyes.

Eventually, the artist called us over. The man in this sketch had a thin face and dark, curly hair. I recognized him, too. Only this guy I had met in the flesh. It was Joey DeMarco.

Tom turned to Jason. "If you want, get yourself a cold drink. Then you'll need to look at some more photos, like earlier." Tom signaled to a police officer. "Look after our guest."

Tom turned to me. "What's the scowl about?"

"I'm concerned about Jason's safety."

"Not buying it. You recognize the guy in this sketch."

"I don't want to prejudice the ID." I looked away.

"You mean you're not going to gloat that you're a step ahead of us?" Tom laughed. He and the other officers finished a photo array of men who resembled DeMarco.

When Jason returned, he pointed DeMarco out from the photo array without hesitation.

"Jason, we want to take you where you'll be protected." Tom explained about Villanova. "We need to keep you safe while these men are still on the street."

Jason looked over at me, and I saw fear in his eyes. "I'm not staying with you anymore?"

I smiled. "Don't worry. You'll be well looked after. Besides, we can arrange to have your schoolwork sent to you at the university. That way, you won't get further behind."

"How long do I have to stay there?"

Tom and I looked at each other. I sure as hell didn't want to tell the kid he could be there long enough to begin college courses.

"We'll get these guys into custody as soon as possible," Tom said.

Jason nodded and seemed to accept that. I handed him my card. "Call me if you need me." He gave me a sudden, embarrassed hug and quickly walked away escorted by two uniformed officers.

After Jason left, I told Tom what I knew about DeMarco. "He worked at McFarland's Riverfront site, and he got paid four thousand, allegedly for a scaffolding accident. I think it was for the warehouse job."

"We'll look into it," Tom said. "Is that all?"

"That's it." I still didn't mention the drive-by. I wanted to use whatever leverage I had with DeMarco before the cops took him into custody.

"Then isn't it about time you went home?" Tom said.

"Don't worry. I'm on my way. I've been thrown out of better places, but never so politely."

I drove home worrying about Jason. But Tom was right. The kid would be safer at the university. I wasn't so sure how safe I was since these goons had me on their radar and I lacked police protection.

CHAPTER FORTY

As I drove down my street, I surveyed the block looking for the Dodge Charger or any unfamiliar car. The only parked cars belonged to my neighbors. Was I right that the gunshots were a warning meant only to scare me? But I thought about Nate, who died from multiple gunshot wounds. I needed to stay vigilant.

I checked the outside perimeter of my house. The downstairs doors and windows remained locked. The new porch lights, timed to come on at dusk, illuminated the front and back of the house. Everything looked secure.

I unlocked the side door to the vacant upstairs unit. I checked to make certain the windows and back door were secured, then relocked the side door. I hadn't rented to a new tenant, waiting to see if Aunt Roseanne would be paroled and could come to live upstairs.

Back inside my apartment, I poured a glass of Chianti, sat on the living room sofa, and worked on a crossword puzzle. My way of relaxing my mind before I made any major decision. Like whether to own a gun again. With my history, I wanted a weapon about as much as I wanted the Ebola virus.

The following day, I stood in front of the gun shop for the second time. The first time I went in, I started hyperventilating as though I were having an asthma attack.

"Are you okay there?" the clerk called from behind the counter.

"Need some air," I managed to say before I bolted out the door and walked around the block, breathing from the diaphragm the way I learned in yoga class. The night before, I had a nightmare that DeMarco and Miller were both aiming weapons at Jason and me. And I couldn't protect either one of us. I inhaled once again and returned to the store.

I popped a piece of peppermint gum into my parched mouth and pushed the door open to the tingling of a bell. The same clerk was selling a hunting rifle to an old guy in a wool cap.

I nodded to him and forced a smile as I approached the counter.

"I'll be with you shortly. Feeling better?"

"Much," I lied. I stared at the cracked gray linoleum at my feet. Visualize a pleasant image, Fabiano. I pictured the Atlantic Ocean, its soft waves rolling onto a sandy Cape May beach. Peaceful, serene. The salty air caressing my face.

A bell rang. The ocean vanished. I looked up and saw the old guy walking out the door.

The clerk said. "Now, what is it that I can do for you?"

Perspiration beaded up on my forehead and upper lip.

"I need to purchase ..." My voice cracked. I paused and wiped my forehead. "I'm interested in a Glock pistol." I showed him my city license to carry a concealed weapon. "I prefer a side holster."

The clerk disappeared into a back-storage room.

I paced. I walked to the window to check out the street traffic. I considered escaping again, but the clerk reemerged and placed three handguns on the counter.

"This one here is the G26 Gen 4." He handed me the weapon.

I held it like it was a hand grenade. I gripped the Glock, turned to the sidewall, and aimed at a framed federal license. In my head, I heard the constant pop of bullets. I hadn't touched a gun since my aborted training at the police academy. I already knew how to inflict harm with my self-defense skills, but those injuries were rarely fatal. With a gun, I had the means to kill another human being.

"How does that feel?" I heard the clerk say. "The design lets you customize the grip for your hand size," he pointed out.

I placed the gun back on the counter. "Fine. It feels fine." I wiped my sweaty hands on my jacket.

"It has a ten-round capacity."

Too much firepower for me. "I'd prefer just the standard six rounds."

The clerk pointed to another weapon. "This G43 is our single stack. It's accurate, easy to operate, and has your standard six rounds."

I picked this one up.

"This feels comfortable." I wanted to buy the gun and leave before a panic attack struck. I reached into my tote for my credit card, but the clerk handed me a third choice to consider.

"This one is the smallest Glock pistol. It's a .380 automatic."

I only half-listened to his sales pitch, something about slimline, subcompact. I didn't want to be rude, so I went through the motions of checking out the weapon as he expected me to.

"I prefer the G43." I put the .380 down and handed over my credit card.

"Good choice."

"And I'll take a side holster and ammunition. You've been a great help."

"You need to fill out this background check. I'll put it through while you're here. There shouldn't be a problem."

"No waiting period?"

The clerk shook his head. "It's all done electronically. If you come back clean, you can take the gun with you today."

Ain't technology great? I would have preferred more time to adjust to bringing a gun into my home.

The approval came through. I walked out into the city streets with the Glock in my holster, an unsettling sensation. Despite my misstep at the police academy, I had landed on my feet and earned a decent living sticking to white-collar crime.

Now I was hunting dangerous criminals. I looked down and saw my holster peeking out from under my jacket. Owning a gun should have given me a greater sense of security. It didn't.

CHAPTER
FORTY-ONE

"Come on, DeMarco. Do yourself some good," I said. We were sitting at his kitchen table.

"I don't want you showing up here. You'll make trouble for me." DeMarco sneered.

"I left my car blocks away and came in through the alley."

"You don't give a fuck what happens to me. You're in this for yourself."

"I'm in this, as you say, to find out the truth and get some justice for my clients."

"There ain't no justice in this stinkin' world."

"Face it, Joey, if you don't talk, you could be left to take the full weight. You told me you didn't know about Doyle until you read the newspaper, and I believe you." I lied. "So, give it to me straight. Tell me exactly what happened the night of the arson."

"You think I'm that stupid?"

I leaned in across the table. "You already told me Doyle had something on McFarland. Could Doyle have been demanding money for his silence?" I thought about the cash Doyle left with his sister.

"I might have heard something like that."

"Did McFarland order the arson?"

"I told you before I don't deal with McFarland."

I immediately thought of McFarland's right-hand man. "Bobby Regan?"

DeMarco choked on his smoke. I went to the sink and got him a glass of water.

DeMarco used the back of his hands to dry his eyes. "For a broad, you get around."

"A professional investigator gets paid to find out things."

"Me and Bobby grew up in the same neighborhood. He told me Doyle was getting money out of McFarland. But he never said why."

"It was your pal Bobby who hired you for the arson." Pieces were falling into place.

"I didn't have a choice. He knew I violated my parole, and he threatened to turn me in if I didn't do a job for him."

"And you got paid the four grand for the arson, not the construction site accident."

"I didn't set no fire."

"Don't try to snow me, Joey. You were there helping Miller. You're as guilty as he is."

DeMarco smirked. "If you're so smart, why are you here talking to me and not the cops?"

"I told you I won't press charges against you if you talk to me. I want to know about Nate Warner and how he fits into all this."

"Again. What is it with this guy? You keep asking, and I keep telling you. I don't know who the fuck you're talking about."

"He's a man who was murdered. Shot and left in the trunk of his car."

"Nothing to do with me. I never killed nobody."

I was beginning to believe that DeMarco wasn't involved in Nate's murder, and he wasn't going to be the weak link in nailing McFarland for it. Bobby Regan, however, seemed like my next best move.

CHAPTER
FORTY-TWO

Joey DeMarco was trying too hard to look calm and relaxed as he sat across the table from Tom and Detective Lewis at police headquarters.

Tom had called me earlier, asking me to be there when Jason came for the planned lineup. I talked him into letting me observe his interview with DeMarco from behind the two-way mirror.

"I don't know about no fire," DeMarco said.

DeMarco sat next to his attorney, who I recognized as one of the city's high-priced criminal defense attorneys. Made me wonder who was paying the fee.

"And you deny knowing David Miller?" Tom asked.

"That's right."

"Where were you on the night of the McFarland warehouse fire?" Tom read him the date.

"Too long ago for me to remember."

"It was a few weeks ago," Detective Lewis said.

"I don't remember two days ago," DeMarco said.

"We're wasting everyone's time here," DeMarco's attorney said. "My client knows nothing about this incident. Can we leave now?"

Tom didn't answer. "What if I told you that your client and Dave Miller served time together at the old Graterford state prison?"

I saw DeMarco's eye and cheek twitch.

"Thousands of other inmates were there at the same time," the attorney said.

"Not in the same cell," Tom replied in an even tone. Lewis grinned.

"I don't remember everyone I shared a cell with," DeMarco said.

"Sure. You've had so many extensive stays in our state facilities during your illustrious criminal career," Lewis sneered.

"There's no need to harass my client. If you have nothing further, we're leaving." The attorney stood up and motioned DeMarco to follow.

"I'm afraid I can't let you go, not yet," Tom said.

"This better be good," the attorney said.

"We have a witness that puts your client inside the warehouse owned by Sean McFarland when the fire was started. Your client here fired his gun at the witness, then pursued that witness through the neighborhood but failed to catch him. Then, of course, we have the victim, Paddy Doyle, who died in the fire. Your client is facing charges of murder and arson."

"I didn't know he was in the place," DeMarco blurted out. "I'm not takin' no fall for no murder."

"Don't say another word." The attorney placed his hand on DeMarco's shoulder. "This interview is over."

Tom stood up. "I'm holding your client for a lineup."

Jason looked relieved. "Good job," I told him. He and I were standing in front of a two-way mirror, and he had just picked DeMarco, without hesitation, out of a lineup of seven men.

Tom and DeMarco's attorney had left the room while we waited for DeMarco to be escorted out.

Tom poked his head in. "You can come out now. DeMarco is gone." He shook Jason's hand. "You did good. Two officers are outside to drive you back to Villanova."

After Jason left, I asked Tom, "Is DeMarco in custody?"

"For now. I'm sure his attorney will make a bail application. As soon as we get a judge's okay, we'll execute a warrant at his house. I want to see if we discover other evidence that will convince a judge to yank DeMarco's parole."

"And DeMarco didn't give you any idea where Miller is?"

"Not a hint."

Perhaps DeMarco wasn't snowing me when he told me he had no idea where Miller was.

When I told Keenan, SEPA Financial's attorney, that the warehouse fire was, in fact, arson, he sank into his chair, his shoulders slumped. "The police are certain?"

"A witness has identified two men who started the fire. One man, Joey DeMarco, is in custody. He was paroled from state prison this year. The other man is still at large. He's known as Miller the Griller, for obvious reasons."

"This witness is credible?"

I kept Jason's name out but told Keenan that he picked DeMarco out of a lineup.

"Have the police linked this crime to Sean McFarland?" Keenan asked.

"DeMarco isn't talking. All we know at this point is that DeMarco worked at one of McFarland's construction sites, and he and Miller served time together."

"But no proof McFarland hired them?"

"Who else would be interested in torching the place, and who would have the bucks to pay a professional like Miller?" I pointed out.

"I don't see a successful businessman like McFarland breaking the law to collect thousands when he owns properties worth millions."

"What if the warehouse wasn't the first arson at his buildings? Maybe now upper management will give the green light to investigate the earlier fires."

"I'll speak with the management committee and let you know."

"The question is, what will you recommend?"

"That, Ms. Fabiano, comes under attorney-client privilege."

"Have you considered that McFarland might not be as financially successful as he presents himself?"

Keenan made no reply. The atmosphere turned noticeably chilly. Still, I pressed him.

"The loan application for his mortgage firm could tell us about the state of his finances," I said.

"Ask Paul Cameron."

"I did last week, and I'm still waiting. How difficult is it to get someone to print out the damned documents and hand over a copy?"

"I don't like your tone," he paused. "I'll look into it."

"You need to do better than that. What's wrong with that computer on your desk? Let's have a look right now."

"I can't ignore our protocols."

"What's going on here, Jim? Pushback like this makes me wonder what SEPA Financial has to hide."

Keenan's energy and forcefulness returned. "I resent your implication. We're a reputable company and have been for decades."

"I've thought so too, until now. You warned me off talking to McFarland from the beginning. And you and upper management put those earlier fires off-limits. Now neither you nor Cameron are willing to cough up McFarland's financials that got him his loan."

"I've already told you I would look into it. I don't need a dressing down from you." He stood. "I have another meeting to go to."

"This is the last time you're going to stall me." I left and slammed the door.

CHAPTER FORTY-THREE

I worked out on the elliptical for forty minutes, attempting to tame my anger and compensate for the Triple Mocha Frappuccinos from Starbucks that were becoming a daily habit. Another sign that my investigations weren't getting me where I needed to go fast enough. I wiped perspiration from my neck and headed to the shower.

My cell phone rang as I was drying off. It was Michael Shea, the attorney who filed a negligence suit on behalf of the workers injured at McFarland's building site.

"You may be right about McFarland's financial situation. I contacted his investors in the Riverfront project. Several agreed to talk with you, and they tell an interesting story. I can email their names to you."

"Thanks. Appreciate the help. But McFarland's financial difficulties can't be good news for your clients."

"He's got enough insurance for our purposes. And besides, I'll shed no tears if he turns out to be the cheat that I think he is. Oh, and our pal Bobby Regan is an investor, too."

Not at all surprising to me that Regan had skin in the game. I figured he'd only hang around if he had a sizable stake in McFarland's business. I finished dressing while I waited for Shea's email. When it arrived, there were four investors on the list willing to talk to me.

My first call once I returned to my office was to the owner of a popular bistro. I told him Michael Shea had given me his name. "Like I said to him, I'm glad someone is finally looking into Sean and that Riverfront project. It's been a disaster. I warned him about taking on the kind of development he knew nothing about, but Sean wouldn't listen."

"But you invested in it anyway?"

"I went to college with Sean. I couldn't say no. Besides, I've made money on his other projects. This time, though, I didn't put in as much as he wanted. I invested the amount I was willing to lose."

"Why so negative about the condos?"

"Way out of his league. I told him to stick with what he'd been doing for years. Mid-rise apartments and office buildings. They were financially sound investments."

"Those were the projects you invested in?"

"Sure. And like I said, I made money, and I was happy. Then Sean decides on the harebrained idea to build a huge condo project with a rooftop supper club. He was obsessed. It was the only thing he talked about. At the time, I had doubts about his mental state. I knew he was having marital troubles. They could have put him over the edge."

"Any idea of the extent of the losses?"

"Millions." He paused. "What concerns me more is that my distributions from Sean's profitable buildings started to drop when his precious condo project was getting off the ground. It smells like three-day-old fish to me."

He was confirming what Caroline found in McFarland's financials.

"Did you ask Sean about that?"

"We stood face-to-face, and he made some excuse about rising costs and the need to spend more on upgrading and refurbishing his buildings. Claimed he couldn't raise the rents. But he was lying. I found out later that he did raise the rents at his apartment and office buildings."

"You're sure?"

"I like to keep tabs on my investments. You're free to check. Last year the rents on Sean's apartments went up twenty dollars a month for the one-bedrooms and thirty for the two-bedrooms. I have my lawyer looking into things. Sean may be a college buddy, but if he's cheating me, I'll sue him just as I would anyone else."

After we hung up, I confirmed that the rents on McFarland's apartment buildings had been raised. And then called the next investor who had agreed to speak to me.

"Sean invited my husband and me to the supper club the night before it was scheduled to open," one of the city's top hairstylists told me. "Let's just say it didn't go well. We waited an hour for our food, and when it arrived, it was not only cold but inedible. We were promised top entertainment, and we got a third-rate lounge singer. Anyway, the opening was postponed for weeks."

"It seems Sean has turned things around," I offered. "From the ads I see around the city, the supper club is booking major talent now."

"Absolutely. My sister and her husband went two weeks ago and raved about the show and the new chef. But, like I told that attorney, my returns on the investments I have in two of his office buildings dropped while he was pumping money into the supper club. I don't think that's a coincidence."

Sean McFarland had to have coughed up big bucks to book named stars and attract a top-notch chef. Where was he getting that kind of money?

The last two investors on the list also told me they saw a drop in their distributions in investments from earlier, successful properties.

I called Shea. "Thanks for the help. I have another request."

"Why am I not surprised?"

"I'd like to see the entire list of investors."

"They won't talk to you."

"I'm okay with that. I want to see if anyone from my investigation pops up."

"Okay, I'll send the list, but let me know before you reach out to any of them."

I took a break, grabbed a half-pint of milk and a chocolate

Kind bar to get a bit of calcium and protein along with the chocolate.

By the time I finished my snack, Shea's list was in my inbox. My instincts were right. Besides Bobby Regan, I recognized one other name. Greg Saunders, whose driver's license Paddy Doyle had stashed away at his sister's house.

My instincts told me Saunders was connected to all this and might have a story to tell. I decided to call and let Shea know later. Easier to apologize than ask permission. My call went directly to voicemail. A woman's voice said: "The Saunders are not available to take your call. Please leave a message." I did, simply saying I wanted to talk to Greg Saunders.

CHAPTER
FORTY-FOUR

I phoned Tom, concerned that DeMarco would make bail.

"DeMarco's not going anywhere. We found a SIG Sauer in an upstairs closet. His attorney isn't going to be happy that his client was stupid enough to violate his parole."

It occurred to me the bullets from DeMarco's gun might match the one I had stowed in my safe, the one my handyman dug out of the wall of my front porch. I opened my mouth to tell Tom, but quickly reconsidered. I might still be able to use it as leverage with DeMarco and his attorney.

"You were about to say something. I thought we agreed to share information. You're holding something back."

I gulped. "Not about the case," I lied. "Sonny is optimistic that Aunt Roseanne will get parole this time."

"You don't seem pleased."

"I'm happy for her."

"But."

"The thought of her coming home has brought back the whole nightmare. I'm having flashbacks and panic attacks again."

"Maybe you should go see that therapist of yours."

"Maybe I will." But I knew I wouldn't. I learned I could manage, not cure, the effects of trauma.

The next morning, I roamed the city, trying to work out what I'd overlooked in searching for Nate's data. After three hours I gave up, went back to the office, flopped onto my sofa and kicked off my boots. I was considering whether I needed an aspirin or a chocolate bar or both when my phone rang.

"We've brought Dave Miller in for questioning," Tom said.

"We nabbed him at the airport when he got off a plane from Florida. He flew to Miami the day after the warehouse fire," Tom said, "and got back into Philly this morning."

"What's he got to say?" I asked.

"Nothing so far. I left Lewis with him and stepped out to call you."

"What's up?"

"Jason's already here for the lineup. He's been asking for you. I thought you could stay with him while he waits, keep him calm. We want to keep at Miller a bit longer before we hold the lineup."

"On my way."

When Jason saw me walk in, I saw the tension in his face ease. He had gained a bit of weight since I had seen him last and had gotten a haircut.

"I'm glad you came," he said.

"How are you doing?"

Jason shrugged his shoulders. "Detective Volpe convinced my parents to let me board at Penn Wynn."

"Getting back to normal school life. That's got to be good for you," I said. "Which reminds me ..." I handed him a shopping bag. "This is for you."

"What is it?" he said.

"Open it. I thought you could use a new one."

He looked inside and pulled out a Philadelphia Union hoodie and hat. His face broke out in a wide grin. "Thanks. This is great." He leaned over and gave me an awkward, tentative hug, his cheeks red with embarrassment.

"I am glad to be back playing soccer. But coming here reminds me that I'll have to testify at a trial."

I pointed him to a bench in the hallway and we sat.

"Jason, take one step at a time," I said. "Today, you're here to see if you can pick one of the arsonists out of a lineup. That's all you need to do. You've been through this routine before. Don't get too far ahead of yourself. A trial could be a long way off. So, tell me what's been going on with you." I would have asked about his parents, but I figured that would only add to his nerves. After we talked about school, his friends, his soccer team, I asked him if he knew where Tom was.

"They told me he's interviewing someone."

Shit. Tom wasn't letting me in on Miller's interview. Okay, he wanted me to keep Jason calm. I didn't mind. I liked the kid and knew he wasn't having an easy time with being a witness. Still, I wanted to learn what Tom was getting out of Miller.

Several hours later, Jason and I were brought in to view a lineup behind the two-way mirror.

Tom, Lewis, and a silver-haired man in a thousand-dollar gray suit, who I figured was Miller's attorney, were already in the room. I spotted Miller standing in the middle of a group of men as bulky and rough looking as he was. Jason was right. His dark, fierce eyes could give me nightmares, too.

"Who is she? And what's she doing here?" the man with silver hair asked.

"Jason's a minor. She's here as his guardian," Tom said.

"Just so long as she knows not to interfere."

"Not a problem," Tom said.

"Okay, son. I want you to step close to the mirror, take a look at these men, and tell us if you recognize anyone," Tom said.

I watched as Jason looked at each of the men, one at a time. He seemed so young to me to have such a heavy burden.

"The man in the center. Number four," Jason said.

"And where did you see this man before?"

"I saw him set fire to a warehouse."

"And where was the warehouse?"

"Down the street from Ferguson's auto body shop."

Tom nodded to me. "You can go now."

"Not as bad as you thought, huh?" I said, as Jason and I walked to an elevator bank where two officers were waiting to take Jason back to school. One of them held Jason's bag of Union gear.

"It was okay," he smiled. "Thanks for coming."

"You take care of yourself now." I shook hands, knowing I would embarrass him if I gave him a hug in public.

"Oh, and thanks for the Union gear," he said.

After Jason left, Tom took my arm. "Let's get some fresh air."

Despite the bright sun, a brisk wind made the forty-degree temperature feel much colder. Tom pulled up the collar of his jacket to cover his neck. I put gloves on.

We walked along Broad Street toward City Hall. "Jason tells me he's back at prep school," I said, "and his parents are allowing him to board."

Tom nodded. "He'll be safe there. The DA will oppose bail for Miller. We'll argue he's a flight risk since the guy does jobs all over the country. In fact, Lewis told me the Miami police like Miller for a restaurant arson that occurred while Miller was down there."

"Have torch, will travel. Did Miller give anything up? Or anyone?" I asked.

"The guy knows his way around the law. He gave us nothing. Only ..."

"Only what?"

"When I questioned him about Paddy Doyle, Miller tried to deny he knew anything about the guy," Tom said. "But for a half-second, I saw real fear in his eyes. He knew he'd be facing a murder charge, so he lawyered up. End of interview. And that attorney of his is almost as good as your pal, Sonny. And his type of talent doesn't come cheap."

"I'd bet you neither Miller nor DeMarco have deep enough pockets to pay for their attorneys," I said. "Miller's arson for hire business could be lucrative, but DeMarco makes union wages, when he gets work, that is."

"Who would fork out for their legal bills?"

"Someone paying to keep their mouths shut."

"Like McFarland, you mean?"

"I do."

"But you say he's in financial trouble."

"How much is it worth to him to stay out of jail?"

Tom paused, looked around and said quietly. "Miller told us he received a $15,000 settlement for a worksite injury where he claimed to be working as a carpenter."

"At McFarland's condo construction site?"

Tom nodded.

"That man is no more a carpenter than I am," I said. "McFarland paid him for the arson and tried to hide it as a settlement for injuries. The guys who got seriously injured have to sue him for compensation."

CHAPTER FORTY-FIVE

Sunday morning, I woke before four, ate a quick breakfast, and got on the road to visit Aunt Roseanne. I drove straight through with no pit stops and got to the prison in record time.

My aunt looked paler than the last time I saw her, and she still hadn't gained any of the weight she had lost during her hospital stay.

"Have you seen the doctor?"

"Last week. I'm okay."

"What did he say?"

"What he always says. I have heart damage, and I need to stay on my medications."

"What about the meds for your depression?"

"Don't worry. I'm still taking them. I won't try anything again."

When my aunt was first convicted and went to prison, she tried to slash her wrists with a homemade shiv she bartered from another inmate for two packs of cigarettes. The blade, however, wasn't sharp enough to do fatal damage. She was given various anti-depressants over the years but remained in a deep depression until eventually, the docs found meds that helped.

We hugged and cried when I left her for the long ride back to Philly.

On my way home, Russ called, and we arranged to meet at Barcelona, a Spanish restaurant on East Passyunk, an area of South Philly burgeoning with new restaurants offering diverse cuisines. We ordered an assortment of tapas to share and a pitcher of sangria.

"You look tired and frazzled. What's going on?" Russ asked once we were seated at a window table.

I wanted to confide in him about my work. But I wasn't sure I was ready to risk telling a reporter. "It's always hard seeing Auntie and then abandoning her to that hellhole."

"I'm sure this time she'll get paroled. She's not a danger to anyone."

"She's had a heart attack. I just hope they release her before she dies."

Russ reached for my hand. "When's the hearing?"

"We don't have a date yet, but it should be soon."

As we ate, Russ talked about his trio and how well they were playing. "We're getting a lot more work now that we have a great bass player."

Earlier in the year, Russ had been reassigned to the business beat. He hesitated to switch from hard news, but when I pointed out that he'd have his evenings and weekends free for his gigs, he took the job.

"Awesome," I said, smiling. I decided to feel him out. "What do you know about real estate development in the city?"

"Some, not much. That's an abrupt switch of topics. Is this about one of your cases?"

"It's complicated." It wasn't a great idea to tell him about my suspicions of fraud inside McFarland's operations and certainly not about the possible involvement of my client, SEPA Financial. But I was stuck, and Russ might have insights into McFarland.

"Try me." Russ chewed on a marinated sardine and sipped his wine.

"Does the name Sean McFarland mean anything to you?"

"As far as I know, he develops and rehabs apartment and office buildings. The new condo development on the Delaware River is his, too."

"That's about right."

"Obviously, you suspect something, or we wouldn't be having this conversation."

"You can't write about anything that I share with you because none of it is nailed down. If, and when, I get to the bottom of things, you'll have an exclusive. But you can't move out ahead of me."

Russ reached for a forkful of calamari, giving him time to consider my offer.

"Okay by me." He signaled the waiter for another pitcher of sangria. I told him the general outlines of what I suspected about McFarland's fraud, leaving out any details about Caroline Hewitt and avoiding any mention of the arson and murder.

"If you can prove the fraud, it would be a major scandal," Russ said. "People in this city admire McFarland, coming from a working-class background and succeeding big time." Then he added. "But this isn't only about fraud, is it? You think this is somehow connected to Nate Warner's murder, or you wouldn't be so interested."

"You know I can't touch an open murder investigation," I said.

"Don't even try to con me. This is me, Russ. Remember. You might have bitched and complained about how Nate got on your nerves, but you have a higher sense of loyalty than anyone else I know. You'd find a way to go after his murderer, even though your own relative is heading the investigation."

I drank a mouthful of sangria, and it went down hard. No way could I deny what Russ said. I whispered, "Alright. I'm looking into the murder, too." I took another sip of wine and cleared my throat. "I think Nate's death is somehow related to the fraud and the arson at McFarland's warehouse."

"Arson? I thought it was ruled an accident."

"Not anymore. The cops have a witness."

"So, why do you think this warehouse arson is connected to Nate's murder?"

"I haven't worked it all out, but I'm getting closer. I can feel it." I didn't mention the gunfire I had attracted.

"Then you better watch your back."

"Don't worry, I am." My side holster still felt like an extra appendage, but I kept it on every day.

After dinner, we went back to my apartment and Russ stayed the night. Our relationship filled our needs for now. Nothing complicated. No talk of future plans. We were comfortable with each other, more than passionate. I fell asleep with a feeling of contentment that I hadn't felt since Nate Warner called me to investigate a suspicious fire.

CHAPTER FORTY-SIX

Late Monday morning, I called the Saunders residence again, and once again, my call went to voicemail. I spent the next few hours finalizing yet another background report. This one concerned a potential hire at a Center City law firm. Background checks were far from the most challenging aspects of my job, but they helped keep my bank account healthy.

When I took a break, I scanned my cell phone pictures to take another look at Greg Saunders' driver's license. He was fifty-three and lived in a high-rise condo building near the Philadelphia Museum of Art. His license had expired in June.

I did a quick Internet search and found news articles reporting that Saunders, a bank executive with a seat on the Chamber of Commerce board, had disappeared in May. I remembered reading about the disappearance at the time, but I didn't remember the details. Follow-up articles indicated a lack of police progress in the investigation, and Saunders remained missing.

I called my contact in missing persons. "We never got a lead on that one," she told me. "He went to work in the morning and never arrived back home. Since he walked to and from work, we had no car to trace."

"Cell phone?"

"We traced his phone to a trashcan in Rittenhouse Square."

"Who reported him missing?"

"The wife, Claire Saunders. She still lives at the same address. And she calls me from time to time. She hasn't given up hope. But you know the probability of us finding him alive after all these months. What's your interest? Did Mrs. Saunders hire you?"

"Greg Saunders' name cropped up in connection with another case, and I wanted to talk to him."

"Good luck with that."

I called the Saunders condo again, and this time a woman answered.

"Claire Saunders?"

"Yes, may I ask who's calling?"

I identified myself and asked to see her.

"You're the person who left messages asking for my husband."

"I've since learned he's disappeared. I'm so sorry." I paused. "I found something that belonged to him."

"Oh, my God. Do you know how long the police have been looking, but still no one can tell me what happened to Greg? Please come over as soon as you can."

"I can be there within a half-hour."

Claire Sanders was in her early fifties, with porcelain, wrinkle-free skin. She wore black crepe slacks, a black and white cashmere sweater, and Jimmy Choo heels. I figured her outfit cost about as much as my car insurance policy.

She showed me into the living room and we sat down on an elegant cream-colored sofa. "Please tell me what you found out about my husband," she said, her voice trembling.

I handed over my phone with the pictures of her husband's driver's license, wallet, and credit cards. As she scanned through the images, tears streamed down her cheeks.

"This tells me he didn't leave me for another woman or run away to live somewhere exotic." She sobbed and took a tissue from a silver dispenser on a side table. "Seeing these means he's dead, doesn't it?"

"It could, but we'd need to know more in order to be sure whether he's alive or not."

"Forgive me for forgetting my manners. I've prepared tea for us." She left the room and returned with a tray holding a tea service and scones. "Please help yourself to a scone. I'll pour the tea."

"Mrs. Saunders, I've brought you upsetting news. I'm sorry."

"I thought I'd been preparing myself during these past months, but it is still a shock. We've been married for thirty years." Her eyes grew moist once again. "I miss him every day. Please call me Claire."

I chose one of the scones, already halved, and spooned on clotted cream and raspberry jam. I took one bite, and the taste and smell took me back to when I was ten, enjoying afternoon tea at the Four Season's hotel with my mom. A treat for just us two after seeing a performance of the ballet, Swan Lake. A precious memory. She died a year later.

"I'm glad to see you're enjoying the scone," Claire said. "My neighbor is a retired pastry chef, and he keeps me supplied." But she didn't take one. She leaned back and sipped her tea.

"Where did you find Greg's things?" she asked as she replaced her teacup onto the table.

"In the possession of a man who was killed in a recent fire. His name was Paddy Doyle. Did you or your husband know him?"

"I certainly didn't. What can you tell me about him?"

"He worked construction jobs and had a drug and alcohol addiction."

Mrs. Saunders shook her head. "I can't think of any connection between him and my husband. He must have killed Greg. Otherwise, why would he have my husband's license?"

I ignored her question.

"I understand your husband invested in Sean McFarland's Riverfront development?"

Claire Saunders frowned. "I don't understand. What does an investment have to do with any of this?"

"I'm not sure. But you see, Paddy Doyle knew Sean McFarland and worked on the project." I poured another cup of tea.

"Greg's known Sean for years." She stared out the window. "But he never mentioned any Doyle." Then she placed her hand across her mouth.

"What is it, Claire?"

"I hadn't thought about this until now. Greg told me he believed that Sean was cheating his investors."

I nearly choked on the hot tea. "Did your husband ever confront Sean McFarland about his concerns?"

"Greg did tell me that he planned to see Sean, but I don't know if he ever did. He disappeared shortly after we talked."

Neither of us spoke. I was considering the possibility that McFarland had a hand in Greg Saunders' disappearance and probable murder. Looking at Claire Saunders' face, pale, lifeless as a marble sculpture, she might have been considering the same possibility.

Finally, she broke the silence.

"Why are you interested in what happened to Greg?" she asked.

"I've been working on another case. When I saw your husband's name on a list of Mr. McFarland's investors, I connected it to the driver's license Doyle had. That's why I called you. I haven't gotten any farther along."

"You've done better than the police, and they've been at it for months."

She offered me another scone. This time I chose the jam without clotted cream. It couldn't hurt to save a couple hundred calories.

"What are your next steps?" she asked me.

"I'm not sure. But I'm going to do my best to find out what happened to your husband."

"He must have been killed," Claire said.

"I'm afraid that may be true, but how and why would anyone want him dead?"

She grabbed another tissue, dabbed her eyes. "I have no idea." She walked over to a Queen Anne desk near the window. "I'll pay your fee to find him alive or dead and a bonus if his body comes back to me so I can give him a decent burial."

I left the Saunders' apartment with a goodie bag of scones

and a check with an amount that made me smile. Claire Saunders and Helena Warner deserved to know the truth about their husbands, and somehow, I was going to get it for them.

CHAPTER
FORTY-SEVEN

"I'm here to see Sean McFarland." I handed my business card to his secretary, a twenty-something, who looked like a wannabe Miss America contestant with her coiffed hair and perfect makeup.

"I'll let him know you're here." When she picked up the phone, her red metallic nails, long and sharp as bayonets, glistened in the light. I wanted to ask how she managed to shower and dress without impaling herself but managed to restrain my curiosity. She spoke into the receiver, too low for me to hear.

McFarland came out of his office. He looked much the same as he did when I had him under surveillance. Except now, I was close enough to see pockmarks etched deep into his cheeks.

"I thought my lawyer told you to stay away from me and my properties."

"I'm here to talk about an entirely different matter."

"Which is?"

"I'm looking for a missing person who I understand you know."

"Who are you talking about?"

"I think it's best if we speak in private."

McFarland frowned, then led me through his office door. "This better be quick."

We stood face-to-face.

"I'm looking for Greg Saunders."

McFarland turned away, swayed, and gripped the back of a client chair to steady himself.

"Are you alright?"

He didn't reply and went to sit at his desk. "Why come to

me?" His voice tensed.

"His wife hired me to find him. She told me that you knew her husband for years. I thought you could tell me something about him that might help me locate him. I understand he was one of your investors."

McFarland took a deep breath. "He was an investor, yes. One among many. I didn't know him well."

"Surely you must know something about a loyal investor?" McFarland hadn't offered me a chair, but I sat down anyway.

"He was wealthy and interested in real estate investing. But I know nothing about his personal life." He stood up. "I can't think of anything to tell you."

I remained seated. "Before he went missing, Mr. Saunders told his wife that he had concerns about his investments with you and was going to speak to you."

McFarland gave me a closed-lip smile. "You'll find investors never like a decrease in their returns."

"He talked to you about his concerns, then."

McFarland turned his face to the window, paused long enough to make me wonder if he would answer, then without turning to face me, he said, "I never spoke to him. Now, I'm sorry that he's missing, but I really can't help you." He turned and pointed me toward the door.

I left and closed the door behind me. As I walked down the corridor, I thought about McFarland's reactions. Like DeMarco, he'd make a lousy poker player. Too many tells.

When I mentioned Saunders' name, he nearly collapsed. And I never said what Saunders' specific concerns were. But McFarland knew it was about a decline in the investment returns.

Tom and I sat on a bench in Rittenhouse Square eating roast beef sandwiches with horseradish, Tom's favorite. The wind whipped dried leaves in circles around our feet. The sun warmed the air, but when it disappeared behind clouds, the temperature felt as if it dropped ten degrees. I wrapped my hands around my coffee cup to keep them warm.

"You're telling me Sean McFarland could be guilty of income tax evasion and defrauding his investors," Tom said.

"That means he could face prison in addition to civil liabilities for restitution and damages," I pointed out. "All of which might give him a motive for murder."

"Nate's?"

"McFarland's business seems to me to be the key to unraveling not only Nate's murder, but the warehouse arson and the murder of Paddy Doyle." I didn't mention my suspicions about Greg Saunders' fate. "Maybe you could have Doyle's body re-examined?"

"We might need to do that to get a murder conviction during the commission of an arson," Tom said. "Right now, Nate's murder is my priority. I'd buy the idea McFarland could be involved in killing Nate only if Nate had serious, incriminating evidence against McFarland and McFarland knew it," Tom said.

"Nate had proof. Evidence that he stashed away and asked me to find."

"But you don't have any evidence in your hands to back up this theory of yours," Tom said.

"Tom, we can get to the truth if we put both our minds to this."

"At least you know how to treat a guy when you have the nerve to pick his brain on a case that you shouldn't be interfering in." Tom bit into his sandwich.

I handed him a napkin. "There's horseradish on your chin."

"Thanks." Tom wiped his mouth and chin. "Why would McFarland want Doyle out of the way? Doyle worked on a McFarland construction site, but there's no indication they knew each other."

"One of my sources tells me otherwise. Apparently, Doyle knew McFarland well enough to consider him a crook." I wasn't prepared to tell Tom that I got that from DeMarco. I did, however, decide to tell him about my new client, Claire Saunders.

"She hired me to find her husband, Greg. He's been missing since May. You remember it was Saunders' driver's license and credit cards that Doyle had squirreled away at his sister's. Along with a lot more cash than any of our city's homeless."

"What are you thinking?" Tom said.

"Saunders was one of McFarland's investors. According to Claire Saunders, her husband had grown suspicious that McFarland was cheating his investors out of their rightful distributions. Soon after, Saunders disappeared and hasn't been seen again. And somehow Doyle has possession of the missing man's driver's license and more than four thousand in cash.

"I'll try to ignore the fact that you went through Doyle's suitcase because I know you left no prints," Tom said. "Doyle could have robbed Saunders and killed him."

"Somehow, I don't see a businessman like Saunders walking around the city with thousands of dollars in his pockets."

"Point taken," Tom said. "And why would Doyle keep the man's wallet and ID rather than dump it?" Tom stopped eating. "Blackmail."

I nodded. "It would explain the cash. And it would mean Doyle knew what happened to Greg Saunders."

We finished the last of our sandwiches in silence.

"Circles within circles," Tom finally said. "No wonder this case is so damned hard to get a handle on."

"I have confidence that in the end we'll get the answers."

Tom smiled. "An optimist."

I shook my head and nudged his elbow. "I happen to believe in our crime-solving abilities, bro."

"Okay. Keep looking into Saunders' disappearance and Nate's stash. Let me know what you're up to. I'll keep you in the loop as much as I can. But don't press me when I tell you something is off-limits."

"Deal."

He kissed me on the cheek and left to return to headquarters.

Tom was right. I had reasonable theories, but no proof. I needed to nail down McFarland's fraud and show that his fear of exposure led to Nate's murder. Finding Nate's documents could provide the proof, but I was still in the dark as to where Nate had put them.

Since defrauding investors and tax evasion were federal crimes, I had just the person who could help on my speed dial.

CHAPTER
FORTY-EIGHT

I knew Maggie Connors had entered the restaurant even before she arrived at our table. Nearby diners were all staring in the same direction. I turned to follow their eyes and saw Maggie wearing a lipstick red pant suit.

Maggie was one of those rare mortals whose energy glowed like a spotlight that drew attention wherever they went. Today she dominated the room with her custom-tailored suit, her tall, slim frame, and Chanel sling-backs. Her golden hair draped softly across her shoulders, not a strand out of place. Maggie exuded power, intellect, and beauty. I often thought she must trace her ancestry to the Amazons.

She slid into the chair across from me. "Now, what's so important you couldn't discuss on the phone."

After we ordered, I laid out what I knew so far about McFarland's financial dealings.

"And you know about the fraud and tax evasion? How?"

"An informant."

"Someone involved in the fraud?"

"Not directly, no."

"The guy's accountant?"

"Forgive me for not confirming."

"Andrea, I remember our conversation over our chocolate fix."

The waiter brought our glasses of Pinot Grigio and two Cobb salads.

I was starving, so I dove right in. "I promised to keep my informant out of this as long as possible," I said.

"If you want my help, I'll have to speak to whoever it is." Maggie poured ranch dressing over her salad.

"Can't you get a look at McFarland's IRS files with what

I've told you?"

"You know the answer to that," Maggie said. "I need probable cause. And do I need to point out that you have no right to see those tax records?" She ate a forkful of salad and chased it with a sip of wine.

"My informant prepared them, and those records speak for themselves."

"I still need an affidavit to subpoena McFarland's financials and his tax returns."

"I'll see what I can do."

We made small talk over the rest of lunch, then Maggie suggested dessert. "I need a chocolate fix," Maggie said, flagging down our server.

"You always do."

It wouldn't be easy to convince Caroline Hewitt to talk to the U.S. Attorney's office. She knew about Nate's murder. She had every right to be concerned, even frightened for herself and her children. However, I saw no other way for Maggie to begin an investigation into McFarland's activities without Caroline's help.

When I got Caroline on the phone, I took in a deep breath and went into my spiel. "An assistant U.S. Attorney I trust wants to investigate McFarland's finances. Her name is Maggie Connors. I spoke with her at lunch recently ..."

"Absolutely not," Caroline interrupted. "I'm sorry I ever spoke to you about it. She'll have to do it without me. What do you think would happen to me and my children? I don't want my body dumped somewhere like that insurance executive."

"We can protect you."

"Twenty-four-seven? And don't even suggest I uproot my family. I have a thriving practice. My children love their school and their friends. No way am I yanking them away. Besides, my ex-husband would fight me for custody if I tried to move out of state."

Obviously, Caroline had given considerable thought to the downsides of taking on Sean McFarland. And I couldn't really disagree with what she said. But I was counting on the fact that Caroline was a woman with a conscience.

"Maggie Connors is the one prosecutor I know who is good enough to get to the truth behind McFarland's finances and put him in prison if he's dirty. If you don't want to trust me with the evidence you have, you can trust Maggie. She's an officer of the court."

"There are no guarantees that he'll be convicted or ever spend a day in prison," Caroline said. "People like him know how to manipulate the system."

"We could talk to Maggie about protecting your identity as a confidential source."

Caroline sighed. "I can't deal with this now. A client is due in ten minutes."

"At least think about it. McFarland needs to answer for his crimes."

I'd let her have a few days to mull things over then try again.

Caroline called before I contacted her. I was prepared for her to turn me down cold, but she turned out to be the straight shooter I thought she was. She agreed to talk with Maggie. Her only condition was for Maggie to come to Narberth. "I don't want to be seen going into the federal building."

"Can you protect her identity?" I asked Maggie as we drove into the suburbs.

"I'll do my best to convince the judge," she replied. "I can't promise anything."

Caroline's face remained tense when I introduced her to Maggie.

"I know this is a difficult decision for you, so let's take things one step at a time," Maggie said.

We sat in taupe upholstered chairs around a glass coffee table where a pitcher of water and three glasses sat on a tray.

I poured each of us a glass and waited for Maggie to take the lead.

"Tell me in your own words what you know about Sean McFarland's financial reports," she began.

Caroline explained her responsibilities on the McFarland account and how she uncovered two sets of reports. Maggie asked for specific details, such as when the reports were prepared and when Caroline found the second set.

"You didn't know the report you worked on wasn't accurate until you found that second set?" Maggie asked.

"That's right. And I wouldn't have seen the second set if it hadn't been misfiled."

"And your report was the one used to file with the IRS?"

"Correct."

"And you have copies of both reports?"

Caroline nodded. "I took copies to protect myself. I didn't doctor any numbers."

"I understand you no longer work at Hayes and Osborne," Maggie said.

"I didn't feel comfortable staying," Caroline said.

"I'll need to have a look at those reports."

Caroline walked over to a filing cabinet, unlocked it, and pulled out a folder. Her hands trembled slightly as she handed it to Maggie.

"I want to do what's right, but you need to understand I can't endanger my children."

"I have children of my own," Maggie said. "I have no intention of putting you or your family in jeopardy." She began reading the contents.

I started to rise from my chair, eager to have a look, too. But Maggie tilted her head and gave me her "don't even think about it" look.

"I thought …" But Maggie didn't give me a chance to finish.

"We'll talk later." Her tone was as stern as a master sergeant. No wonder her kids were so well-behaved.

So, Caroline and I sat there and watched Maggie take her time going through the documents, page by page. I poured more water and handed a glass to Caroline.

"No, thanks." She bit her lips and fidgeted with her pearl necklace.

I smiled. "You've done a fantastic job with your office. These chairs are extremely comfortable."

"I worked with an interior designer."

I smiled again but couldn't think of any other small talk. Caroline wasn't the only one on tenterhooks. I looked over at Maggie, searching for a clue to what she was thinking. But, after years as a prosecutor, Maggie had perfected a calm, impassive face that no one, especially a juror, could read.

Finally, Maggie closed the folder and looked up. "I want to use this information to get a subpoena for McFarland's financial records."

I put my hand out for the folder. Maggie ignored me. "I'll need to take these with me," she said to Caroline.

Now I was steaming. Maggie was acting like a one-woman band when she wouldn't have gotten those documents without me.

"Do you need to use my name?" Caroline asked.

Maggie repeated what she had told me in the car. "I can't promise the judge will agree, but I'll make a strong case for considering you a confidential source that will make it difficult for the judge to ignore."

I got up from my chair. "If the judge refuses to keep your name private," I said to Caroline, "you can withdraw."

Maggie glared at me. "But then I won't be able to move ahead with an investigation."

"It is your choice," I said to Caroline. "You need to decide what's best for you and your family." I knew what I was doing, and so did Maggie. But then she wasn't playing fair with me.

"I understand," Caroline said, then made copies of the reports and handed them to Maggie.

Once in the car, Maggie ripped into me. "You undermined me in there. What the hell were you thinking?"

"And what were you doing refusing to let me see the folder? You wouldn't have gotten within fifty yards of Caroline without me. I still have enough influence with her to convince her to pull out if you continue to stonewall me."

Red splotches broke out on Maggie's face.

I realized then that I had let my anger jeopardize my own goal of bringing the law down on McFarland.

Before I could apologize, Maggie handed me the folder. "I shouldn't be doing this, but you win." She turned to look at me. "I'm not ungrateful. But as an officer of the court, I need to be careful."

I read the contents as we drove back into the city and saw for myself that Caroline's story was backed up by the documents. The evidence looked solid.

Maggie got her subpoenas, and the judge agreed to refer to Caroline in court documents only as a confidential source. My anger hadn't done any actual harm. No thanks to me.

I phoned Tom to fill him in. "Maggie Connors has started an investigation into McFarland's finances." I told him about the falsified financial filings, but I didn't disclose Caroline's name. "If the U.S. Attorney's office can bring fraud charges against McFarland, he would be facing heavy jail time. We could have found a motive for murder."

"I'd like to know how you persuaded Maggie to go after McFarland," Tom said.

"It wasn't me. It was her confidential source."

CHAPTER
FORTY-NINE

"Andrea, you know I can't discuss an ongoing investigation," Maggie Connors told me. We were in her office, and I asked to see what information the subpoena recovered.

"Are we back to this again?" I tried not to go ballistic, this time, not yet anyway.

"You're taking advantage of our friendship."

"You're damned right. Friends are supposed to help one another."

"I went too far letting you see those financial reports."

"I already knew about them, remember. What if you happen to leave your office and ...?"

"Stop right there, and I'll forget what you're suggesting."

Maggie was incorruptible.

"It's Sean McFarland's bank records relating to his mortgage business that I'm most interested in. Do you have them yet?"

Maggie drew a deep breath. "No comment."

"Bullshit."

"I'm glad neither of us is thin-skinned."

"I need to do my job too, you know. McFarland received a loan from my client, SEPA Financial. I need to know the amount of the loan and see the financial statements he submitted to qualify for the loan."

"It's time for you to step back," Maggie said, using her firm, courtroom voice. "This office is handling the investigation now. Your job is done."

"Not by a long shot. How much was the loan McFarland secured from SEPA Financial?"

Maggie leaned back in her chair and crossed her arms. She shook her head and laughed. "You are relentless, you know."

I smiled. "Occupational hazard. I think Nate was looking into McFarland's financial worth and was suspicious about how he qualified for the loan, which had to be sizable."

"Aren't you forgetting that the Warner murder case is an ongoing police investigation with Tom in charge?"

"I'm not forgetting. In fact, Tom still needs to catch a break in the case. McFarland's financial records, specifically as they relate to my client SEPA Financial, could have a direct connection to Nate's murder."

Someone knocked on her office door.

"That's my next meeting."

I remained in my chair, staring into Maggie's eyes with laser focus. I wasn't about to move an inch, and she knew it.

"Okay, you're right. Nate had a copy of McFarland's loan application. That's all I'll tell you. Now get out of here."

I walked to the door. "One more favor. Talk to Tom. I believe your conscience allows you to share information with a fellow officer of the law." I left and slammed the door.

When I returned to my office after lunch, I listened to a message from Tom telling me Maggie had filled him in. "Thanks, kiddo."

I called Tom back. "One favor deserves another."

"Now what?"

"How much was the loan Sean McFarland's brokerage business received from SEPA Financial?"

"I can't say."

"Try. Just a slight hint."

"I can't reveal his financial records."

"Fair enough. I won't ask you to. Just tell me if someone with a similar balance sheet would qualify for the loan?"

"No financial institution I know would lend twenty million dollars on the basis of the balance sheet I saw."

Twenty million! "Thanks, my favorite brother."

"I'm your only brother. But I'm beginning to wish you had other relatives to pester."

McFarland lacked the assets to back up such a substantial loan. That's what caught Nate's attention. And was likely the reason I wasn't being given access to the loan application. Someone at SEPA Financial had approved the loan either without performing any due diligence or despite knowing McFarland lacked sufficient assets. It had to be a high-level executive. Both Keenan and Cameron came to mind.

I started to call Keenan when my phone rang, and Maggie's name popped up on my caller ID.

"Hey, Maggie. Change your mind about filling me in?"

"Not on your life. I need you to go over to Caroline's office. She's received threats. The local police are there now."

"So now it's okay for me to get involved."

"Isn't this your kind of work? Helping to protect people like Caroline."

"I'll go and see what I can do." I paused. "Could her name have gotten out somehow?"

"I don't know. I hate to think there might be a leak in this office. Make sure Caroline and her children are safe."

Two police cars were outside Caroline's office when I arrived.

"We got a heads-up from the U.S. Attorney's office that you were coming," the officer in charge said. "We're looking at two threatening notes and the gift of a dead rat on the doorstep of Ms. Hewitt's office."

"Any threats made to her children?"

"None. We sent an officer over to their school and no one's been near them."

"I'd like to see Caroline first and then have a look at the notes," I said.

Caroline's red-rimmed eyes were the only color in her face. "I knew this would happen. Why did I ever listen to you?"

"I'm going to find whoever is doing this."

"You said I'd remain anonymous. But you and that attorney friend of yours didn't keep your promises."

Caroline's words caught me in the chest. I didn't reply. Whatever I said would sound lame. Instead, I walked back toward the officer and asked to see the threatening notes.

"You mean you don't want to see the present?" He grinned.

"I've seen others like it before."

He handed me two plastic evidence bags with the notes. Both were hand-printed in black pen on plain white paper like you'd buy at any Staples.

"Snitches have a short life," one read.

"That was left under the windshield wipers of Ms. Hewitt's car," the officer told me. "She saw it this morning on her way to work. It could have been left there any time after she returned home last night and before she left for work today."

"Then whoever it was knows where she lives," I said.

"The box with the second note and the rat was left at the office door," he said.

The note read: "Rats like you make clients angry. Watch your back."

"Anything from the surveillance cameras?" I asked.

"We're checking now. Any idea who may be targeting her?" the officer asked.

"None," I lied. I wanted to get to the culprit before the cops. If only to alleviate my feelings of guilt.

"These notes aren't much to go on," the officer said. "We'll check fingerprints, of course. But our best bet is if the security cameras here and at her home give us anything useful."

"Give me a call if you have any luck. Can your department keep a lookout at her office and home?"

"We'll send a patrol car around to check during every shift."

I thanked the officer for his help and left, satisfied that Caroline was as well protected as possible.

What puzzled me was how Caroline's name could have been leaked. Who would have access to the identity of an anonymous source?

CHAPTER FIFTY

It was after eight when I pulled up to my house. The lights inside my living room, timed to come on after dark, were visible through the curtains. But my front porch was in darkness. The timed LED light the handyman recently installed was out. My next-door neighbor's porch light was out as well.

I tensed. I drove into my driveway and saw that my backyard was also in complete darkness. One long-lasting LED light bulb might be defective, but not two.

I removed my Glock from its holster, took a flashlight from my tote, and stepped out of the car, my heart pounding. I started to walk toward the front of the house, where there would be light from the nearby streetlamp.

Suddenly I was hurled to the ground, tackled around my knees from behind. My face hit the ground with an impact that stunned me, lights bursting in my head. I managed to keep hold of my gun, but the flashlight was gone. My attacker dragged me toward the backyard, my face burning against the concrete pavement.

We stopped. I spit out a mouthful of dirt and pebbles, and my attacker dropped my legs. I managed to jam my gun into my jacket pocket as he flipped me onto my back. He punched me hard in my face and ribs. I couldn't breathe without feeling sharp, knifelike stabs in my lungs. I hurled wild punches into the air, hoping to hit his face, wherever it was. One of my jabs hit his jaw, but he came back at me with another powerful punch to my gut. Stomach acid rose in my throat, and I gagged. I took another swing, but he grabbed my wrists and immobilized them with a powerful grip and punched my face.

By now, my eyes had begun to adjust to the dark, and I could make out the outline of his head. I butted heads with him; he jerked back, and his grip on my wrists loosened. I felt dizzy but managed to free my arms. I opened my fist, splayed my fingers, and aimed for his eyes, but missed. I went for them again. This time I felt the soft, wet surface of an eyeball. My attacker fell back and hit the ground, moaning in pain. He was lucky I didn't have nails like McFarland's secretary. I scrambled to my feet, holding onto my ribs. When he started to get up, I kicked his groin and then his head with my heavy boot. He dropped onto the ground with a thud. I pulled out my Glock and bent over him. He was breathing, but unconscious.

I ran to my car and turned on the headlights. In the arc of light, I recognized Bobby Regan. He was dressed in a dark-colored jogging suit with a metallic stripe along the side of the legs. I kept my gun on him and reached for my cell in the back pocket of my jeans to call 911.

"What's going on down there?" My neighbor across my driveway called out from his upstairs window. "Is that you, Andrea?"

I turned to see Mr. Rossi at his open window. A sharp crack and then a searing pain in my arm. I dropped to my knees. I'd failed to check if Regan was armed.

"Call 911, Mr. Rossi," I shouted.

I managed to get to my feet. Regan's gun was pointed straight at me. I aimed at his shooting arm and fired. His gun lowered, and he ran into the street, holding his arm. I fired after him, but he disappeared into the darkness.

I sank to the ground and wiggled out of my jacket, using it to stanch the blood oozing from my arm.

By now, my neighbors were gathering in the street.

Mr. Rossi came out in his bathrobe and fur-lined slippers. "The cops are on their way. *Madonna*, you're bleeding."

CHAPTER
FIFTY-ONE

I woke up in the emergency wing of the hospital, my left arm bandaged. I must have dozed off. When I opened my eyes again, I thought I saw a woman, with long black hair wearing a magenta sweater. I closed my eyes then opened them again, trying to focus my vision. Then I recognized Julia Volpe, Tom's wife, standing next to my bed.

"How are you feeling?" Her hand reached for mine, her large dark eyes revealing her concern.

"How did you know I was here?"

"Tom called me. He's over at your place, checking with the officers there."

"How long have you been here? Shouldn't you be at work?"

Julia was a professor of Art History at University of Pennsylvania. "It's after midnight, Andrea. I promised Tom I'd call to let him know how you're doing."

"How am I doing? Right now, I'm having a hard time keeping my eyes open but I don't feel a thing. Except your warm hand."

"You're going to be fine. The doctor told me he removed the bullet."

"The doctor was here?" My voice sound far away.

"You're still in recovery," Julia said. "The anesthesia hasn't worn off yet."

"I want to go home." I raised my head and the room spun around.

"You're not going anywhere. You're being monitored and you have an IV drip. We're waiting for you to be taken to a room."

Then I remembered. "It was Bobby Regan. I need to tell Tom."

"Don't worry. Tom will come to see you. But now you need to rest."

I woke up when I felt my bed moving. Julia was gone. I was being whisked down corridors, into an elevator, and then into another room. I drifted back to sleep and didn't wake again until a medical technician arrived to draw my blood.

"What time is it?" I asked.

"It's five-thirty."

"At night?"

She smiled. "It's morning. The doctor will be making his rounds soon."

I had just dozed off when the doctor woke me.

"Good morning. How are you feeling, Ms. Fabiano?"

"Fine, thanks." I wanted to scream out, "Like I've been shot," but stopped myself.

"I have good news to report," he told me. "The bullet missed any bone, and we removed it easily. Your face has lacerations, but you didn't need stitches. Two ribs are cracked, not broken. Overall, you were lucky."

Funny, the bullet wound, lacerations, and cracked ribs didn't hurt any less despite my so-called luck. I didn't have the energy to rage at him. Besides, I came through the shooting better than most of the daily ER carnage. I merely nodded and gave him the best smile I could manage without disturbing my sore cheeks.

"If you continue to improve, you could go home in a day or two."

"Thanks, doc. Is it okay to shower?"

"Don't let your arm get wet and be careful not to fall." He opened the door, then called back. "Be sure to eat."

I used one hand to put on a pair of hospital booties and padded over to the closet, looking for my cell phone. All my clothes, my cell phone, and my Glock were missing. The cops took the gun into custody.

Without my cell, I couldn't call Tom, and the phone in my

room hadn't been connected. Without any clothes, I couldn't spring myself. I felt marooned.

I managed to walk to the shower, swaying like Uncle Dom after finishing off a bottle of Canadian Club. I was careful to keep my injured arm away from the water but felt revived as its warmth cascaded over the rest of my body. I struggled with one hand to coax lather out of a bar of soap, but it fell before I succeeded. A small bottle of shampoo sat on a shelf, and I considered prying it open with my teeth. But I didn't think I could stand long enough for a shampoo. Instead, I massaged my hair and scalp with one hand, forcing the excess dirt down the drain.

The hospital towels were thin and skimpy, and my body still felt damp when I put on a fresh hospital gown and slipped another on as a robe. I crawled back into bed, cold and exhausted.

When my breakfast arrived, I ate slower than I bathed. The coffee was lukewarm and weaker than tea. Before I ate a half slice of my French toast, it was ice cold. I gave up, leaned back, and closed my eyes.

It was a little after eleven a.m. when I woke. I must've been exhausted if I managed to sleep on a rubber mattress, so thin and flat that I wondered what could have been used for fill. A sleeping bag would have been more comfortable.

About an hour later, another nurse came in. "Let's take a stroll in the hall."

I figured I had nothing else to do and could use the exercise. It was the first time I left my room and the first I realized a security guard was seated outside.

He smiled. "Out for a walk, then?"

I smiled back. The nurse and I made it once around the floor without me falling. But my injured arm felt like it didn't belong to me.

When we got back to my room, I told the security guard I needed to reach Tom and gave him Tom's number. "It's important."

The rest of my day alternated between nurses' visits, untempting food, walks in the hall, short naps, and recurring dreams. Nightmares, really, about Nate and Aunt Roseanne reaching out to me, begging for my help, but I couldn't get to them. The painkillers were messing with my mind. Or not. It could bc my unconscious mind dwelling on my real guilt and fear.

When I woke up from one of my naps, Tom was standing by my bed, holding a tiny teddy bear. "From the kids. They said they miss you and to get well." He leaned over and kissed me on the forehead.

I smiled. "How sweet. How did they know I never owned a teddy bear?"

"I'm not sure they did. Bears are their favorite." Tom pulled up a chair. "How are you doing?"

"I'll be fine once I get out of this place and sleep in my own bed."

"Feeling up to telling me what happened?"

I nodded and told Tom everything I remembered. "Bobby Regan was the shooter. I fired back and grazed his arm, but he ran away."

"We'll get him."

"Tom, I don't have my cell phone."

"Almost forgot." He handed me my cell. "The lab guys are finished with it. It's charged."

I held my phone to my heart. I hadn't realized until that moment that I had grown almost as fond of my phone as I was of my Subaru, Bella.

"Will I be charged with firing my weapon?"

"The DA's office hasn't made any decision yet. They want to check the ballistics and the other evidence." Tom paused and gave me the stare that must be effective when he questions a suspect. "Andrea, when did you buy the gun?"

"I got it to protect Jason."

"Bullshit. You're up to your neck in my murder investigation." He paused. "Listen, you're the only sis I have. I don't want to see you hurt or, God forbid, killed. And I don't want to see you ..."

"Hurt anyone else?"

"I don't want to see you in trouble."

"Am I?"

"I believe what you told me, and so will the DA's office. Regan came after you at your home, not the other way around. So don't worry. Just rest and get well."

"When do I get my Glock back?"

CHAPTER
FIFTY-TWO

During the night, I tried to sleep but kept waking up. I had a headache from the rock-hard pillow. I was too hot with the blanket, too cold without it. At five in the morning, when the medical technician woke me to draw yet more blood, I gave up trying to doze.

"What do you guys do with all this blood?"

"Didn't you hear?" He grinned. "Some of us drink it."

When I laughed, my cracked ribs revolted, and my lungs couldn't take in air. "Don't joke. It hurts."

"Laughter is good for the soul."

"But not for my ribs. At this point, sleeping in my own bed will be my best cure."

"I hear you, but you don't get out of here until the doc makes sure all your tests are normal."

I fell back to sleep and when I opened my eyes, breakfast was sitting on my tray. The scrambled eggs were cold and congealed. I skipped them, ate a piece of dry toast, and sipped cold coffee that wouldn't have tasted any better if it were hot.

The doc was at the door of my room when I'd finished.

"When am I getting sprung from this place?"

"You sound like it's a prison."

"Similar, but with legal drugs."

He laughed. "Let's have a look at you, then I can tell you when you'll be released."

After the doc left, I showered as best I could, took a stroll in the corridor, and managed to remain vertical. Then I phoned Julia. "I'm going home tomorrow."

"What are those doctors thinking, releasing you so soon?"

"Saving money for the insurance company?"

"You need more time to heal."

"I can rest better at home. This place is noisy, the bed sucks, and all kinds of people come in at all hours to poke and probe me. Can you do me a huge favor? I need clothes from the skin out. Everything is ruined. Even my jacket's gone."

"I'll stop by your place and pick up what you need."

"You're the greatest. You'll find a loose-fitting wool cardigan in the closet. It'll be easier for me to wear over my injured arm."

Dealing with life with only one usable arm gave me an acute appreciation for people with permanent disabilities. My arm would heal eventually, and I kept telling myself that as I struggled to bathe and dress, fix a meal, and use my cell phone.

Julia Volpe, as usual, was a godsend. She brought care packages of homemade meals that I could heat and eat, and she cleaned my bathroom.

"Don't you have enough to do?" I asked.

"My flexible schedule is one of the great advantages of teaching at Penn. Besides I feel better knowing you're eating healthy protein," she smiled as she packed my freezer with containers of chicken soup and beef stew. "And it's always more pleasant to use a clean bathroom."

I hugged her with one arm.

"Do you think you could do me one favor in return?" Julia said. Again, a look of concern crept into her face.

"Whatever you wish, my dear friend."

"Don't try to do anything heroic."

I pointed to my injured arm. "I don't think that's in the cards right now."

"Good. Keep it that way."

When I was alone, I took my antibiotics and two of the painkillers the doctor prescribed, went to my desk, and turned on my laptop.

The Narberth PD had sent me a file with frames from the security camera outside Caroline Hewitt's office. The camera had caught a figure in a dark jogging suit placing the box at her door. The face was obscured, but when the figure turned, I noticed a stripe along the side of the jogging pants. Regan was wearing a similar jogging suit when he assaulted me. And the man's height and size resembled Regan. If McFarland wanted to frighten Caroline, he couldn't turn to DeMarco or even Miller. The two were in custody. His buddy Bobby, however, seemed to be active. I decided not to call the Narberth PD and instead give Tom time to pick up Regan on the more serious charge of shooting me.

I began catching up with emails, voicemails, texts, and my social media pages. So much for the theory that the digital world saved time. Nausea hit me like a sharp left hook. I ran to the bathroom and vomited. I felt dizzy, and my body shivered. Once the retching stopped, I rinsed my mouth and washed my face, then went to lie down on my sofa, slipping under my comfy wool afghan. I fell asleep until the pain in my arm and ribs woke me. But no way was I taking any more pain meds. Instead, I took two Tylenol, which managed to take the edge off and didn't make me sick.

Later in the afternoon, I was lying on my sofa in clean sweats, exhausted after taking the first decent shower I had in days. My doorbell rang.

I peered through my living room window. Russ Hanley was on my porch holding a bouquet of freesia and carnations, wrapped in green tissue.

"I wanted to see for myself that you were alright."

"The flowers are lovely, thanks." This was the first time in the years that we've known each other that Russ had brought me flowers. "I'm doing fine. Come on in."

He gave me a peck on my cheek. "Do you realize that you always say that you're fine even when you're obviously not?" He pointed to my wounded arm. "That man could have killed you."

"He didn't. All my vital organs are intact. I'll still be able to work."

"It's your job that worries me. I spoke to Tom about what's been going on."

"What exactly did he tell you?"

"Enough. Don't worry. I won't write about any of the financial stuff while the investigations are going on." He looked around like he was casing the place. "Tom thinks this guy could come after you again. He's still out there."

"I can take care of myself."

"With only one usable arm?"

"I'll be careful."

"What about getting protection?"

"I'm not a rock star. I can't afford a bodyguard," I said with a half-smile.

"Be serious. You're in danger."

"I've taken precautions here and at my office."

"What about when you're out on the street? Like you were when this asshole shot you." He took my hand. "Maybe I can help with the investigation. Take some of the burden off you."

"Let me think about that." No way did I want to put Russ in any danger, but I felt touched by his offer and obvious concern. "I was about to have lunch. Join me?"

After lunch, Russ left, and I returned to the sofa. Who was I kidding when I said I was okay? I had a gunshot wound and couldn't move without pain. The heavy-duty painkillers made me sick. And I was sleeping away the day. How was I going to get any work done? Or be ready to fight off any thugs heading my way?

Was I too quick in refusing Russ's offer? He was a thorough reporter and had won awards for several investigative series. He wouldn't only be helping me. I'd be giving him the inside track to an important news story. But then I thought about Nate's murder and dismissed the idea. No way did I want another death on my conscience, least of all Russ Hanley's.

Lucky for me, the next morning, I had a follow-up appointment with my doctor. Since I couldn't drive myself, Julia took me.

"Why didn't you call me about your reaction to the painkillers?" the doctor said. "I would have prescribed an alternative."

"I tolerated the drugs I was given in the hospital. But the painkiller you prescribed was different and seemed strong. I don't want to be doped up so I can't function. I need to get back to work."

"You're in pain. Your arm isn't healed yet, and your body's been weakened by the loss of blood." The doctor began tapping the computer keyboard. "I'm giving you a prescription for a milder medication at a lower dose. I want you to go home, finish your course of antibiotics, and take the pain medication before even thinking of working."

"I'm in the middle of an investigation and can't be sidelined."

"If you go back to work too soon, you risk re-injuring your arm," the doctor said. "I can't force you to follow my instructions, but I strongly advise it if you want to get your health back.

I walked out of the examining room and down the hall to the waiting area where Julia was reading a magazine.

"Why the gloomy face?" she asked.

"I've been told to go back home and rest."

"That sounds reasonable. You were shot."

The other patients in the waiting room turned away from the TV screen and stared at us.

"We can talk outside," I said. In the car I turned to Julia. "Sonny Waite called to remind me that Aunt Roseanne's parole hearing is tomorrow. I had promised to be there for her, but now I can't."

"What does Sonny say?"

"He said I didn't need to testify. The warden, the prison doctor, and psychiatrist all agree to her release. The DA's office isn't opposing it. Those are the people who count whenever the parole board decides on a release. Not a relative."

"Andrea, I know how much you care about Roseanne. But I have eyes, and I see that you are not up to traveling. You're pale and you have dark circles under your eyes. You need to think about yourself. Follow the doctor's advice. Your aunt will understand."

"Julia, I can't tell her I've been shot."

"Tell her you have the flu. Say you're praying for her release and that you'll see her when you're better."

I nodded.

At my apartment, Julia heated up chicken soup for me and propped me up on the sofa before she left.

I called Tom while I ate my soup. "Any news on Regan?"

"We checked the hospitals and no one fitting his description was treated for a gunshot wound. It looks like he did a runner. His car was found in the lot at 30th Street Station. But there's no record that he bought a train ticket. He could have used an alias. Any ideas where he might go?"

I thought of his girlfriend Tanya but kept it to myself. "Not off the top of my head, but I'll stay in touch. By the way, when do I get my weapon back?"

"I'll let you know when we're done with it."

"You're not deliberately keeping it from me? I want it for personal protection."

"I'll get back to you."

Next, I called Maggie. "I've been out of the loop. How are things with Caroline?"

"Out of the loop is one way to describe it. Tom gave me the details of the shoot-out in South Philly. How are you?"

"Recovering nicely, thank you. But I called to ask about Caroline. Any more threats?"

"Nothing. The local police continue their patrols, and it's remained quiet."

"Glad to hear it." My mind immediately turned to Regan. I doubted it was a coincidence that when he went underground, the threats against Caroline stopped.

"Caroline, however, is still upset, blaming us for letting her name get out," Maggie said.

"She's probably right."

"I can't imagine someone in this office doing such a thing, but I'm looking into it personally."

A light bulb went off in my head. "If I were you, I'd look at an attorney named Arthur Newman."

"Any particular reason?"

"I'll leave it up to you feds to figure it out. Talk to you later."

I spent the next two days resting and taking my new meds, which managed my pain without ugly side effects. By the third day, I felt good enough to get back to work.

CHAPTER FIFTY-THREE

To say that Tanya Powell was not pleased to see me would be a gross understatement. She tried to slam her front door in my face, but I kicked it in, chipping the black paint.

"We need to talk," I said. "I know your husband isn't home."

"Why can't you leave me alone? What is it that you want?"

"What I've always wanted. Bobby Regan."

"Can't help you."

"Or won't. I want you to get a message from me to Bobby."

"I don't know what you want to lay on Bobby, but you've come to the wrong person to help you."

"He shot me." I pointed to my arm. "And now he's disappeared. Where is he, Tanya?"

"No idea. And even if he did what you say, I wouldn't help you get your revenge."

"It's not revenge I'm after. I want justice for Nate Warner, Paddy Doyle, and Greg Saunders."

"I don't know who the hell you're talking about."

"Three men who were murdered." I didn't know for sure about Saunders, but hell, the number three sounded good. "And your lover is involved up to his eyeballs."

"You want to talk to Bobby. Find him yourself."

Strike one.

"Wake up, Tanya. When the cops find him, he'll be headed for prison. And you could be considered an accomplice. If you know anything, now is the time to speak up. Or you may find yourself facing jail time yourself."

"I know nothing about any murders. All I did was fall in love." She began to sob. Her whole body trembled so badly I thought the seams in her skinny jeans might pop open. I removed a pocket pack of tissues from my tote and handed it to her. I waited while she mopped her face and the crying subsided.

Strike two, but then I pushed.

"You need to help yourself here. Help me, and I can keep you out of all this." I took my cell from the back pocket of my jeans and showed her photos of DeMarco and Miller. "Have you seen these men?"

She kept her head down and blew her nose.

"Come on, Tanya. This isn't hard. Look at these photos and tell me if you've seen either of these men with Bobby."

Tanya dried her eyes and raised her head. I held my phone close enough for her to see.

"They came to the office a few times," she said. "But Bobby always closed his office door, so I didn't hear what was going on. They seemed like buddies. That's all."

"When did they come to the office?"

She frowned. "What?"

"When, what date?"

"I only remember they came one day when it was hot because I was wearing a sleeveless maxi dress. Could have been August. I don't know for sure. They stayed for about an hour and then went to lunch. Bobby didn't come back for hours."

I was no longer striking out. Bobby Regan, McFarland's man, knew the two men who set the warehouse fire that killed Paddy Doyle, who, in turn, held a grudge against McFarland. As Tom said, circles within circles. But finally, proof of a connection that led back to McFarland.

"I need a cigarette." Tanya walked over to a nearby table and took out a pack of Marlboro and a book of matches from a gold metallic handbag.

"So how many times did these men stop by to see Bobby?"

"Maybe two or three times."

If Tanya's time frame was correct, the men were meeting before the warehouse fire.

"Do you know their names?"

"Don't you?"

"I want to know if we know them by the same names."

"Joey DeMarco and Dave Miller. Do I pass the test?"

I ignored her attitude. "Tell me what sort of work goes on in your office?"

Tanya's hands shook when she put her cigarette to her lips. After she took several deep drags, she seemed to calm down along with her hands. "They paid me very nicely, so I didn't ask questions."

"I'm asking now. What was the office a cover for?"

She sneered at me.

"I'm not buying the talent agency shit," I said. "And I doubt it's a coincidence that you're not at work now that Bobby is AWOL."

"I don't know what Bobby did," she snapped. After a few more puffs, her voice became less shrill. "Bobby needed someone at the front desk, so I got transferred over. At Bobby's request, of course."

"Of course." I smiled. "What do you mean transferred over?"

"I worked for Sean for about four years."

"Sean McFarland?"

"Yeah. First, in the office and then as his secretary." She inhaled and let the smoke out through her nostrils. "I didn't have much to do for Bobby except answer the phone."

A bit of private office duty, too, I thought.

"So, the girls at McFarland's would send me some of their work to keep me busy and help them out."

"What kind of calls did you get?"

She flicked ashes into a crystal ashtray and took another puff. "The girls from McFarland for me. Sean would call to speak with Bobby. Some of the foremen at McFarland construction sites. And one of those guys you showed me called a couple of times."

"Which one?

"It was Joey."

"Bobby never gave you a hint about what he and Joey talked about. Not even when you were in bed together?"

"We had more important things to do."

Tanya crushed out her cigarette stub and lit another.

I had breathed in more than enough secondhand smoke without a filter. I held out my hand. "I'll borrow your keys to Bobby's office."

"That would be breaking in."

I grinned. "I'd have the keys. That isn't a break-in."

"You're a god-damned pain in the ass."

"I'll be out of your way once you hand over the keys."

Tanya stood up and grabbed her handbag from the table. She fumbled through whatever was inside, stalling.

"You found your cigarettes quick enough," I said.

"Shut the fuck up."

"What time will your husband be back?" I asked.

"Bitch." She threw a set of keys to me. "You can figure them out for yourself. Now get out of here."

I removed the sling and forced my wounded arm into the sleeve of my sweater. A security guard would remember a woman with a bandaged arm.

Lucky for me, the guard at the desk at Regan's building hadn't been on duty when I visited before. I said I was from Regan's employer, who wanted me to check on things while Regan was in the hospital.

"Sorry to hear that," the security guard said. "How's he doing?"

"He's had back surgery, so it may be a while before he comes back." I lied. If it were up to me, he'd never return.

I popped a Tums into my mouth before I entered the elevator, but thankfully, the ride to the fourth floor was an express. At the office door, I managed to slip a latex glove on my right hand with the aid of my teeth, then located the key that opened the front door. Inside, the reception area looked much the same as when I had visited earlier. The furniture and potted plants were still there, but the phone, computer, and printer were gone from Tanya's desk.

I scanned the area again. Nothing else seemed to have been moved or disturbed. I shrugged out of my sweater. Slowly I managed to force a glove onto my other hand. My arm throbbed, but I wasn't going to allow the pain to interfere with my search.

As quickly as I could, I unlocked Regan's office door. No phone or computer on his desk, either.

Did Regan come here and remove whatever might be incriminating? Or did someone do it for him? Like Tanya? Or another of McFarland's lackeys?

I walked around the office, looking for anything at all that might be helpful.

No clutter on the desk, no paperwork, no pens. The only other furniture in the room was a brown sofa by the window, a side table, and lamp. No file cabinet or credenza. I unlocked Regan's desk but found nothing to enlighten me. In one of the bottom drawers, I saw a power cord for an HP laptop, the same brand that I had seen on Tanya's desk, and a half-dozen take-out menus. In other drawers, I found pens, a letter opener, and a half-used bottle of glue.

Searching using only one reliable hand was taking much too long and proving fruitless. It looked as if the office had been abandoned.

The pain in my arm kicked in with a vengeance. I needed my meds. I sat down on the sofa and reached into my tote for my water bottle and painkillers. Even as I struggled to open the pill container, I knew it would be easier to use the level surface of the desk, but I was in too much pain to move. Finally, the lid popped off, but the container tilted over, spilling pills onto the sofa and floor. It was turning into a bitch of a day. I took a swig of water and downed two of the tablets still in the container. Then I started picking up the pills that had fallen. I didn't want to leave any behind for someone to find. Besides, the damned meds cost more than a month of groceries.

I scooped up all I could see. In case any had fallen into the sofa, I removed the cushions and saw that I had been sitting on a sofa bed. A favorite spot for Regan and Tanya?

I rescued more pills, then opened the bed, thankful for all the hours I spent building muscle in my right arm. I flipped the mattress over to inspect the carpet beneath. I didn't see any of my meds. However, a manila envelope was taped to the underside of the mattress. I took a deep breath, then carefully remove it without tearing the envelope or tape. I brought it over to the desk and used a nail file from my tote to pry open the envelope that I held in place with my injured arm. Inside were black and white photographs. I snapped each one with my cell camera, returned them to the envelope, and resealed it using the glue from the desk drawer. I returned the packet to the underside of the mattress, managing to reuse the same tape to fix it in place as if it hadn't been disturbed. That way, the images could be used as evidence when the cops came with a search warrant. I checked the time. I had been here more than two hours.

Before I left, I rechecked to make sure I'd retrieved all my pills, and made a quick inspection of Tanya's desk, which yielded nothing. I grabbed my sweater, forced my wounded arm back into a sleeve then left, removing my gloves once I closed and locked the door.

On the way down in the elevator, it occurred to me that if Regan had come to his office to remove anything incriminating, he would have taken the envelope so carefully stashed away. So, whoever removed the phones and computers must have known that Regan was on the run but didn't know about the pictures.

CHAPTER
FIFTY-FOUR

The photos were dark, obviously taken at night. The only illumination in the first picture came from bare light bulbs around the roof of a trailer. I recognized the man standing outside the trailer. In the next photo he punched another man whose back was to the camera. That man fell to the ground. The attacker was Sean McFarland. His face was distorted in anger and he wore a barn jacket. The man McFarland decked, however, wore a suit and tie.

The photographer had taken a close-up of the face of the man on the ground. Despite the blood smears, I recognized him from his driver's license photo. It was Greg Saunders. Then a series of photographs showed McFarland and Bobby Regan digging a hole. Finally, the remaining shots were of McFarland and Regan placing Saunders' body into the grave and covering it over.

If Saunders died from the fall, his death might have been considered manslaughter, not intentional murder. But these two guys decided to bury the body rather than go to the police.

Who took the pictures? Someone else had been there without McFarland or Regan knowing their nighttime activities were being recorded for posterity.

I wanted to bring the photos to Tom. I valued his opinion more than anyone else's on something like this. But I couldn't. I had coerced Tanya into giving me the keys to Regan's office and searched it without a warrant.

I called Russ.

"What's cooking?"

"I need your opinion on something I'm working on. Can you stop by my office today?"

"Sounds important."

"It is. I want you to have a look at something and tell me what you think it means."

Russ arrived around two p.m. I handed him a glass of Scotch.

"I need you to look at something. But you need to promise to keep this completely confidential. Can you do that?"

"For you, I can."

"I've been puzzling over these photos and what they mean. Just so you know, I can't take them to the cops."

"You're not going to tell me anything about them?"

"I want an unvarnished opinion."

I handed over my cell with the pictures I snapped in Regan's office.

Russ studied the photos one by one. He remained silent until he came to the picture of the body tossed into the grave. "Oh, my God. They killed this guy and buried him."

"I believe so."

"Who are these people?"

"You don't recognize the man who struck the victim?"

Russ went through the photos again, slowly, and enlarged one of the pictures.

"Shit." He jumped from his chair. "It's Sean McFarland."

"And that's Bobby Regan with him. He's the guy who shot me. The victim is Greg Saunders, whose wife hired me to find him. But where did this happen?"

"The trailer looks like the kind used as an office at a construction site."

I glanced over his shoulder. "That makes sense. It could be one of McFarland's sites. Where else would there be enough space to bury a body? And have shovels lying around to do the digging?"

"They're wearing light jackets," Russ said, "so it can't be wintertime. The ground would be too hard in cold weather to dig a grave with those light shovels."

I straightened up as though I were a soldier called to attention. "Of course." I hugged him around his shoulders. "Greg

Saunders disappeared in May. He told his wife he had a disagreement with McFarland and wanted to talk to him.

"Saunders must have gone to see McFarland to confront him. And he ends up probably buried under a new building. No wonder he hasn't been found."

I explained to Russ about Saunders and Paddy Doyle. Then I sat down and reexamined each photo. "Doyle had possession of Saunders' driver's license and credit cards. He had to have been there and took these pictures. He could have taken the wallet and ID while McFarland and Regan were busy digging the grave."

"I'll buy that theory," Russ said, "but why was he there in the first place?"

"This could be the site of the Riverfront condos. Doyle worked there as a laborer, and he might have been sleeping at the construction site. He was homeless. But where did he get a camera?"

Russ nodded. "Most likely he had a cheap burner phone."

I finally ferreted out evidence that would explain Saunders' disappearance and Doyle's murder. Doyle used the photos to blackmail McFarland. Doyle was killed in the warehouse fire, and somehow the photos ended up with Regan.

Russ left while I was still contemplating the photographs. Why would Regan keep them when Doyle was no longer a threat? Was it his insurance against McFarland ratting him out? Or to prove if he had to that McFarland delivered the fatal blow?

Russ had been gone about a half-hour when Sonny Waite called.

"Roseanne's been granted parole," he told me. "Her age and her health were the deciding factors."

Tears filled my eyes, and I couldn't speak for a moment.

"Andrea? Did you hear me?"

"I did. Thank you so much for all your work. I'm just trying to take it in. After all these years, I can't believe it. She's finally coming home."

"Not just yet," Sonny said. "First, she's being released to a halfway house in West Philly to have time to adjust to life on the outside."

"I understand." I was ashamed to admit I felt relieved. I, too, needed time to adjust.

"The prison doctor expressed concern about her overall health," Sonny said. "He told the board that her heart was severely damaged, and she was clinically depressed. I'm afraid you're going to have your hands full when she does come to live with you."

"We'll figure it all out."

"You might consider getting a home health aide for your aunt."

"Good point."

I thanked Sonny again and hung up. My heart raced. Suddenly, I struggled for breath. The sensations were all too familiar. I was having a panic attack. I went over to my office sofa, lay down, and closed my eyes. I concentrated on taking deep breaths. After my uncle's death, I suffered from panic attacks for years. But eventually they subsided and then finally stopped. That is, until I went to buy the Glock, and now that I learned that my aunt would be coming back.

I lifted myself from the sofa and made a cup of soothing chamomile tea. I worked for a few more hours but couldn't concentrate, so I left and went home.

Once I got home, I didn't feel like cooking or eating. I fell asleep in my living room chair, reading. When I woke up thirty minutes later, I called Russ.

"Twice in one day. Anything the matter?"

"If you're not busy, do you think you can come over? I need to talk."

"About those photos?" Russ asked.

"About Aunt Roseanne. She's been paroled, and I need a reality check. I can order a pizza for us."

"I'll pick one up on my way over. What time should I be there?"

"I'm already home, so come whenever you can."

Russ arrived with eggplant pizza, my favorite. "Do we eat, or do we talk?" he asked, giving me a peck on both cheeks.

"Let's eat now, or the pizza will get cold."

I took out a bottle of Chianti and two glasses, and Russ brought dishes and napkins to the table.

Russ had eaten a slice and was finishing another while I was still working on my first.

"I thought this was your favorite?"

"It is, and it's delicious. I just don't have much of an appetite."

Russ went for a third slice. "I thought you'd be celebrating. You've been pushing for Roseanne's parole for years."

I nodded. "But now that it's a reality, painful memories are flooding back. Horrible memories I thought I had put behind me."

"Don't you want her living here?"

"I do. But I'm going to need time to adjust."

"Roseanne will, too," Russ said, reaching over with his napkin to wipe my chin.

"Tomato sauce." He smiled.

"I don't know if I can do it."

"You're one of the strongest women I know. And before you ask, the other woman is my mother. You're both the kind of people that do what has to be done and do it better than most."

I lifted my wine glass. "Thanks for the vote of confidence."

We clinked glasses, and suddenly I had my appetite back.

Russ was already in bed when I slipped in beside him.

"You smell great," he said.

"It's my Tuscan soap from Italy." I smiled.

We snuggled closer. Russ kissed me and caressed my face.

Russ pulled me closer. He kissed my neck and breasts. I stroked his hair and kissed him.

He moved on top of me, and as quick and sharp as a punch, I was back on my aunt's kitchen floor, my uncle on top of me, his blood soaking my white turtleneck, fighting nausea from the metallic odor of his blood.

"No!" I screamed and pushed Russ away. I gasped for air like an asthmatic, and my heart pounded like a drum was beating in my chest. Inside my head, the room was spinning around.

"Andrea. What's wrong?" Russ took my hand. I pulled away and ran into the bathroom.

I knelt on the cold tile floor, vomiting into the toilet, and shaking with chills. After the retching stopped, I reached for my bathrobe on the back of the door, washed my face with warm water, and rinsed my mouth out with Listerine.

I cracked open the door but stopped. I wasn't up to facing Russ. Not yet. What must he be thinking? I had never told him exactly what happened when Uncle Dominic died. I gulped down a glass of water and rewashed my face. My flashback ruined a night of intimacy. Would I ever be able to put that other night behind me?

I looked in the mirror. Stop feeling sorry for yourself. Go back and apologize to Russ.

Russ was dressed, sitting on the chair by the window. "Maybe this wasn't a good idea."

"This isn't about you." I sat on the side of the bed. "I can't tell you how sorry I am … about my behavior. I don't know how to tell you."

"You don't have to. I understand."

"No. I don't think you do. It's about Uncle Dominic and what happened when I was fourteen."

CHAPTER FIFTY-FIVE

Uncle Dominic came into the kitchen. "Where's Roseanne?"

"She went next door to bring dinner to Mr. Pollini."

"Giving away more of our food. She's more worried about that old man than me."

I looked up from my book. "He's ninety. He needs help."

My uncle grabbed the book I was reading. "Make me coffee. You spend too much time with your nose in stupid books."

My stomach felt queasy from the smell of his breath, sour with the odor of stale beer. Since he lost his job, Uncle Dom got drunk every day. I yanked the book out of his hand. "Don't ruin the book. It's my teacher's."

He slapped me hard across the face. "Don't you get fresh with me. I only took you in because of Roseanne, and it's my house, so I can throw you out anytime I want."

"You're drunk, and you stink," I shouted. "It's not our fault you lost your job or that my parents died. Make your own coffee." I turned to leave the room.

Dominic grabbed me by the back of my white turtleneck, the one Aunt Roseanne had given me for my birthday. I started to gag. He spun me around and hit me in the face again, first with an open hand, then with his fist.

Blood from my nose oozed onto my new sweater, no longer clean and white. He ruined it. He always ruined everything. I hated him. "Stop, you're hurting me."

He slapped my face again. I was so mad I wanted to hurt him. His fat stomach made an easy target. I jabbed it hard. He groaned and wobbled but held onto my shoulders. I tried to pull away to run next door for help. I could outrun him when he was drunk.

I kicked at his shin, again and again, until he teetered backward and lost his grip. I ran to the door, but he grabbed me, spun me around, and with his massive hands on my shoulders, he threw me to the floor. My back slammed onto the cold, hard tile, and I yelled out in pain. Uncle Dom held me down, and his fist pounded my face, ribs, and stomach. I tried kicking him as hard as I could. I wiggled and shimmied, trying to get up, but he kept pushing me back down, and each time my head hit the tile. I felt dizzy and closed my eyes. God help me. Don't let him kill me. When I opened my eyes again, I saw Aunt Roseanne standing in the kitchen doorway.

Uncle Dom's back was to the door, so he didn't see her come in. Aunt Roseanne stood without moving like her shoes were glued to the floor, her face twisted in anger. Then slowly she removed a large carving knife from the bag she'd brought over to Mr. Pollini's. She plunged the blade into Uncle Dom's back. He screamed and, for a moment, seemed suspended in mid-air. He tried to turn to see who had struck him, but Aunt Roseanne stabbed him again, and he fell to the floor, pinning me down.

Blood gushed from his back, the warm red liquid spilling onto me. I felt my sweater and wool skirt soaking up the blood. I tried to scream, but no sound came out of my mouth.

"I won't let you do to her what you've done to me." Roseanne's voice was high-pitched and eerie. She stabbed him again.

I was gagging, struggling for breath under the weight of my uncle's body. I used all my strength to push my uncle away, but I couldn't. He was too big, too heavy. I started to sob and found my voice. "Aunt Roseanne, please help me. I want to get out."

My aunt ignored me. She kept stabbing him, over and over, until the knife handle broke off in her hand, but the blade was still in his back.

I felt the room spinning. I couldn't see where Aunt Roseanne was, but I called out anyway. "Auntie, help me. Please, I need to get up."

Finally, I managed to bend one knee, lifting his body enough to slowly squeeze one leg free. Then I used my foot to shift his *body inch by inch until I freed an arm. I used my arm and leg to push aside Uncle Dom's body until I managed to wriggle out completely. I rolled over onto the floor and vomited. Smelling and tasting the pumpkin pie I had eaten at dinner.*

When I looked up, my aunt was standing over Uncle Dom, holding another knife. This time it was a bread knife with its sharp, uneven blade.

"Aunt Roseanne. Aunt Roseanne, he can't hurt us anymore."

Aunt Roseanne seemed not to see or hear me. She knelt over Uncle Dom, her arms in blood up to her elbows, her dress wet as if had been dipped in red dye. And still, she stabbed him.

"Stop. Stop." Now I was screaming and shaking my aunt by the shoulders. "You have to stop."

But Aunt Roseanne didn't stop. I ran out the back door and banged on Mr. Pollini's kitchen door. "We need help."

CHAPTER FIFTY-SIX

Russ didn't leave. He held me in his arms until I fell asleep. And he was there the next morning when I woke up.

"You going to be alright if I go to work?" he asked.

"I'll be fine."

"Maybe you should see a doc."

"I've had more years of therapy than I can count. I'm afraid what I'm dealing with never goes away."

"Call it what it is, Andrea. Trauma. You experienced extreme trauma." He put his arm around me. "I know you were embarrassed last night. Don't ever be." He kissed me on my forehead and went into the bathroom to shower.

I put arabica coffee on and set out bagels and cream cheese. Russ was more understanding than I ever hoped a man would be. I felt grateful to have him in my life.

Russ came into the kitchen fully dressed, with his hair still damp.

"Do you have time for breakfast before you go?" I asked.

"Can't ever refuse your coffee."

I poured a cup for him, and he smeared a thick wad of cream cheese onto his bagel.

"It was kind of you to stay with me," I said, feeling awkward.

"Least I could do. I'm glad you finally trusted me enough to tell me the truth about what you've been through." He squeezed my hand. "We've broken a major barrier between us."

We finished eating, and Russ brought the cups and dishes to the sink. We kissed at the front door when he left. "I'll call you later to see how you're doing," he said.

I walked up the steps to a stately gray stone house in West Philly, near the University of Pennsylvania, and rang the bell.

Inside, I registered at the desk and received a visitor's badge.

"Your aunt's in the library." The receptionist gave me a tight smile.

Aunt Roseanne sat in a faded club chair reading a tattered-looking paperback of *Jane Eyre*. On the other side of the room, a young woman with striped hair like a CATS cast member was leafing through an *InStyle* magazine and ignored us.

When Aunt Roseanne spotted me, she closed her book and put her arms up to reach out to me.

"The nightmare is finally over," I said. "You're out of that god-awful place forever."

"Thanks to you and Mr. Waite. What a lovely man."

I hugged her with one arm.

"*Cara Mia*, what happened to you?"

"I had a little accident, but it's healing nicely."

"It's dangerous work you do," Roseanne said. "First, the police force and now a private investigator. I worry you could end up dead."

"Fabianos are made of tougher stuff. Enough about me. I came here to see how you're doing. Is this place treating you right?"

Aunt Roseanne dismissed me with a wave of her hand. "Compared to where I've been, it's a vacation. But the food. They never heard of olive oil." She wrinkled her nose.

I took hold of her hand, its blue veins visible beneath paper-thin flesh. "You'll be coming home soon, and we can cook together like old times."

"I never thought the day would come." Tears welled up in her pale brown eyes. "I thought I'd die in that prison. And maybe I should. I deserved to for what I did."

"Don't talk that way. The judge was way too harsh with your sentence. You deserved to come home years ago." I smiled.

"How about we go outside, take a walk?"

"It's too cold, *Cara Mia*."

"The sun's out. The fresh air will do us both good."

"I'll go outside tomorrow. Sit down. Talk to me."

I sat in the chair next to her, still holding her hand. "I hope you'll like your apartment. I've spruced it up a bit, but you can add your own touches whenever you like."

Aunt Roseanne sighed. "You're so good to me. Even when I put you through all this. You did enough, visiting me in that terrible place. I don't want to be a burden to you, not anymore."

"You're not. You're the only aunt I have, and I want you near me."

"I should have left that uncle of yours years before."

"It would have been a hard thing to do, auntie."

"I brought much harder times on both of us for staying."

"We survived."

"At my age, it's okay for me to say I survived. It's not good enough for you. I want you to find real happiness, like your mother and father would have wanted if they lived. God rest their souls. Not the pain I've brought you."

"It's okay. We're both doing okay."

CHAPTER FIFTY-SEVEN

I watched from my car as Tanya's husband left their South Philly home for work. She was at the door in a robe to see him off. He was a big guy, wearing a puffer jacket and carrying a lunch pail.

The morning was gray and chilly with a gusty wind. I had turned off the car heater a half-hour earlier, so Bella and I were cold. I pulled my woolen scarf tighter around my neck to keep the cold, damp air out. Thankfully, I still had a mouthful of hot chocolate left in my thermos and finished it off.

"Okay, you and I need to buck up, Bella, and wait for Tanya to come out." It was my third day on surveillance. With Regan MIA, Tanya wasn't going into the office. I also figured she was lying about not knowing where Regan was, and she'd lead me to him, eventually. But not so far. The day before, Tanya left the house and met two friends for lunch at Marra's on East Passyunk. When she returned home, she remained inside for the rest of the day and night. Her husband came home at five-thirty p.m. Hopefully, today I'd see more action.

An hour later, Tanya came down her front steps and got into a red Mazda parked farther down the street.

I put on my newsboy's hat to change my appearance.

Tanya drove to a supermarket on Oregon Avenue. I kept my engine running and the heat on while she went inside. She came out wheeling a cart with four bags of groceries and placed the bags in her trunk.

I removed my hat, put on sunglasses, and followed her. Tanya didn't drive in the direction of her house. Instead, she took Broad Street into Center City, then drove down the Ben Franklin Parkway toward the Philadelphia Art Museum and took Kelly Drive, along the east side of the Schuylkill.

"This looks promising, Bella, my girl." I fingered my Glock to make sure it was there if I did find Regan. Lucky for me, Tom had returned the weapon when he told me the DA concluded I acted in self-defense.

Tanya turned right on Midvale Avenue into East Falls. She drove into a side street off Ridge Avenue and double-parked outside a house in the middle of the block. I drove past the house and watched from my rearview mirror. Tanya unlocked the front door and began to bring the grocery bags inside, one at a time, leaving the front door ajar.

As she brought in the last bag, I ran from my car, leaving it double-parked, leaped up the front steps, and kicked the door wide open, my Glock drawn.

Regan jumped off the living room sofa. He was growing a beard and his right arm was bandaged.

"You stupid bitch," he shouted to Tanya and slapped her in the face so hard she dropped the grocery bag and fell to her knees, sobbing. I saw him eye his gun on a nearby side table.

"Stay where you are, or I'll shoot," I said. "I can't miss this close."

He hesitated, then pulled his hand back toward his side.

"Smart move, Bobby."

Tanya was still sobbing and moaning.

"Get up off the floor, Tanya, and go sit in that chair where I can see you." I nodded toward a chair near the window, out of reach of Regan's gun.

"What about the groceries? I have things for the freezer," she said.

"Tanya, forget about the food. Stay out of this. I'm not here for you, but I can shoot you as easily as your boyfriend if you interfere."

She obeyed and sunk into the chair. "Can't you put the gun down? It frightens me."

"He's already shot me once. I'm not stupid enough to give him another chance."

"You told me it was a frame," Tanya said to Bobby.

"Shut your stupid mouth," he said.

"You really don't know you've been sleeping with a murderer?" I said.

Tanya opened her mouth to say something, but instead, held her cheek where Regan had struck her.

Regan moved toward the sofa.

"I told you to stay where you are."

"I wanna sit down. I lost a lot of blood when you shot me."

"Too bad."

"You're crazy. You've got nothing on me."

"Remember Paddy Doyle, Greg Saunders, and let's not forget Nate Warner. And then there's your attempt to kill me."

"You have it all wrong."

"Let's have the cops decide."

Regan laughed. "How you gonna call the cops and keep that gun on me too? You only got one good arm."

He had a point. I transferred the Glock to my left hand, which was weakened by the wound in my arm, and reached into my pocket with my good arm to retrieve the phone. It was risky, but I had no choice.

Regan made a dash for me, wrenched my injured arm behind my back, and yanked the gun from my hand. I grimaced but refused to give him the satisfaction of calling out in pain.

He tightened his grip and pulled so hard I thought my arm would pop out of its socket. "Big man. You like beating up on wounded women, you coward."

"Shut up, or I'll break it," he yelled.

I kicked him in the shin.

He held the gun to my temple. "Drop the phone," he said.

I obeyed.

He held both my arms around my back and dragged me into the kitchen. We stopped in front of the cellar door.

"Get over here and open this god-damned door," Bobby called out to Tanya, still in the living room.

"What are you going to do, Bobby?" Tanya stood in the doorway.

"Just open the door."

"Your boyfriend has already killed," I said. "He has nothing to lose by killing me. If you help him commit another murder, you'll go down with him."

"I don't want to get involved with a murder." Tears ran down Tanya's cheeks.

"If you don't open this door this minute, you'll be going down there with her," Bobby said, his anger building into rage.

"He can't hurt either of us if you don't help him."

Tanya, pale and trembling, didn't move.

"Fucking stupid broad." Regan turned the gun on Tanya.

She fainted.

I mustered my strength and used my back to push Regan away from the cellar door. He stumbled, fell over a chair, and we both landed on the floor. I broke free, grabbed the gun, scrambled to my feet, and moved out of his reach. Then pointed the gun at him.

He struggled to get up, but he must have been dazed by his fall and fell back down. I didn't want to shoot him. I needed him alive. But I had to phone the cops and couldn't chance him interfering again.

I slammed the tip of my boot into his temple. When he passed out, I used the heel of my boot to stomp on the metatarsal bones in his foot. That would keep him out of my way.

I heard a moan behind me. Tanya was coming around, her body blocking the doorway. I climbed over her, retrieved my phone from the living room floor, and called Tom.

While waiting for the cops, I helped Tanya off the floor and onto the sofa. I went back into the kitchen to check on Regan. He looked like he was still out, but he could have been faking. No way did I want to take the chance he'd come to before help arrived. I kicked him on the other side of the head.

I brought Tanya a glass of water and a handful of ice wrapped in a dishcloth. "Thanks for helping me out," I said.

"He was going to kill us both, wasn't he?" Tanya said,

"Like I said, he has nothing to lose."

"I thought we loved each other."

I didn't reply. Men like Regan don't know the meaning of the word. I handed her the dishcloth.

"What's this for?"

"Your face. You're going to have a nasty bruise, but this may help."

"Thanks."

"Listen up, Tanya. Let me do the talking when the police get here. It'll be better for both of us."

"You tell them whatever you want, honey. I don't like talking to cops."

"I knew you were holding out on me," Tom told me after two officers had taken Regan into custody. "You knew about the girlfriend."

"I did. But I called you as soon as I could." I briefed Tom on what happened.

"You should have called before you came into this house."

"I wasn't certain Regan was here."

"You could have gotten yourself killed."

"I didn't, thanks to Tanya. Go easy on her."

"Go home and get a good night's sleep tonight. You look beat. Come in tomorrow to sign your statement."

Tom was right. I felt exhausted. I went straight home, took a shower and my pain meds. An hour later, I woke up on my sofa. Taking naps was getting to be a bad habit, but then again, until now, I had never been shot, mauled, and threatened with death in a cellar.

I went into the kitchen, my afghan around my shoulders, and made myself a hot cup of tea.

I may have been nursing my wounds, but I felt relieved that Regan, Miller, and DeMarco were all in custody. I felt proud that I helped put them where they belonged. But now Tom and the police would take over. And I'd be left out in the cold when I wanted to stay involved.

Sipping my hot tea revived me. I considered using DeMarco's bullet as leverage to stay in the game. Earlier I had offered not to prosecute DeMarco for his drive-by, which he rebuffed. Now that he was arrested, DeMarco's attorney might go for the deal and get his client to talk to me.

I found the name of DeMarco's attorney in the court records from his arraignment. It was not the same high-priced lawyer that had been at police headquarters for the lineup. This new attorney I recognized. He was a reasonably priced, hardworking defense lawyer, who I'd seen often around the criminal courts. The type of attorney DeMarco could probably afford to pay – without McFarland's help. My call went straight to voicemail, and I left a message.

CHAPTER FIFTY-EIGHT

The following day, I woke up late, sore but rested. I decided to make myself a decent breakfast of omelet, toast, and coffee before leaving for police headquarters to sign my statement and to see what I could drag out of Tom.

When I arrived, I learned Tom was out executing a search warrant.

"Detective Volpe wanted to talk with you when you came in," one of the detectives told me. "You can wait if you'd like, but I don't know how long he'll be."

"I'll wait and get some work done." I took a seat and pulled out my tablet. About an hour later, Tom came in holding an evidence bag containing a manila envelope.

Tom placed the bag on his desk, and one of the officers handed over more evidence bags.

"Regan's place?" I asked.

"You're here to sign your statement," Tom said. "That's all."

"I like to be of help. What do you have there?"

Tom took my statement out of a file and handed it over. "Read this and sign. Then get on your way and be sure to have a nice day."

I took my time reading and making corrections. Stalling, knowing Tom wanted to inspect the contents of the envelope that I figured were the photos from Regan's office.

He leaned back in his chair and started going through the photos, one by one. When he finished, he sat erect. "Lewis, take a look at these."

"Jesus," Lewis cried out. "Who the fuck is the victim?"

"Gentlemen, I might be of some help," I said.

"It's none of your business," Lewis snapped.

I ignored him and tried my luck. "I understand you were

searching Bobby Regan's digs."

"And who told you that?" Lewis said, looking at Tom.

"One of the officers mentioned it when I arrived," I lied. "Tom knows I've been investigating Regan and his activities. When you said victim, my ears perked up. I figure it can't be either Paddy Doyle or Nate Warner in those pictures because you'd recognize them. But Regan and Sean McFarland have connections to another man, Greg Saunders, missing since May. Tom knows I've been hired by his wife to find him. With your permission, I'd like to see the photos?"

"Absolutely not," Lewis said.

"You did say victim. Tom, it might be the man I'm looking for," I said.

"Let her have a look," Tom said to Lewis.

"Are you nuts?"

"She may know something that could help us."

Lewis threw the photos onto the desk. "Have it your way." He walked away.

I took my time reviewing all the photos as if I'd never seen them before. I tried to look shocked and surprised as I leafed through. When I put the pictures down, I rubbed my forehead.

"Let's have it," Tom said, his voice firm, his eyes stern.

"That's Sean McFarland, striking the other man. The victim is Greg Saunders, the missing executive I've been searching for. And you must have recognized Regan, who helped bury the body."

"Who could have taken the pictures?" Tom asked.

"Paddy Doyle seems the logical choice," I said. "He used the photos to blackmail McFarland."

"That could explain the cash Doyle left at his sister's house," Tom said.

I nodded. "And it would explain why Doyle ended up dead."

Tom leaned in and whispered in my ear. "You got to these pictures before us. Don't try to deny it. I watched you looking through them. I know you've seen them already. You're not that good an actor."

"What are you going to do?"

"I'm going to use these in evidence, and you're going to keep your trap shut, Andy."

"Right." Tom was most definitely furious with me.

I signed my statement with the corrections I made and left without saying another word.

I figured he'd forgive me once Regan and McFarland were convicted. At least I hoped he would.

CHAPTER
FIFTY-NINE

It took three more calls with Joey DeMarco's new attorney before he and his client agreed to talk to me.

The attorney and I met in the parking area of Curran-Fromhold Prison in the Northeast section of Philadelphia. We went through the security check together and were placed in a small interview room. Five minutes later, DeMarco was escorted in by two correctional officers.

"How's it going, Joey?" I asked.

"How do you think?" He sneered. "I only agreed to this because he said it could help me out." DeMarco tilted his head toward his attorney and sat down next to him across the table from me.

"I'll come straight to the point," I began. "I'll agree to withdraw my charges against you if you tell me what I want to know."

"I've heard that before, but here I am," DeMarco said, gesturing at the locked room.

"You're in for arson and murder," his attorney pointed out. "I know Andrea's reputation. She does have influence with the DA's office. If you talk to her, things may go easier for you."

"So, you talk first," Joey said to me.

"Tell me about your relationship with Bobby Regan. You said you grew up in the same neighborhood."

"Yeah, we lived in the same block in Mayfair. But Regan was luckier than me. He went to community college and got a degree. And went to work for McFarland. Me. I had to scrounge around for any kind of work and ended up serving time. Whenever I got out, Regan got me construction work at a McFarland site. And from time to time, I'd do odd jobs for Regan."

I had an idea about the kind of jobs they were, but I didn't need the details. Except for one. "It was Regan who recruited you for the warehouse job."

"Right. And he hired me to tail you and try to frighten you off. Okay?"

"What did Regan tell you about the warehouse job?"

"He had me introduce him to Miller, so I knew what he wanted done. But I swear to God, I never knew Doyle was anywhere near the place."

"Why would Regan want the warehouse torched? Or, for that matter, why would he want Doyle dead?"

DeMarco looked over at his attorney.

"Keep going."

"Regan and I were out having a few beers one night. He got a call from McFarland. He said, 'What photos? I'm fucking sick of cleaning up your messes, Sean.' Then Bobby slammed his phone on the table so hard I thought he'd break the screen. I asked him what was wrong. 'McFarland never makes things easy,' was all he said. It was after that Bobby asked me to put him in touch with Miller."

"You did good, Joey. I have what I need for now."

"Shit. She's going to the cops." DeMarco stood up and pointed his finger at his attorney. "You told me to trust her."

"Calm down. I'm not going to the cops with any of this." I stood up. "You've been straight with me. So, I'll be straight with you. I won't be pressing charges against you."

"I didn't ever mean to hurt you," DeMarco said, "only scare you off."

That was about the only apology I was likely to get from DeMarco.

On the way to our cars, DeMarco's attorney thanked me. "You got more out of him than I've been able to. Do you believe him that he didn't kill Paddy Doyle?"

"Joey had no reason to kill Doyle," I said. "Can I give you a piece of advice? It's up to you if you want to take it."

"I'm listening."

"I'd ask your client what Regan had on him to convince him to commit an arson while he was still on parole."

"Besides the money, you mean?"

I nodded. "Regan had something over him. I'd bet on it. And if Regan was involved, it's something illegal. Another piece of evidence your client can use against Regan."

"I told my client it was Regan you were after."

"Your guy is in the trenches taking orders from above. I'm after the top brass."

CHAPTER SIXTY

I found Tom at his desk, talking on the phone, and waited until he hung up before I sat down.

"The answer is no before you ask," Tom said. He looked around. "You're coming here does no good for my reputation."

"It doesn't do much for mine either," I said, grinning. "Clients don't like a PI who talks to the cops, but I have something to share."

"Depends on how you obtained whatever it is you got."

"In this instance, it doesn't matter. DeMarco may be able to enlighten you about Sean McFarland's ties to Paddy Doyle."

"I've got this, but thanks for the info," Tom said.

"Regan talked," I said. "So, what did he tell you?"

"Nice of you to drop by, but I need to get back to work," Tom said.

"So much for gratitude." I slammed a fist into my sweater pocket. "Without me, you wouldn't have gotten Regan and you know it." I speed-walked to my car, letting off steam. If I were a police officer, I'd have been at that interview. By the time I was behind the wheel, my mind had turned lucid enough to remember there was no way I'd get back on the force even if I wanted to. And I didn't want to. Not now, not ever.

My cell phone rang. It was Tom. "Where are you parked? I want to come down and talk to you."

I unlocked my passenger door to let Tom in. "I may live to regret this. But you're right, you have helped nail this guy. Regan had nothing to say until we showed him the photos."

"I'm glad you can use them."

"Let's hope they'll be admissible in court. Anyway, Regan confirmed that Saunders and McFarland argued about the drop in the investment returns. Saunders died and McFarland panicked. So they buried the body."

"Where is Saunders?"

"Buried on the Riverfront site."

"Can I let his wife know?"

"Better let me take care of that. Regan did confirm that Doyle was blackmailing McFarland about Saunders' death."

"So, Doyle was there that night taking the pictures?"

"Right. Regan said McFarland was paying up, until Doyle came to his house and demanded more. According to Regan, McFarland called and told him he needed help. When Regan got there, Doyle was already dead and McFarland said Doyle fell and hit his head while they were arguing."

"Do you believe that?"

"I'm going to request an exhumation and an autopsy to confirm how Doyle died. Regan told us he moved an already dead Doyle to the warehouse and paid Miller and DeMarco to torch the place."

"Then maybe those two guys didn't know Doyle was there."

"Or didn't care enough to check if anyone was there when they set the fire. We know that Jason Kramer was asleep at the time."

"I hope they all rot in prison," I said.

"I have to get back."

"Thanks for filling me in."

"Just pray no one finds out we spoke." Tom opened the passenger door to leave.

"Tom, did Regan say anything about Nate?"

"Nothing. Claimed he didn't know who he was."

"I don't believe him, do you?"

"I'm keeping an open mind."

CHAPTER
SIXTY-ONE

"I prayed my husband would come back to me alive," Clair Saunders said, her voice trembling.

I had waited until Tom relayed news of her husband before I phoned. "I'm so sorry. I can't image how painful this is for you."

"We both doubted he was still alive after all this time," she said. "At least now I can give him a proper funeral thanks to you." She sobbed into the phone. "The detective who came to see me said you provided the information that helped them find Greg's body."

"I was doing what you hired me to do."

"I'd like to stop by your office to thank you in person, if I may."

"I'll look forward to it," I said.

DeMarco's attorney called me several weeks later to tell me that Joey and Dave Miller reached agreements with the District Attorney's office and entered guilty pleas. Both confessed to setting fire to the warehouse and agreed to testify that Bobby Regan hired them for the job. DeMarco also pled guilty to aggravated assault for firing his weapon at Jason.

"DeMarco won't be sentenced until after he testifies against Regan," his defense attorney said. He didn't reveal the prison term agreed to. "Joey's getting credit for telling the truth. Thanks again for not pressing charges against him."

"I believe in keeping my word," I said. "What did they have to say about Doyle?"

"Both men insisted they knew nothing about Paddy Doyle

being in the warehouse," he said. "And he was dead before the fire was set."

"I get that," I said. Doyle's body was exhumed and the autopsy concluded he was killed at McFarland's home when his skull was crushed with a baseball bat. "But they never bothered to look to see if anyone else was in there." I thought of Jason.

"By the way, I did ask DeMarco numerous times about the Nate Warner you wanted to know about," the lawyer said.

"Anything?"

"DeMarco insists he never heard of Warner and I got the same story from Miller's attorney. Both men claim Regan never mentioned the name."

"Thanks for trying, and I appreciate your call."

"And you were right that Regan was holding something over DeMarco. I can't reveal what it was, but my client was coerced into the warehouse job."

When I hung up, I danced around the office singing Patti LaBelle's "New Attitude." *"I'm feelin' good from my head to my shoes."* Much more fun than drinking.

I decided to congratulate Tom in person. On my way, I felt a sense of relief for Jason Kramer. With DeMarco's and Miller's guilty pleas in place, Jason wouldn't need to testify at a trial. He could get on with his young life.

"DeMarco was one of your sources, wasn't he?" Tom said. "That's why you didn't press charges when you knew he was the one who shot at you."

"You got him on more serious crimes, and he'll be in prison for a long time. That's all I cared about. What's happening with Bobby Regan?"

Tom considered his answer. "I see no harm in telling you at this point. Regan knows Miller and DeMarco gave him up.

So, he lost no time ratting out Sean McFarland," Tom said.

"He confirmed that McFarland provided the money to hire Miller and DeMarco for the arson, and he agreed to testify against McFarland in Doyle's murder," Tom said. "But there's no plea agreement between Regan and the DA's office. Not yet anyway."

"You have enough on him to get a conviction, so if he's smart enough, he'll make a deal before McFarland does. You did great." I gave him a high five.

"So did you. Even if you came painfully close to interfering in a police investigation."

"Just doing my job."

"Be more careful in the future. Other police officers would have gone after your license."

"I hear you," I said.

"Do you want us to pursue the charges against Regan for shooting you, or do you want to drop the charges as you did for DeMarco?"

"I'm not that generous. Even if it only adds months to his sentence, I want him charged." I paused. "Tom, Nate's murderer is still out there. You've got to consider McFarland." Before I could finish, Tom interrupted.

"Weren't you listening just now?"

"We already know McFarland had no hesitation eliminating people who got in his way," I said.

"I have no evidence connecting McFarland to Nate."

"You and I both know Maggie Connors is likely to indict McFarland for fraud and tax evasion. I know in my gut Nate had the goods on McFarland's activities and that's what got him killed."

"It's a theory still without proof."

"You're forgetting Nate's missing documents. I'm still being paid to find them. I'm not stopping until I do."

"Alright, but ..."

"I know, Tom, you've told me enough times. Stick to my lane."

"Good, so we're clear then."

As I walked to my car, I cursed myself for being an ungrateful bitch. Without the Volpe family, I'd be dead or in prison. They treated me with kindness and patience. They got me counseling and encouraged my education. And now my arrogance was alienating Tom.

I needed to figure out how to patch things up with him. Bringing him a roast beef sandwich wouldn't do the trick anymore. But for now, I still had my obligation to Helena Warner. I'd have to find a way to apologize to Tom later.

Technically, looking for Nate's documents wasn't interfering in the murder investigation. I'd just have to be careful.

CHAPTER
SIXTY-TWO

What still nagged at me was why Nate didn't put his information on a hard drive and lock it in his desk at home. Why make it so hard for me or anyone to find? Of course, Nate wasn't expecting to be killed. It was clear to me that Nate was protecting his information from someone within SEPA Financial. After all, McFarland's ex-wife had overheard Regan say he had a contact inside the company. If McFarland used his henchmen to deal with Doyle and Saunders, why not with Nate? But neither DeMarco, Miller, nor Regan acknowledged knowing Nate Warner.

I couldn't get any further in my thinking without finding Nate's stash. Where would he hide something of value that he also needed access to? I'd already ruled out mailbox stores near SEPA Financial's office.

I decided to check the mail stores near the Warner home in West Mount Airy. I tried two establishments and used my envelope ploy to con the clerks into checking their records. But Nate's name didn't pop up.

I walked to my car, staring at Nate's note. I stopped in my tracks. All the PO boxes and the boxes in the mail stores I'd visited used keys, not combination locks. I'd been looking but not observing. And then I remembered I'd seen Nate frequently carry a tan briefcase with a combination lock.

I phoned Helena Warner. "I'm still searching for Nate's missing files. I was wondering if you know what happened to Nate's leather briefcase, the tan one with a combination lock?"

"I'd forgotten about that," Helena said. "I haven't seen it since he died. I only have his black lightweight Tumi and we've already looked through that."

"Any idea where that tan briefcase could be? It might be

what we've been searching for."

"No idea."

"Is it possible the burglars took it?"

"I don't think so. No. It wasn't here when my attorney and I went through all of Nate's records and that was before the burglary."

I was beginning to despair until Helena Warner phoned a few days later.

"I received a statement from a mailbox store. Nate rented a box there for three months and the renewal date is coming up. Do you think this is what we've been looking for?"

My pulse quickened. "Where's the store?"

"It's near Thirtieth Street station."

"Are you calling from your home?"

"Yes, my new living room furniture was delivered yesterday and I'm here putting things back in order."

I'd forgotten about the destructiveness of the burglary.

"I'll come to pick you up. Bring the statement, Nate's death certificate, and your picture ID. And look to see if you can find a key that looks like a mailbox key."

"Why would we need all that? I thought you had the combination."

"The combination I have is for the briefcase. The mailbox opens with a key. Nate must have placed the briefcase inside the mailbox. If we can't get the store to open up the box, then we'll have to get your attorney involved and that will take time and money."

I drove as though I had a woman giving birth in the back of my car. My brakes screeched when I stopped outside the Warner home. Helena was waiting for me at the curb.

"Why did Nate go all the way to Thirtieth Street to rent a mailbox?" Helena asked on our way into Center City.

"He didn't want anyone at the office to know what he was looking into."

"But someone did find out, and you think that's why he was killed."

"Afraid that's a strong possibility."

On the drive, Helena told me she couldn't find any new, unfamiliar key that might belong to the mailbox.

A clerk with spiked red hair and a nose ring glanced over Helena's paperwork.

"A death certificate. Weird."

"Mrs. Warner's lost her husband, and she needs access to his mailbox. Nothing weird about that," I said.

A woman sitting at a desk behind the counter walked over to us. "What seems to be the problem?"

Again, Helena explained why we were there.

"Please come with me." She led us to her desk and examined Helena's papers. I crossed my fingers, hoping she'd accept our documents and not force us to get Helena's lawyer.

"If you could wait here, I'll be a few minutes." She went into a back room and emerged with a master key.

"His box is on the side wall," she said. We followed her to a row of boxes, wider and larger than a normal-sized letter box. I held my breath as she unlocked the mailbox.

Inside was Nate's tan briefcase with the combination lock. "That's it," Helena said. "It has his initials on the front."

We thanked the manager and went to sit in my car. I slowly entered the numbers that Nate sent in his note. When I punched in the last digit, I heard the distinctive "CLICK."

I smiled at Helena. "Nate would be proud of us."

I pulled out three file folders and an external hard drive. "Let's go to my office and see what we have here."

CHAPTER
SIXTY-THREE

The contents of Nate's briefcase proved worthy of the long pursuit. He had bank records for Sean McFarland's Mid-City brokerage firm, which showed insufficient funds to qualify for or make payments on the twenty-million-dollar SEPA Financial loan. In fact, SEPA Financial records showed that Mid-City never made a single payment and defaulted on the loan months ago. There was every indication that Mid-City Brokerage had no clients and no revenue. But SEPA Financial took no legal action against McFarland.

"Nate would never let anyone get away with that sort of thing," Helena said.

"Knowing Nate, he must have been livid," I pointed out.

"What do we do with this now?"

"Use what we have to trap Nate's killer."

"How?

"Don't worry. I'll work something out."

I took Helena home and then returned to my office.

I considered taking the briefcase to Tom, but the District Attorney had strict rules regarding the chain of custody of evidence in criminal cases, and I had interfered with that chain.

In my mind, I began playing out various scenarios of what Nate would have done with his information. Did he confront Paul Cameron, the SEPA Financial executive responsible for approving such loans? Did he go to Keenan, the corporate attorney? And if he did approach those men, what happened?

Neither Keenan nor Cameron had coughed up the Mid-City loan application when I had asked to see it. Both worked in the same building with Nate. They would have known when he arrived in the office and, more importantly, when he left to drive home.

I waited until an hour before closing, then entered the SEPA Financial building. The security guard on duty at the desk recognized me. I signed in, indicating I was there to visit Nate's assistant, Diana. "Enjoy your evening." I waved to the guard and headed to the elevators.

Diana seemed glad to see me. "How have you been? What happened to your arm?"

"I'm good. Fell off my bike. I came by to see how you were getting on."

"It's been difficult. All of us on Nate's staff were given a week leave, which did help. It's funny, though, I still expect Nate to walk through that door any minute."

"That doesn't surprise me. You worked with him every day for years," I said.

"More than seven," she said.

"Any idea who your new boss will be?"

Diana leaned across her desk toward me. "Nate's office has been cleaned out, but so far, no word on his replacement. Have you heard anything?"

"It's probably still too early." I couldn't think of any other safe topic, so I said goodbye. I considered going to Cameron's office but didn't think I would get by his fearsome secretary. I opted instead for Keenan's office.

"He's at a meeting in the building, Ms. Fabiano," his assistant said. "Was he expecting you? I don't have you on his calendar."

"I spoke with him by phone this afternoon." Lies and more lies. "He asked me to come at four-thirty. He said there was something confidential that he needed to talk to me about."

"He should be back shortly, if you care to wait."

I smiled and took a seat in the waiting area. I reached into my tote for my computer tablet and began answering emails.

By five o'clock, the offices were emptying out.

"I didn't expect Mr. Keenan to be this long. He told me he'd be back in ten or fifteen minutes."

"I'll wait a bit longer since he did say it was important," I said. "I have work to keep me busy."

"I usually stay until six, but Mr. Keenan said it was okay to leave early tonight. It's my husband's birthday." His assistant looked around nervously. "I don't know what to say. I really shouldn't leave you alone."

"I'll be fine. I'm sure he won't be long. I noticed he's left his jacket on the back of his chair."

His assistant stared at me and then looked through the open door into Keenan's office. "You're right."

I kept pecking away at my keyboard while Keenan's assistant shut down her computer, locked her desk, and put on her coat.

"I won't lock his office," she said. "I'm not sure he has his keys. Besides, no one else is likely to come by."

"I'm sure you're right." I smiled. "Have a good evening." And I bent my head down toward my keyboard.

I waited until she got into the elevator and then made a quick reconnaissance of the other offices and cubicles near Keenan's office. No one was around. I headed into his office.

Besides leaving his jacket behind, Keenan had left his computer on. His screensaver was up. I clicked the mouse and the screen he'd been working with came into view.

It was the application for McFarland's Mid-City loan. Keenan must have been reading it before he left his office. I looked it over and saw what Nate saw. The value of McFarland's assets had been inflated to secure the loan. And Cameron had approved the loan.

As I worked, the lights on the floor and in the office went out, leaving me in darkness except for the lamp on Keenan's desk. I listened for any sounds outside the office. Then I remembered that motion sensors controlled the lights. Since no one had been moving around the floor, the lights had kicked off. I stood up, left the office, and walked a few paces. Sure enough, the lights came back on.

I went back to Keenan's computer. The database of loan applications had a search function. On sheer instinct, I searched the commercial loan applications over the last two years. I was curious if there were other suspicious loans in addition to McFarland's.

A message box popped up. Keenan's session had timed out. I needed to reinsert a passcode. I thought about trying possible options, but quickly dismissed the idea. I would get locked out if I failed too many times.

I searched through desk drawers, under the mouse pad, and under the lamp. Nothing. I eyed his granite pen set. It was so heavy I had to stand up to lift it with my one working arm. Underneath was one of Keenan's fancy note cards. I opened it and saw what had to be his passcode.

I keyed it into the password window, and *Finalmente!* I was back in. This time when I entered my request into the search bar, up came a list of more than one hundred loans. I printed out the list.

The lights went off on the floor again, but I ignored it and read the list using the light from the desk lamp. My eyes widened when I saw a one-million-dollar loan to R. Regan Associates, a consulting business, with an address at Bobby Regan's home. I pulled up the loan application and printed out all the documentation. The financial statement showed income and revenue just enough to meet the loan requirements. The numbers looked suspect to me. I had checked out Bobby Regan thoroughly and never came across a consulting business. Cameron, however, approved the loan. I stapled the papers together and stuffed them in my tote bag.

I was so engrossed in my research that I realized I had forgotten about Keenan. I looked at my watch. It was six-thirty and Keenan hadn't come back, which meant I could continue my research undisturbed. But I was unsettled. He wouldn't have gone home without his jacket.

I scarfed down a Kind bar for energy and continued down

the list.

The next-to-last loan was for a restaurant I recognized. Its owner was mobbed-up. Turned out he received a five-million-dollar loan, also approved by Cameron. I printed out the documentation.

I was reading the material when the lights came back on in the office. I looked up and saw Paul Cameron standing in the doorway.

CHAPTER
SIXTY-FOUR

"What the hell are you doing here?" Cameron stared at me, his eyes hard, cold. "You shouldn't be in Keenan's office alone. You're not an employee."

I stood up. "I have Jim's permission. Did you want me to let him know you were here?"

"You've been going through confidential company records, haven't you? Keenan has no authority to let you do that."

"He gave me computer access." Not technically a lie. He conveniently left a note with his passcode. "I am a fraud investigator for this company, after all."

I moved to the front of the desk.

"What fraud? I don't know what you're talking about."

"Sean McFarland's twenty-million-dollar present." Then I went for broke. "I see that McFarland's loan was not your first fraud."

Cameron's face blanched.

"Somehow, I doubt your friend Bobby Regan's nonexistent consulting firm has the assets to qualify for your very generous loan. And then there's your mobster pal. Should I go on?"

Droplets of sweat appeared on Cameron's forehead, but he remained silent.

"Why do it? You have a job and a salary most people would envy. Why jeopardize it all?" I kept talking, hoping he'd give himself away. "You must have known you'd be found out sooner or later," I said. "Especially with Nate Warner in charge of fraud protection."

"You're too clever for your own good," he spit out. Cameron removed a SIG Sauer from his jacket and aimed it straight at me.

I had disobeyed another of my unwritten rules. Never confront a suspect when you don't know if he's armed. I stopped and scanned the room for something I could use as a weapon.

I spotted a paperweight on Keenan's desk and hurled it, hitting Cameron in the chest, winding him, and causing him to lose his balance. I went for him, but not fast enough.

"Get away or I'll shoot," he shouted, the gun still in his hand.

I moved back toward the desk.

"Put your gun on the floor and kick it over to me," he said.

"I don't have one."

"Don't lie to me. I saw the holster when you came around the desk."

I removed the Glock from its holster and kicked it over to him. He picked it up and put the weapon in his pocket.

"It was you who killed Nate," I blurted out. "You knew if Nate learned about the McFarland fraud, he'd find the others and you'd be heading to prison for a long time." As I spoke, I slowly inched forward, trying to get close enough to stomp on his foot or break his nose.

"Come closer and you're dead."

I stopped in my tracks.

"You would have known when Nate left his office the night he was killed," I said, keeping my voice steady. "And you park your car in the same garage. You could have easily followed him when he pulled out."

"Shut up." Cameron pointed me toward the office door. "We're going for a walk."

"Don't make things worse for yourself."

Cameron was too far away from me to try to kick the gun out of his hand. Then I spotted Keenan's heavy granite pen set, strategically placed near the edge of the desk.

"Move," Cameron said, his nostrils flaring.

I did what I was told. As I walked toward him, I snatched the pen set and hurled it with as much force as I could muster with one arm, aiming directly into Cameron's face. My improvised weapon hit its mark. The chunk of granite spun like a ball, and caught Cameron in the forehead, between the eyes, near the hard ridge of his brow.

He staggered, reeling back onto his heels. His hand holding the SIG Sauer trembled, the barrel jerking out of control, pointing first at the floor, then the wall, then the ceiling. He clamped his forehead with his other hand, trying to stop the flow of blood oozing through his fingers, down his nose and cheeks, and onto his silk tie and crisp blue shirt.

I reached out for the gun and got hold of it. I twisted his wrist, working to wrest the gun from him. But he held on. Suddenly, Cameron's finger jerked the trigger.

The blast of a single shot shattered the air. It startled us both, and we tumbled onto the parquet floor.

As we fell, the SIG Sauer rolled across the room and skidded to a stop in front of a bookcase. Cameron began crawling to retrieve his gun. I jumped onto his back and slammed his bloodied face into the hardwood floor.

He yelled out in pain, but managed to jerk his backside into my stomach, throwing me back onto the hard floor. I winced from a sharp pain in my injured arm.

Cameron tried to get up, but I sat on his back again to keep him down. I had no handcuffs, no gun, and only one working arm. While I was considering my options, he grabbed me by my sweater and I tumbled onto the floor. I looked up to see his shoe aiming for my face. I turned away and the kick landed on my temple.

I felt dazed and my vision was blurred, still I saw him running out of the office. Despite the dizziness, I forced myself to stand and darted out the door after him. With the lights back on, I saw him opening a door into the stairwell. At the pace he was going, I figured I could catch him. But then I remember he had my Glock in his pocket. I ran back into the office, picked up his SIG Sauer, and returned to the stairway.

When I cracked open the stairway door, I heard footsteps heading down. I entered and leaned over the railing. Cameron was several flights below, panting and wiping blood from his face with his tie.

When I reached him, he was breathing heavily, sweating from exertion, and pulling open the door to the twenty-fifth floor.

"It's over," I shouted, aiming the gun at him.

But he didn't stop. He ran onto the office floor, the steel door closing behind him. I lost seconds struggling to reopen the heavy door. I saw him running along the corridor. Our movements had turned the lights on. His back made an easy target. But I aimed at the ceiling and fired a warning shot.

"Stop and turn around," I yelled.

He fired at me, missed, and ran into a maze of office cubicles. I took cover behind a filing cabinet. I remained still. I waited. Eventually, the lights on the floor went out. It was dark and quiet, except for the humming of a ventilation fan.

I began to creep alongside a row of cubicles and the lights came back on.

I spotted Cameron crouched down under a cubicle. He fired at me as he ran, but I ducked and the bullet missed me. I returned fire, but I was never good at hitting a moving target. By now alarms were blaring, and blue emergency lights were flashing. Security or the police would be coming to find us.

He had reached the door to the stairwell. I fired again just as he opened the door, placing it between us, and the bullet bounced off the steel.

I paused, then cracked the door open slowly with the SIG Sauer drawn, figuring he'd be on the other side ready to shoot. Sure enough, I recognized my Glock before I saw him, and I kicked it out of his hand. The weapon slid against the wall. He tried to slam the metal door into me, but I leaped out onto the landing, pushed him up against the wall, and pointed the SIG Sauer at his temple, blood still oozing down his face.

"I'm close enough now that I can't miss your big fat head," I said.

From the terror in his eyes, I could tell he believed I would kill him. And I grew frightened because I had worked up enough rage to pull the trigger.

The thought of my aunt stopped me. I didn't want to be imprisoned for decades because I killed this greedy bastard.

"It's over. I'm handing you over to the cops."

I read Cameron's eyes. He realized I wasn't going to shoot. He punched me in the chest. Winded, I stumbled, hitting the small of my back against the railing. The jolt knocked the SIG Sauer from my hand. It tumbled over the railing and down the stairs.

Cameron ran after his gun. I followed, but tripped, twisted my ankle, and slid down the flight of stairs. As I hit the landing, I heard a bone in my foot snap and felt a surge of pain in my leg. I didn't have time to recover when I heard his footsteps climbing back up toward me. Cameron must have found his gun. He was coming for me. I was unarmed. My Glock was still on the landing above. If I could make it up one flight, I could get the gun, take cover on the office floor, and let security know where I was.

I struggled to stand, but when I put weight on my foot, I had to hold my mouth to avoid screaming. I sat down and tried again.

"Now it's over for you." Cameron, his eyes on fire, stood on the landing below the steps where I was sitting, pointing his weapon at me. The landing was narrow. The stairs heading down were to his right.

I steadied myself as best I could and stood on my broken foot, feeling a bone move. I used my good leg to jam the point of my boot into his groin.

Cameron, startled, bent over at the waist. I kicked again, hard, at the side of his hip causing him to tumble over sideways down the stairs. His body hit the lower landing with a thud. He was out cold, the gun next to him.

I sat on the stairs and went down on my fanny, step by

step. I retrieved his SIG Sauer and held it on him. He wasn't moving, but I felt for a pulse. He was alive. As I watched him, he morphed into Uncle Dom, and I wanted to pull the trigger to get him out of our lives.

I shook myself back to reality and called Tom. I told him where I was and what happened. "We're in the stairwell between the twenty-second and twenty-third floors."

"On our way."

I collapsed onto a step, still holding the gun this nasty piece of work used to kill Nate Warner.

The police and paramedics took Cameron away on a gurney.

"Cameron killed Nate." I gave Tom the short version of why.

"Then McFarland had nothing to do with it," Tom said.

"I wouldn't go that far. He didn't kill Nate or hire goons to do the deed for him," I said. "But he's still guilty as hell in my mind."

"You need to have a doc look at you," Tom said.

"It's just my foot. I'll be okay."

Tom got on his phone and asked for another gurney. "Medics are coming up for you."

I was on a gurney riding down on the elevator when I jumped up.

"What's wrong? You still have claustrophobia?" Tom asked.

"Keenan. The attorney. You need to find Keenan. He was supposed to return to his office and never did. He may or may not be involved with Cameron."

I was in the hospital emergency unit waiting for my x-ray results when I saw Keenan brought in on a gurney.

Tom followed behind him and came over to me. "How are you doing?"

"My foot is probably broken. So, what's with Keenan?"

"We found him tied up and gagged in Cameron's office. Keenan said he went to talk to Cameron about the McFarland loan and Cameron went ballistic. He pulled a gun, and Keenan thought Cameron was going to kill him. But then, Cameron tied him up and ran out of his office and didn't come back."

"That was when he came to Keenan's office and found me," I said. "He must have thought Keenan had the incriminating evidence Nate put together. The stuff Cameron couldn't find when he killed Nate. He was tying up a loose end when he found me. Another loose end."

"You could have been killed confronting a suspect on your own." Tom frowned.

"I wasn't, and we got Nate's killer."

A nurse came up to my bed. "We're going to put your foot in a walking cast."

CHAPTER
SIXTY-FIVE

Paul Cameron had a bandage on his broken nose and blotches of red bruises on his face. "I tried to get Nate to cooperate. I promised him a cut. I even told him I'd pay the tuition for his kids' college. But Nate was holier than thou. He told me he wouldn't be able to live with his conscience." Cameron, ignoring the advice of his attorney sitting next to him, was answering Tom's questions.

I was listening once again on the other side of the two-way mirror. Tom had agreed to let me observe when I reminded him that I had gotten the goods on Cameron at the risk of my own life.

"So, you killed him. And added murder to your fraud," Tom said.

"The way I look at it, Nate sealed his own fate."

Cameron seemed only too happy to relate how clever he'd been. I guess when you know you're heading to state prison or death row, you want to have your moment in the spotlight.

"Tell us about the murder," Detective Lewis said.

"We left the office in the same elevator. I said I wanted to talk with him and suggested a coffee shop. He agreed and we drove there separately. But when Nate got out of his car, I put my gun to his back and forced him down an alley. He turned to face me, telling me that fraud was bad enough. Shooting him would make things worse. I walked up to him and I shot him. I was lucky. Nobody heard a thing. It was too noisy. At the other end of the alley a trash truck was loading dumpsters and sirens from a fire engine were blaring from the next block." Cameron laughed. "I couldn't believe my luck."

He leaned back, his arms across his chest. "I left my car where it was, pulled Nate's car into the alley, and put his body in the trunk, then left it in a downtown garage where you found him. It was perfect. Except that I couldn't find the evidence that Nate said he had on me."

"It was you who burglarized the Warner home?" Lewis asked.

"Yeah. But no luck. I was starting to think Nate didn't have the goods until that pest of an investigator started snooping around. I thought I could stall her, get her to lose interest."

Tom glanced toward the mirror. "But the McFarland loan wasn't your only fraud that would have come to light."

"You seem to know everything, so you can understand I had nothing left to lose."

"What about your family?" Lewis asked.

"My wife took the children and left." Cameron shook his head. "Nate and that PI screwed me good."

CHAPTER
SIXTY-SIX

Weeks after Cameron's arrest, I received an early morning call at home from Maggie Connors. "We're holding a press conference later this morning to announce that we're charging Sean McFarland with fraud and tax evasion."

"Way to go, girl. I have to say, though, he deserves harsher punishment than a stretch in Camp Fed."

"Andrea, his life is ruined. He's losing everything. Isn't that enough?"

"Not for me. The man not only committed fraud, but he also cost people their lives."

"With charity for none, with malice for all," Maggie said, misquoting Abe Lincoln.

"Too funny, but I'm not laughing."

"I didn't think you would. But sometimes you need to lighten up on this mania of yours for what you call justice."

"I'll bear that in mind, doctor."

Maggie laughed. "Have to go. Thanks for your help, my friend."

Was Maggie right that I wanted revenge? She could be. I couldn't help thinking it was too bad the feds didn't use chain gangs.

With the cast on my foot and my arm still healing, I had been staying home. In the afternoon, I decided to go into the office to clear up mail and other administrative tasks. I had been working at my desk for an hour when Tom came through the door.

"What the hell are you doing here?" Tom said.

"It's my office. The question is, what are you here for?"

"That's the thanks I get for wanting to tell you that we charged McFarland with both the Doyle and Saunders deaths."

I limped over and gave him a hug. "Bravo. What did the crook and murderer have to say?"

"He signed a confession last night, and the DA is working out a plea agreement."

I kissed him on both cheeks. "Now he'll do serious time." I stepped back. "At least I hope so."

"He's charged with murder in Doyle's death. But manslaughter for Saunders. Although he'll face other charges for concealing the corpse."

"And Regan?"

"He's decided to go to trial for the arson, for helping to dispose of two dead bodies, and for shooting you. He's too arrogant to admit any guilt."

"That's okay. He'll get convicted and hopefully get a tougher sentence than the DA would have offered. But, Tom, you haven't mentioned Cameron. I'd have thought he'd plead guilty after he was eager to spill his guts to you and Detective Lewis."

Tom frowned. "That's really why I wanted to see you in person."

"What's happened?"

"Cameron hanged himself in his cell. I wanted to let you know before the news got out."

I sat down. "I wouldn't have expected that. He showed such bravado when you interviewed him."

"Turns out he had a gambling problem. Even with the kickbacks he got from people like McFarland he was drowning in debt."

"He did say his wife and kids left even before you arrested him."

"He was about to lose their house, and his wife said she had enough," Tom said.

"We got justice for Doyle and Saunders, but Nate?"

"We did. Cameron paid the heaviest price for his crimes. We did our jobs. But I haven't forgotten the liberties you've taken."

"You don't seem angry at me anymore." I smiled.

"Not angry. Frustrated and worried for your safety."

"I'm fine."

"With a gunshot wound and a broken foot?" Tom led me to the sofa. "Listen, Andrea, I can't deny I'm grateful for your help. Between you and me, we couldn't have closed these cases without you. But don't ever do this again. Stick with white-collar crime. Agreed?"

"Agreed." I didn't remind him that it was my usual insurance investigation that got me involved in murder. But the next time he said I overstepped his boundaries, I would remind him that he admitted my help was invaluable.

Two days later, I was making beef soup to help rebuild my strength when my doorbell rang.

"Come on in, Jason." He had texted me the day before and asked to come to see me.

He had grown taller and put on weight.

"You're looking well," I said.

He leaned over and gave me a peck on the cheek. "I had to come to thank you. I never wanted to see you get hurt because of me."

"You and I got mixed up in something way more complicated than either of us could fathom. Come on in and sit down. Have you eaten lunch?"

Jason nodded.

"How about a cup of beef broth? I'm making soup, but the veggies aren't ready yet."

Jason sat at the kitchen table, and I poured both of us a cup of broth. "It's hot, so be careful," I said.

Jason took a sip and wiped his mouth with his napkin. "There's something I wanted to let you know." He paused. I listened.

"My parents have separated, and my mom's filed for divorce."

"How do you feel about that?"

"Okay. I think it's for the best. My mom and I moved into an apartment and my dad's in rehab."

"That's where he needs to be," I said. "I hope he gets help."

"I don't think my mom would have decided to divorce my dad without your influence."

"I'm not at all sure about that. As far as I could tell, things hadn't been good between your parents for a long time."

"Right. But she saw how you stood up to him."

"You did, too."

Jason had a hint of a smile on his face before he looked away.

"Jason, I'm glad you felt I helped. But you and your mother helped yourselves. You're growing into a fine man. You have brains, honesty, and courage. Any parent would be proud of you. I know I am."

I gave Jason a hug at the door. "Take care of yourself."

"You, too," he said, pointing at the cast on my foot. Then he opened the front door and turned to face me again. "Can I text or FaceTime with you?"

"Of course. I'd be glad to hear how you're getting on."

CHAPTER
SIXTY-SEVEN

I sat on my back porch, wrapped in my afghan, sipping hot chocolate. Thanksgiving was next week, and Aunt Roseanne would be coming home to visit.

I lifted my face toward the morning sun and breathed in the brisk, invigorating air. I had relinquished my arm sling and bandage, and the cast on my foot had been removed.

These days I eased into the day. No rushing to the office before eight. Instead, I had time to relax, catch up on the news, including Russ's stories on the McFarland case. Russ got his exclusive before word got out to the competition and he continued to publish stories that broke new ground. I was impressed and so was his editor, who told Russ the stories were award material.

"Andrea," Mr. Rossi called to me from his yard. "Glad to see you resting."

"Morning, Mr. Rossi. How are your yams doing?"

"Don't worry, we'll have plenty for the holiday. When's your aunt coming?"

"She'll be here Tuesday."

Mr. Rossi waved and went back into his house.

I went inside, showered and dressed for my physical therapy appointment. Then poured another mug of hot chocolate while I filled in a crossword puzzle. I was a lady of leisure. I could decide what I wanted to do and when I wanted to do it. A new experience for me, who always had to work, go to school, or both.

My successful results in the McFarland investigation had bulked up my bank account to the point that I didn't have to worry about new clients until the new year. I received a hefty bonus from SEPA Financial plus a renewal of my yearly retainer with a raise. Claire Saunders did come to visit and added an extra twenty percent to my fee. Helena Warner, unlike her late husband, was generous beyond the slim fee we'd agreed to earlier.

My front doorbell rang. When I opened the door, a gust of wind and Russ came through. "Right on time." We kissed and embraced. "Want some hot chocolate before we head out?"

"I'm all set."

Russ offered to drive me to the physical therapy appointments I needed to strengthen my weakened leg.

"I told my mom I'd be coming to your house for Thanksgiving. She agreed if I went to her for Christmas."

"Seems fair."

"You sure you want me?"

"Of course, I asked you, didn't I?"

"It's just with Aunt Roseanne. I thought it might be difficult for you."

I touched his arm. "I want you here. The Volpe family will be here, too. You'll enjoy meeting them all and we'll have a nice celebration. Aunt Roseanne and I will have a few days together, and we'll see how we adjust. It will be good for all of us."

"Which reminds me. Have you decided to join me in New York? Playing a New York gig is a big deal for the trio."

"Wouldn't miss it for the world."

"Then I'll book a hotel room for us."

"That will be lovely."

ACKNOWLEDGMENTS

Writing is solitary work but publishing a novel becomes a group endeavor.

I am grateful for the writing community that I am privileged to be a part of.

Thanks to C.J. McGroarty, Gus Cileone, Pam Stratton, and Matt Corso, writers and friends, who offered invaluable critiques throughout numerous drafts.

And to Philadelphia professional writers, known as the Liars' Club, including Merry Jones, Kelly Simmons and Greg Frost for their expert advice.

I am also fortunate to have a faithful cheering section, my sister, Marguerite Marcus and friends Ginny Kurz and Claire Piscapia.

And a huge thanks to Atmosphere Press, its editors, proofreaders and graphic artists for their professionalism during the entire publishing process.

ABOUT ATMOSPHERE PRESS

Atmosphere Press is an independent, full-service publisher for excellent books in all genres and for all audiences. Learn more about what we do at atmospherepress.com.

We encourage you to check out some of Atmosphere's latest releases, which are available at Amazon.com and via order from your local bookstore:

Icarus Never Flew 'Round Here, by Matt Edwards

COMFREY, WYOMING: Maiden Voyage, by Daphne Birkmeyer

The Chimera Wolf, by P.A. Power

Umbilical, by Jane Kay

The Two-Blood Lion, by Nick Westfield

Shogun of the Heavens: The Fall of Immortals, by I.D.G. Curry

Hot Air Rising, by Matthew Taylor

30 Summers, by A.S. Randall

Delilah Recovered, by Amelia Estelle Dellos

A Prophecy in Ash, by Julie Zantopoulos

The Killer Half, by JB Blake

Ocean Lessons, by Karen Lethlean

Unrealized Fantasies, by Marilyn Whitehorse

The Mayari Chronicles: Initium, by Karen McClain

Squeeze Plays, by Jeffrey Marshall

JADA: Just Another Dead Animal, by James Morris

Hart Street and Main: Metamorphosis, by Tabitha Sprunger

Karma One, by Colleen Hollis

Ndalla's World, by Beth Franz

ABOUT THE AUTHOR

Chris Quarembo is an award-winning former reporter, who also worked as a speechwriter and ghostwriter for corporate executives. Killer Deals is her debut novel. Her short stories in the crime and mystery genre are available on Amazon.

When she is not reading or writing, Chris loves live theater, art museums and traveling, especially in France and Italy. She is also a volunteer docent at the Barnes Foundation, an early modern art collection in Philadelphia.

Website: www.chrisquarembo.com